M000103233

SCORPION DOWN

A DAN ROY THRILLER
DAN ROY SERIES, BOOK 7

Mick Bose

SCORPION DOWN
Copyright © 2018 by Mick Bose
All rights reserved.

No part of this book may be reproduced in any form or by any electronic or mechanical means including information storage and retrieval systems, without permission in writing from the author.

This book is a work of fiction. Names, characters, places, and incidents either are products of the author's imagination or are used fictitiously. Any resemblance to actual persons, living or dead, events, or locales is entirely coincidental.

ALSO BY MICK BOSE

Join the Readers' Group and get Hellfire, a novella introducing Dan Roy, FREE!
Visit http://www.subscribepage.com/p6f4a1

HAVE YOU READ THEM ALL?
Hidden Agenda (Dan Roy Series 1)
Dark Water (Dan Roy Series 2)
The Tonkin Protocol (Dan Roy Series 3)
Shanghai Tang (Dan Roy Series 4)
Scorpion Rising (Dan Roy Series 5)
Deep Deception (Dan Roy Series 6)
Enemy Within (A stand-alone thriller)

CHAPTER 1

The night of the kill had arrived.

The Scorpion slipped the US-made Fox USMC kukri knife into the leather pocket of her black tights. The kukri knife, with its eight-inch curved blade, had become her weapon of choice. A man called Dan Roy had taught her how to use it, and as she secured the knife against the side of her lower leg, the memory made her lips twitch. She curled the strap around the six-inch butt and left it loose so the kukri came into her hands easily. The inward-curving blade of the kukri was made for decapitating, and in the Scorpion's hands, the enemy barely saw it before the blade slashed down on them.

Her black tights looked like yoga pants, but they were made of a polyethylene mix that stopped most sharp objects. Bullets were a different matter, but she relied on getting up close and personal to her targets before the kill. Her outfit was skintight and padded out in places to protect her vital organs. On top, she slipped on a flimsy blue vest. She lowered the zipper on the undergarment to accentuate her cleavage. All the men she had killed looked at her face then her breasts. Generally, that was the last thing they ever laid eyes upon.

Light was fading from the sky in Porto Cervo, Sardinia. The turquoise-blue water shimmered in the dying rays of the sun, and purple-gold clouds shrouded the horizon in a festival of colors. Palm trees moved gently in a refreshing breeze that came with sunset. The Scorpion watched out of the restroom window on the second floor of the Bimini Big Game Club Marina restaurant. The place was closed now, and the yacht owners and crew were in the bars of the resort and golf club. She was the only one in the marina restaurant, charged with closing and cashing out the counters. She had been in the manager job for six weeks now. A fake resume and references had got her the post. Her seductive green eyes, full lips, and high cheekbones hadn't hurt much either. Natasha was her real name, but only a few people knew that.

Through the fronds of a palm tree, she watched two servicemen walk leisurely across the courtyard. They would have checked on the gas and electricity and would now change uniforms and take over guard duties with the marina police. Security was tight, given the one-hundred-sixty-foot yachts berthed in the deep-water bays of the marina. The men turned a corner and vanished from view. Natasha took a breath. She worked with these guys and didn't want to kill them, but she would if she had to. Without hesitation.

She checked her appearance one last time. Hair done for an hour in the resort salon and curling nicely around her shoulders. She patted the black curls once. Bright-red lipstick that made her luscious smile more inviting. Sparkling gold chain placed strategically above the enticing depths of her cleavage. Skin tanned to honey gold. Killer looks.

Natasha missed her .22-caliber Glock. But it wasn't easy to smuggle a weapon in here, and it wasn't worth the risk. Adrenaline surged inside her, spreading fire into her limbs. Streetlights were flaring up outside. It was time.

She left the restaurant through a side entrance that led to the living quarters. Walking easily on her flats, she came to the marina berths quickly. A guard came out of the hut, hand on the open holster of his weapon. Behind him, she could see two more men, one with an AR-15 semi-automatic slung around his back.

"*Belissima.*" The guard in front smiled, relaxing his hand. His name was Raul Benitez, and he liked flirting with her.

"*Come sta, signor?*" Natasha smiled easily, flicking her hair to one side with a light toss of her neck.

"Doing anything this evening?" Raul asked, flashing his yellow teeth.

"Oh, just saying hi to you guys." She waved at the taller man standing at the hut's mouth. "Hi, Alejandro."

"We should really have a drink sometime," Raul said.

"Wish I had the time," she said. "But soon, I promise." She needed to keep the boys sweet just for a little longer. They wouldn't search her. She knew that much.

"Where are you off to?" Raul asked.

"I need to give something to Mr. Andreyev, in berth C. It was left for him

2

at the restaurant today. Came in the mail." Natasha indicated the bag in her hand.

Raul furrowed his brows. "That's the *Varvara*, right?"

"Correct."

Raul indicated the bag. "We need to have a look."

"Sure." She held the bag up, and he took it from her hands.

"Any personal items?"

"Nope."

He ran the metal detector along the outside then took it inside the hut. There was a parcel inside, and Natasha knew it would be put through a scanner. She wasn't fussed. The parcel was packed with some souvenirs from the tourist shop. Raul came out in a few minutes and handed the bag to her. It was getting darker now, and a light came on inside the hut.

"He's on board," Raul said.

Natasha nodded, although she knew perfectly well he was. The gates opened, and she blew Raul a kiss, which made him grin. Natasha walked along the tarmac road, yachts of various sizes moored in front of her. The bigger boats were farther out, and it was a ten-minute walk. She took her time, sauntering. Evening's closed fist was snuffing out the last vestiges of light over the salmon-pink horizon. The egg-yellow sun smoldered and spluttered as it sank beneath the line where sea met sky.

Natasha took a left on the road and headed down berth C. Far ahead, she could see the sleek, shining white hull of the one-hundred-sixty-foot yacht. The *Varvara* was named after Boris Andreyev's older daughter. The swells of the sea barely moved the massive boat. As Natasha came alongside it, she flicked her eyes around for signs of life. There were none.

A quick glance behind her showed the coast was clear. Silently, she stepped onto the rear deck then darted up to the partition doors.

CHAPTER 2

A gentle nudge showed the door was locked. Natasha removed a hairpin from her head, and the latch slid back in less than a minute. It was dark inside, and yet she knew that Andreyev was there. The entire yacht was silent. The only sounds were the creaks as the hull rubbed against the mooring slip. Natasha didn't like it.

She was in the living area of the lower deck. Ahead of her, across sofa sets wrapped around corners, was a fully stocked bar. She crouched down by instinct, but the place was empty, anyway. She took off the blue vest and wrapped it around her waist. With thumb and forefinger, she flipped open the clasp of the kukri but didn't take it out. Her customary weapons were tied in a belt around her waist: razor-sharp needles of various sizes. The handle ends were round for easy grasping. She used them as knives, but they flew like arrows too. She stepped out of her rubber flats. Bare feet made less sound.

Stealthily, she advanced. On either end of the bar, doors led to the outer deck. But there was also a door behind the bar. She vaulted over the bar, crouched on the floor, and examined the door. She tried the handle. It turned. There was a light coming from above, and it showed a metal staircase. Natasha listened carefully for ten seconds. Staying near the floor, she craned her neck up. The staircase led to a corridor, with doors opening up on either side. One of the doors was ajar, and a sliver of light came through.

She slipped inside the landing and waited. The low murmur of a voice came from above then faded. A male voice, speaking on the phone. Natasha paused. If Andreyev was on the boat, then so was a bodyguard. Maybe two or more. Andreyev never went anywhere without his security detail. Well, her orders were not to leave any loose ends. She tightened her grip on a needle and stole softly up the stairs. She planted herself to one side of the door and listened. The voice was speaking softly still. Opposite and ahead were two more doors, both closed and dark. The corridor spiralled off to another section, which led to the stairs for the upper deck. She knew this from having memorized the plans.

She leaned across and peeked inside. A man's body rested on an armchair, his side facing her. Her eyes flicked from him to the corridor. The way this man spoke and his relaxed posture told her he was the boss, not a guard dog. His voice was similar to the audio files of Andreyev that she had listened to.

It was best to get him while he was still absorbed in the phone call. Also, the guards wouldn't be that far away. Natasha took a deep breath. She moved like lightning. One hand pushed the door open, and her body twisted then rested inside the room, back to the door. A leg pushed the door closed but didn't click the latch. While she'd moved in, a quick glance had told her the room was empty bar its sole occupant.

Boris Andreyev's mouth opened in surprise. His wide eyes met Natasha's for a fraction of a second. Then she was on him, needle jabbing straight below the angle of the jaw. The soft tissue there hid the carotid artery and jugular vein, and both were severed immediately as the needle ripped through, penetrating the base of the skull and fracturing the soft bones there. Blood gushed out, and a strangled cry came from Andreyev's lips, but Natasha's left hand was already on his mouth. The needle withdrew then dived into the neck again, this time crunching the trachea. She moved the needle from side to side, smashing the trachea completely, then pushed harder into the pharynx. With a longer blade, she would have severed the spine.

The entire process had taken seven seconds. Andreyev's dilated, red-rimmed eyes stared at her in panic. His fat body convulsed as if it were being electrocuted, and the chair shuddered. Natasha put one knee on his chest, pinning him to the chair, and swatted his feeble hands as they came up. His brain was getting drained of blood and oxygen, and blood pumped out as if it were coming out of a hydrant. There were five to six liters of blood in a human body. Roughly half was out already, Natasha knew. As the light in his eyes died, and the fixed, dilated pupils stared right through her, Natasha relaxed.

Then she heard the sound behind her. Steps coming up the stairs. Natasha spun the chair around, making the dead body face the wall. She stood next to the door, heart beating in her mouth. A new and longer needle was in her hand, sharp tip glistening in the light. The steps came up to the door then paused. Natasha swallowed. The next three moves were planned already. Pull inside, neutralize, escape.

She heard a hand grasp the door handle. There was a pause, as if the person on the other side was hesitating. Then the handle turned slowly. Natasha tipped forward on her toes, ready to hurl herself at the body that stepped inside.

In painful slow motion, the door opened. Natasha couldn't see anything, and it made her frown. She should have seen the shadow of a human figure by now.

The door opened further, and below her line of sight, a brown-haired head appeared. Natasha choked back the gasp that arose in her throat. The door opened further.

"Daddy?" said the little boy who stood on the doorstep.

CHAPTER 3

Natasha stared, transfixed, as the boy gaped at the back of the armchair. He still hadn't seen her.

"Daddy?" the boy repeated. He stepped inside the room. His eyes moved to the left and then jerked upwards as he saw Natasha. She still had the needle in her hand, ready to strike. And she had to strike. No loose ends. But what if the loose end was a child?

The boy was about seven years old. He gaped at Natasha with frank curiosity. He closed his mouth, swallowed, and asked, "Who are you?"

Her frozen brain wouldn't allow any words to be uttered. This was not the intel she had received. Andreyev was here to complete a business deal. He was not meant to be travelling with his family. But he was. And now a child had seen the face that remained hidden from every known intelligence and law enforcement agency in the world.

She knew what she had to do. A quick, clean kill. One blow would be all it took. Her palms were sweaty as she gripped the needle tighter. She could see the angle of his jaw as his face was upturned to her, those wide, innocent eyes asking her a question.

Who are you, Natasha?

Her breath came in fast, short jerks. A pressure built inside her like a volcano erupting, only this geyser of hot, molten emotion had nowhere to go. Her hands became like claws, and a silent scream forced its way out of her open mouth. Her teeth bared in rage and impotent frustration.

The boy looked around him and left Natasha for the chair. It was then she knew her time was up. She scrambled out the door and ran down the staircase. The scream came as she was at the foot of the stairs. The boy screamed again, just as Natasha reached for the door. It swung open and away from her.

A burly, barrel-chested man in a suit blocked the doorway. His height and width were big enough to fill the small landing. His eyes widened when he saw Natasha. He paused for a moment, and that was all the time Natasha needed. She flew at the guy, her left arm karate-chopping the hand holding the gun. With a suppressed whistle, the weapon went off. She used her momentum to bend her knee and slam him in the chest, making him stagger back. She grabbed hold of his collar as he did so and brought the needle down with savage force into his left eye. The man saw the blow coming and parried it, but his thick, meaty arm was slow moving. He screamed in pain as the needle punctured the eyeball and burst the fragile bones of the eye socket.

Natasha let go of him and ducked as she saw another figure materialize at the partition door she had gotten in through. A suppressed round flew above her head and smashed into the well-designed bar. Glass burst into a shower of fragments and rained down on her. She shielded herself with both hands and desperately searched for the gun the man had dropped. It was behind him, and as she grappled for it as she heard the other guy rushing in.

Natasha swore and dived for the bar corner. Her fingers had touched the butt, but there was no time to retrieve the gun. She went around the edge just in time as two rounds whistled into the woodwork. More bullets followed, then they stopped. The guy on the floor was still screaming, and Natasha knew the language well. Russian. A few heated words were exchanged, and she heard the rack of a gun being slid. She didn't wait for the new magazine to get slapped in.

Using the bar as cover, Natasha lifted her head. This man was good. To rack the slide, get the mag in, then aim, all in less than five seconds, was no mean feat. That amount of practice meant he was ex-Spetsnaz. Her eyes didn't meet his stare, because she picked up a piece of dislodged wood and threw it at the man. He fired immediately, and chunks of wood flew up above her head as she ducked down and rolled over four times. When she was up on her knees, he was jerking his pistol the wrong way. Natasha saw him stiffen as he realized his mistake.

It was the last mistake he would make. Natasha hurled her needle like a spear, and it embedded itself with a sickening squelch into his left cheek. He roared in anguish but didn't drop the gun. He managed to squeeze out three more rounds, but Natasha had moved already. The kukri was in her hand.

Staying low and using the bar counter as cover, she flew at the guy, who was distracted and howling in pain. He didn't realize how close she was till too late.

The kukri sliced like a curved machete and almost chopped off his gun wrist. She aimed at the wrist joint, and with proper aim, she would've cleaved the hand from the arm. The man screamed, dropped the gun, and lurched back against the bar. More bottles toppled overhead. Natasha charged at him and sliced at his neck with the kukri.

The blind man was trying to stand up, but Natasha stepped over him, lifted the kukri over her head, and brought it down with all her strength onto the base of his spine. The cervical spine popped at the back of his neck, and his head lifted backwards. His remaining eye turned glassy, and he slid from sitting to prone.

Natasha circled around. The door behind her, leading to the staircase, was open, but the landing was empty. She retrieved both handguns from the floor and checked the mags. Both still had rounds in them. They were Makarov PMMs with twelve-round mags, standard Russian Army issue. Well, that settled it. Andreyev's personal bodyguards came from his military contacts. Not surprising, as he was one of the largest defense contractors for the army.

Natasha moved fast. There was no telling who else might be on this boat. There was no way she was going back the way she came. Her stay at the marina was over. Holding one of the Makarovs in her right hand, elbow ramrod straight, she stepped out onto the rear deck.

She crouched and looked over the side. The rigid inflatable boat was tied to the yacht by ropes, a decidedly low-tech solution that she had noticed on one of her surveillance rounds. She jumped onto the RIB, trying to make as little sound as possible.

With the kukri, she hacked at the rope. It was almost severed when she caught the glint of a flashlight from the boat, aimed at her.

CHAPTER 4

It was a light mounted on the night scope of a rifle. That much she knew almost unconsciously as the kukri fell from her hand. She dived forwards, but the rifle fired. Natasha felt the hot, acrid burn of metal as the round grazed her upper back and then another sharper pain. She tumbled down but managed to bring the Makarov out as she fell. Someone jumped on the RIB behind her, and she twisted to fire. The round went in the air as her hand was kicked hard, then a pair of boots landed on her chest with savage force. Air burst from her lungs. Light dimmed in her eyes. But her hands were free, and she got one of the needles out by reflex. She slammed the needle into the man's leg, and he grunted. Another shadow jumped on the boat. Natasha pushed the man's legs, and he lost balance. Her chest was bursting, pain raging in her shoulder where she had been grazed.

She managed to stand up. There was a sharp sound behind her, like air from a bike tire exploding under pressure. She cried out this time as the round went into her left shoulder. She felt the sting of metal and the warmth of blood. Her vision rocked, and her legs suddenly felt as if they were made of stone. The deck, marina, and sky merged into one as her knees folded and she crashed. Her body hit the side of the RIB. She tried to turn as she felt the shadow loom behind her. The blow rapped against the back of her head, and pain mushroomed in a yellow-orange fireball. Her neck snapped forward, and she fell headlong into the water.

Natasha didn't even hear the splash. Her limbs were loose all of a sudden, flaccid like the tentacles of a jellyfish. She couldn't see anything, but even as consciousness faded, the little boy's wide eyes came to her mind.

Who are you?

Then she was falling, silent, rushing headlong into an amniotic darkness. Ice poured in her veins, numbing her to the core. She breathed sluggishly and inhaled brackish water. She choked, and her open mouth swallowed more water. A deep, primitive instinct inside her sparked up like a fire in a desert. She wanted to move, fight, but her body was unable to act. As her eyes began to close, she wondered if she was dying. Then she didn't remember anymore.

CHAPTER 5

Dan Roy was climbing down a mountain. Green-and-brown spruce-fir forests carpeted the slopes around him, as far as the eye could see. Wave after wave of hills undulated to the distant horizon, their color turning to a pale shade of blue, till they merged with the sky.

No wonder, Dan thought as he stepped down the dirt trail, they were called the Blue Ridge Mountains—his favorite mountain range in the world. Here, he had isolation and peace. He was back home in Virginia, and it seemed as though he had spent a lifetime away. The silent splendor of these hills was music to his ears and Kool-Aid for his soul—a soul ravaged by a lifetime of war.

He was coming down Whitetop Mountain, his old, favorite climb. He had run up half the way with his twenty-pound backpack. It was hard, sweaty work but a fantastic workout. While he was at home, his day included a four-hour-long exercise regime followed by an hour of practice at the shooting range.

He had last come to Whitetop with his father, and the memory was both a benediction and a searing pain. He would never see his old man again. Nor his mother, and maybe not even his brother, Rob. He had only himself left in this world. But was he happy? The heaviness of his heart spoke otherwise.

He inhaled deeply. The fragrance of the fir trees mingled with the trail dust was invigorating. The backpack was light on his back, and his weapon of choice, a Sig Sauer P320, was on his belt at his back in a cloth holster, with his shirt over it. As he walked, Dan wondered how he had been on a mission in the Hindu Kush Mountains, near the roof the world, the Himalayan mountain range. But these gentle hills of Virginia, the breeze sighing through the tall trees, the way the sunlight danced on the leaves—it gave him a feeling of peace he had not known in years.

His phone beeped. Dan frowned.

No one knew where he was. He didn't stay in touch with anyone and hadn't forwarded his new cell number to anyone either. By reflex, his eyes darted around. He took in the slopes of the mountain, the white trail, and the forest below him. There was a large boulder by the side of the road, tall enough to hide two men. He stepped inside its shade and took his phone out. He did a three-hundred-sixty-degree sitrep. He was alone. Only the wind, dust, and forest stretched for miles around.

The screen showed no caller ID. Dan didn't answer. The call continued to ring. He was about to put the phone back in his pocket when a text message beeped.

It's Me.

Dan froze. This time, the number was visible. He knew that number by heart and would till the day he died.

But that didn't mean he had to answer. He put the phone away and carried on down the hill. His GMC Yukon was parked in a shady nook at the base of the river that ran along the mountain, behind the parking lot of the park region. The vehicle was invisible in the foliage to the untrained eye. There were no tourists at this hour. Dan approached his vehicle carefully. He didn't like the fact that his security had been breached.

He took out the Sig as he got within ten feet of the Yukon. He waited for five minutes behind the shade of a tree, watching his vehicle. Then he stepped out and slid underneath. The oil and gas pipes didn't show any signs of being tampered with. He ran his hands down the sides of the door. Nothing. He stood well back and pressed the button to unlock the car. Gingerly, he opened the door. Too often, he had seen or heard IEDs exploding inside cars in Afghanistan and Iraq as either the door opened or the engine started. Hell, in Iraq, the enemy even tied IEDs to the backs of cows and dogs. One of those animals would run amok once in a while, and it was comical to watch battle-hardened Marines jumping for cover as a street dog chased after them.

He shook the memories off and focused on the task ahead. He didn't expect an IED in the Yukon. This was home, for heaven's sake.

But old habits were like war wounds. They never really went away.

When he was satisfied the Yukon was clear, he slid inside. There had been no wires visible, so he started the car. The engine growled to life without incident. He took off, scanning the rearview mirror as he drove.

It took him half an hour to drive back home to Montrose, a small town nestled in the mountains. He drove past the drugstore and closed shop fronts. The town had its share of bars and some nice restaurants. There was some old money here and a large community of veterans who wanted peace and seclusion more than anything else. It was a blessing that the real estate developers hadn't found the place as yet, building their McMansions in the hills. *Only a matter of time,* Dan thought wryly. It might mean he could sell the family home for a profit. That was pretty much the limit of the upside.

He didn't stop outside his home. He drove past the two-story redbrick seventies building similar to the rest of the single-family homes on the street.

He parked two blocks down then walked, pulling his baseball cap low over his head. It wasn't much of a disguise, and hiding his big frame wasn't exactly the easiest of tasks. But Dan knew everyone here by name. Most of his old school friends had moved away, but their elderly parents remained. And some houses were boarded up with no one to care for them. He knew the cars and kept his eyes peeled for a new one.

He came up to his door but hesitated before he went in. He moved to the left and went down the side of the property. Halfway down, there was a window about six feet from the ground, near his head height. It was a bathroom window, and he couldn't see through it.

With his kukri knife, he scraped away the putty that held the glass in its frame. He took the frame off slowly, careful not to make a sound. He reached in and turned the handle then opened the window. Gripping the sill, he levered himself up and over and dropped as lightly as possible on the balls of his feet. He listened, but the house was silent.

He removed the bottom panel from the shower. Below the shower tray, there was a long, thin rectangular box. A red digital keypad glowed on top. He punched in the code then pulled out his Heckler and Koch Special Ops Modified (SOM) 416 rifle. He shut the box and slid it under the shower.

Adjusting the telescope butt against his shoulder, he got up slowly. With one hand, he opened the bathroom door. The hallway was empty. It stretched out to the front door, which was also shut. Two sitting rooms opened out on either side, and the kitchen lay to Dan's right. He turned right, pointing his weapon inside the large open-plan space. A long dining table was placed before the folding wooden doors that led to the backyard outside.

A man was sitting at the table, a drink next to him. It looked like a glass of whiskey, with ice from the fridge. The man had his back to Dan and was facing the backyard. He seemed to be enjoying the view of the hills that rose in the distance. The salt-and-pepper hair on his head was buzz-cut. He lifted the glass to his lips to take a sip.

"Come in, Dan," the man said without turning around. "And for God's sake, put that gun down."

CHAPTER 6

Dan didn't lower his weapon. He moved it from side to side as he checked the space. Then he did a three-hundred-sixty-degree sitrep. It was all clear. Only he didn't believe the man was alone.

"Where are the others?" he asked.

The man sighed and took another sip. "Mighty fine bourbon, I have to say. Will you just relax? If I wanted you picked up, it would have happened already."

Dan lowered the gun and crossed the space quickly. He kept the rifle in his hand, pointing down.

"What are you doing here, McBride?" he asked roughly.

Dan's mentor from Team B, Special Forces Operational Detachment-D, or Delta, and later his handler at the black-ops company, Intercept, smiled.

"What, no hello?"

James "Fighter" McBride was closer to seventy than sixty. He had deep lines etched on his face from age and travel. But age had not dulled the sharp glint in his calculating slate-gray eyes. He was also as sparse as a sparrow and as strong as a man ten years his junior. He tended his own farm on the outskirts of Bethesda and, as far as Dan knew, worked full-time for Intercept.

McBride reached inside his pocket, keeping his eye on Dan. He took out a Cohiba cigar, far end already clipped, and lit it with a Zippo lighter. Fragrant smoke enveloped the kitchen. Cohiba cigars were the connoisseur's choice, but they were Cuban and banned in the USA. Dan had long ago learned not to ask how McBride got a hold of them.

A sense of disquiet was spreading inside Dan's mind. "Did you just drop by for some friendly conversation, McBride?"

The older man pointed to Dan's weapon. "Put that thing down, and I'll tell you." He smiled. "You're making me nervous."

Dan sat down opposite McBride and put the rifle on the seat next to him. "What do you want?"

"Does there have to be a reason for me to visit?"

"Cut the crap. We both know you're here for something."

"You know, the older I get, the more I realize life doesn't last very long."

The comment threw Dan. He frowned. Coming back to the family home and seeing all the old photos had made him think along exactly the same lines. He got up from the chair, opened a cabinet door, and got himself a glass. At the table, he poured himself a splash of bourbon. The fiery taste in his throat felt nice.

"It goes by quickly," McBride continued. "All you're left with are memories and a decaying body."

"Since when have you become so depressing?"

McBride grinned. "You're still young. You won't understand."

Dan was pushing forty. "Young? Relative word if I ever heard one."

"Don't leave regrets. Finish what you started."

Dan put his glass down slowly. "What do you mean?"

"Heard of a place called Agadez?"

Dan didn't miss a beat. "In Nigeria, right? South of Libya. We have an air base there, mainly for drones. To keep an eye on terrorists in North and West Africa."

"Correct."

"There's been a lot of activity in North Africa recently. Libya is a lawless state now. It's become a training ground for terrorists."

"It's been that way since Gaddafi was bombed out. What's new?"

"Chechens."

Dan swallowed the rest of the bourbon and poured himself another dash. He swirled the amber liquid, staring at it. Then he looked up at McBride. "Why am I getting a bad feeling about this?"

"Because your gut is telling you that Chechnya has its share of Islamists, being a mainly Muslim country."

"My gut's also telling me you're telling me this for a reason."

McBride smirked. "Just old pals having a chat, you know."

"Yeah, right."

"The head of the Chechens is a warlord called Aliev Daurov. Heard of him?"

Dan nodded.

McBride continued. "He's made multiple trips into the region, and his yacht has also been spotted in the Mediterranean."

"So have the yachts of practically every Russian oligarch. The Mediterranean in the summer is where rich Russians and Arabs come to play. What's your point?"

"Chechens have moved from Libya up north. Into Italy and the smaller islands. Our drones have been marking this."

"Are the Russians involved?"

"They're denying it. We know Russians and Chechens are in the same bed now. Chechens are fighting in Syria for them."

Dan pursed his lips. "But why the move into Europe?"

McBride leaned back in his chair. "You tell me."

"Maybe the Chechens are helping the Islamists launch an operation from Libya. Not far by boat from Benghazi to Sicily."

"Exactly."

"The CIA has plenty of assets in Benghazi after the last mess. In fact, all over Libya. They told you about the Chechens, right?"

"I got it via the National Security Agency, but yeah."

"Tell the CIA director to send in a covert mission. Seek and destroy Chechen capability in the region. That's what the Agadez drone facility is for, right?"

"We could, but there are obstacles. They're hiding themselves well. Also, they have moved up already."

"Where to?"

"Sardinia, among other places."

"Why Sardinia?"

McBride took a deep breath. "This is top secret."

"Then don't tell me."

They stared at each other for a while. McBride spoke in a soft voice. "When you hear who's involved, you'll want to know more."

Dan clenched his jaw tight, and his nostrils flared. The first name that came to his mind was beyond painful. He couldn't go there. But McBride hadn't left him any choice.

Dan uttered one word. "Rob."

"No."

Relief washed over Dan. Of all the wounds he carried, the deepest was the fact that his own brother had gone rogue. No one knew where Rob Roy was or where his allegiances lay. McBride read the expression on Dan's face.

"It's someone else."

"Who?"

"This is on a need-to-know basis only. The CIA have a black prison in Sardinia."

Dan raised his eyebrows. "In Sardinia? Why?"

"The island has always been a route into mainland Italy and then into Europe. That route is now in heavy use by Islamists and Chechens."

McBride paused to push his glass forward. Dan poured another two fingers' worth into the tumbler.

"Two days ago, one of our high-level assets in the Russian government was killed. He was an oligarch called Vassily Andreyev. The man was close to the Kremlin circle."

"Spetsnaz hit squad?"

McBride stared at Dan. "No. He was killed by sharp wounds to the neck. Like he was stabbed by needles."

Dan's face went as white as a sheet.

CHAPTER 7

McBride took a sip of his drink and grimaced. "It gets worse."

Dan didn't say anything. McBride reached inside his coat for the other pocket. He took out an envelope and put it on the table.

Dan stared at McBride and whispered, "The Scorpion. Was it her?"

McBride pulled out three photos from the envelope and gave it to Dan. "The SOG guys who were in the security detail caught her."

Dan stared at the face in the black-and-white photos. His heart constricted, a strange emotion mixing in his blood, spreading into his limbs. A woman whose features he knew all too well looked back at him. He shook his head.

McBride said, "Of course, they didn't know who she was. They sent the photos back to Langley, and I got a call."

Dan looked at McBride sharply. "Did you tell them who she was?"

McBride lit the tip of his cigar again, dropping the ash casually on the table. He shrugged at Dan to apologize.

Dan didn't blink. "Answer my question, will you?"

"If I told the CIA, why would I be here?"

Dan observed his old mentor closely. The old man was crafty, but he was also the only person Dan trusted. He knew too much about McBride—his two divorces and two daughters who didn't keep much contact with him. Dan was surprised the old man had confided in him. Not many in the Pentagon knew much about this former two-star general or the fact that he worked for Intercept. Dan could tell when McBride was lying. He wasn't now.

Still, never say never.

"Where is she now?" Dan looked at the photos. Seeing the face of Natasha, a.k.a. the Scorpion, again had stirred memories that he kept buried—the warmth of her touch, the fierceness of her spirit. They had been lovers once and enemies many more times.

20

"She escaped."

Dan couldn't help a wry grin. "Escaped from a black prison? Jeez, that's got to hurt the CIA."

McBride didn't smile. "Losing face in a foreign country isn't funny, Dan. If this thing goes belly-up and the Italians start asking questions, we look bad. But it's not just that. Why did she kill Andreyev? What's she planning next?"

Dan shook his head, resignation writ large in his tanned, handsome features. "Right. That's what you want me to find out."

McBride lifted his hands up. "Hey, this is just a catch-up. Thanks for the bourbon. I'm not here to ask you anything."

"Sure."

The old man looked past Dan's shoulders into the distance where the mountains slumbered in a sunny haze. "You happy here?"

Dan smiled. "Quit trying. Yes, I'm happy."

"Wasn't trying anything. Simple question. I want you to be happy, son."

They said nothing for a while. Then McBride reached for his fedora. "Remember what I said."

"What?"

"Life goes by quickly. Problem is, you only realize that when you're my age." He stood. "Stay in touch, Dan. I'll see myself out."

Dan watched him go and heard the front door shut. When he looked down at the table, he saw his old lover's face looking up at him.

CHAPTER 8

Melania Stone's high heels clicked on the marble stone floor of New York's Four Seasons Hotel. She had walked the roughly thousand yards from the Rockefeller Center Metro and changed shoes in a public restroom before coming into the lobby. She wore a short black dress with a plunging V-neck, and her makeup was done to be just right without being garish. The push-up bra accentuated her cleavage, and she walked with her shoulders back, hips swinging seductively. She ignored the looks from men who stopped and stared. The art deco lobby was one of a kind in New York. Its onyx ceiling was widely regarded as an architectural masterpiece. But Melania was the person on whom eyes focused today.

She walked up to the reception desk and smiled at the flustered man in a suit. He swallowed and did his best not to stare.

"Mr. Terambutov in the Gotham suite? I believe he's expecting me." She gave him her name.

"Oh yes, of course. Elevators…"

"Don't worry. I know where they are."

She headed towards the left, feeling the reception staff's eyes on her back. She was thankful for the warm weather, without which she would've needed a coat. She rode the elevator to the top floor and stepped out onto the deep-pile carpet, her three-inch heels sinking into it. The two bodyguards outside the suite looked in her direction. She walked towards them. Both were stony faced, with the bulge of shoulder holsters obvious under their suits.

"We have to search," one of them said in a thick Eastern European accent.

This was the part Melania actively disliked, but in her line of work, it was a necessary inconvenience. She took a deep breath and stood with her legs spread. She felt the man's meaty hands move up her legs and linger longer than necessary at the top of her thighs. She clenched her jaw as he moved back and felt around her bra. There wasn't much to her dress, and its revealing look was meant to deter a more thorough and demeaning search. She let out a breath as the man stepped back. His colleague smirked. She gave him a stony, dead-eyed stare then looked straight ahead. Her cell phone and credit card, the only two items in the pocket of her dress, were returned to her.

The door opened, and she was ushered inside. The man who stood at the entrance of the luxurious living room was short and pudgy. He was no more than five feet seven, she guessed, and his belly strained the cloth of his dressing gown. His eyes widened at the sight of her, and he practically licked his lips.

He strode forward and put his hands on her arms then allowed himself to cop a feel. Melania smiled and bent her five-foot-nine, one-hundred-and-forty-pound frame over him.

"Shall we get more comfortable, Mr. Terambutov?" she whispered in his ear.

The fifty-four-year-old almost giggled. "Call me Terry. All my friends do."

They held each other and walked inside. The large space was strewn with comfortable sofas and a wall-hung TV. Curtained doors gave way to a balcony that looked over Central Park. Terry walked over to the bar while Melania glanced around the room. Her eyes fell on the black laptop that was still open on the table.

"What's your poison of choice?" Terry asked. His accent was typical of many south Russian men, thick and guttural.

"Gin, on the rocks," she said, moving closer. She thrust her chest forward, and he dropped an ice cube outside the glass. The escort agency his company had contacted specialized in wealthy Middle Eastern, Asian, and Russian businessmen. They preferred a full bust and hips in a woman. She didn't go to the bar but sat down at the table and crossed her legs slowly.

As he brought the drink over, her eyes scanned the screen quickly. A message board was displayed on it. The letters were in Russian, which she could read and speak fluently.

The photos have arrived.

Good. I will send you the links.

She couldn't read any further as Terry came and sat down next to her. She took the drink and dipped her lip in it without drinking. He leaned forward and shut the laptop. He drained the amber liquid in his whiskey tumbler then smacked his lips.

He grabbed her then kissed her roughly. She arched her neck back, moaning. With her hands, she felt the pockets of his dressing gown. Empty. She untied the cord of the gown. His breathing grew faster.

"Shall we head for the bedroom?" she purred and pouted her lips.

Terry fondled her breasts once more. She gently removed his hands and stood up, holding her hand out to him. He grabbed it and pressed himself against her. Melania laughed and headed for the bedroom, whose door stood open, to the left of a hallway.

He removed her dress quickly, and she took off his gown. He was wearing boxer shorts, through which his erection was clearly visible. She pushed him back on the four-poster bed and straddled him as he whimpered in anticipation.

"Oops," Melania said. "My rubbers and cell phone fell out of my dress. Can I go and get them?"

He stopped and stared at her. "Where are they?"

"On the sofa, where you were just being naughty." She grinned.

He slapped her bottom hard, and she squealed, throwing her head back. He slapped her harder, and she moaned.

"Go get them quickly." He panted. "I can't hold any longer."

CHAPTER 9

Melania rushed to the sofa, naked feet padding on the soft carpet. She picked up her phone and switched it on. From the menu, she activated a Bluetooth protocol that infiltrated all nearby digital devices. Then the protocol unleashed a "reverse worm," a program that mimicked the device's software and accessed all files. She placed the cell phone next to the laptop and tapped her watch. The screen illuminated, and she saw the program was working. The entire process took five seconds. She picked up the condom packet and her credit card then rushed back to the room.

Terry was standing. He was striding to the door and stopped when he saw her flounce into the room.

"Where did you go?"

She waved the packet of condoms at him. He looked at her suspiciously. "Where's your cell phone?"

"I left it on the table. It's safe there, right? This is all we need right now." She gestured to the packet. They kissed, and gently, she pushed him back on the bed and straddled him again. She kissed his chest and moved down.

His eyes were closed, mouth open.

She murmured, "I want you to come all over me." Holding her watch close to her face, she repeated the sentence.

"Yes, yes," Terry whispered.

Melania took out a hairpin from her the back of her head. The titanium pin elongated into a razor-sharp point, becoming a lethal weapon. She jumped on his chest, her knees pressing down into his hands. She grabbed his hair and pushed his head back. The point of the knife was now pressed into his neck.

"Don't move, asshole, or you die."

Terry's eyes flew open. He took a few seconds to readjust, then his eyes filled with hate. He growled and tried to move his hands, but her knees were pressed on them hard. She increased the pressure on her weapon, and it nicked the skin, drawing a bead of blood. He stopped struggling abruptly.

"Saladin Terambutov, I am Melania Stone, CIA agent. Welcome to the USA."

His eyes stared at her defiantly. "I am a businessman. I invest in this country. This is how you treat foreign investors?"

"Your companies are a pipeline for funding money to Dagestani and Chechen Islamist terrorists. That money funds hate preachers in mosques, terrorist cell networks, recruitment, all in this country."

"Prove it."

"The files on your laptop bear code names for known terrorists that we and the FBI have tracked for months. You communicate with them regularly. Money from your companies buys shooting ranges, properties exclusively for the use of these individuals."

"You can't access my laptop. This is entrapment. It's illegal."

Melania resisted the urge to spit in his face. "You get your money from human trafficking. Smuggling Eastern European girls into other countries. Your companies are just a front for that."

Anger blossomed inside her, and a dangerous glint sparked in her eyes. Terry saw it too, and fear showed in his face.

Her left hand throttled his neck, and the right increased the pressure on the knife. "There's enough drone surveillance on your smuggling network to put you away for life, once we connect it to the files on your laptop. But I could just kill you now. Self-defense. My word over yours."

He croaked as blood dripped onto the pillow. "Please, no…"

A crimson tide spread across Melania's face, and an engorged vein stood on her forehead. "Fuck you…"

CHAPTER 10

The doors to the penthouse suite burst open, and loud voices sounded. Boots pounded on the living room floor. Melania slid off Terry and stepped into her dress quickly.

"Over here," she called out. She turned the light on in the room, keeping her eye on Terry. She had checked under the pillows for a gun but not found anything. But she didn't trust him. Terambutov, or Terry, was a high-price target. His human-trafficking business was how he had first come to the attention of the CIA. Hundreds of terrorists were transported to Russia and Syria using that network. Also to the USA. He was a staunch Islamist, a senior member of the Salafist Council, or Council of the Pure, Islamists who believed in their orthodox hard-core branch of Islam prevailing over the world.

Well, Melania thought with satisfaction as she saw the FBI special agent in charge pull him up from the bed, Terambutov wouldn't be doing any more prevailing now. His life was over. She had truly wanted to kill him and would have pushed the knife all the way in if the FBI hadn't arrived.

Now he would face a federal court and jail, but ultimately, he was headed for Gitmo. As the FBI agent read him his charges, Terry glared at Melania. Anger flared inside her again. She stepped in front of him.

"What, asshole? You wanna try me? Free his hands." She went to hit him, but Watkins, her CIA agent colleague, stepped in and grabbed her hand.

"Not here. Let them do their job."

Melania stared at Terry as he was led outside. The FBI agents swarmed inside the suite, three of them in white forensic suits.

Watkins said, "You did well. Growing into your new role?"

She knew Watkins from her days training at the Farm. Melania was now a senior agent in the newly created Human Trafficking Division at the CIA's Directorate of Operations, formerly called the National Clandestine Service.

Undercover work seemed to have become her thing, after she volunteered for the first operation.

"Part of the job, Watto," she said. "Did you get my backpack?"

He handed her the bag, and she went into the bathroom to get changed into a blue skirt suit. They thanked the FBI agents then left for LaGuardia Airport. It was late afternoon by the time they arrived at Langley. When she dropped her bag on her desk, the woman next to her leaned over.

"Chuck from the NSA wanted to speak to you." She gave Melania a number.

Melania thanked her and checked her emails. Chuck Jones had been in touch already on email, but she had been away. She fired off some emails then called Chuck back. He was head of the NSA Signals Intelligence Directorate and had been instrumental in tracking all the phone calls and video signals from Terambutov and his men.

Chuck answered on the first ring. "I hear congratulations are in order."

"Thanks, Chuck. News travels fast. You got anything for me?"

"We put the files you copied from Terambutov's laptop through Echelon and DS-500."

Melania knew the last two names referred to the NSA supercomputers that stored millions of terabytes of data—images, emails, video traces, anything and everything related to terrorist networks. The files would be scanned against the information held in Echelon, and any matches would flash up for the dozens of SID analysts who labored day and night in search of such data.

"Gosh, that was quick. And?"

"It's a gold mine. We have access to all the type-and-erase messaging apps that the jihadis use in the north Caucasus. We got them on lockdown and are tracking their activity in real time."

"Found anything yet?"

"A code keeps flashing up. We got through their basic encryption easily. It's a message delivered to all Islamist and jihadist networks that we know of. Globally." He paused. "It's a significant volume of activity. All the networks are spiking. Last time we saw something like this was before 9/11."

Both were silent. Melania felt the back of her neck prickle, and her chest tightened.

"What's the message?"

"Loosely translated, it says to get ready for the biggest attack ever. An event that will spark a war to bring the world to its knees."

"Where is the message coming from?"

"From south Russia. Chechnya and Dagestan, already on our alarm list."

"Have you called CENCOM?" CENCOM was Central Command.

"The Director of National Intelligence and your boss are already aware. I'm briefing the White House and the Secret Service later today."

"Can I access your networks to stay in the loop?"

"Roger that."

CHAPTER 11

Melania had just put the phone down when she sensed someone standing behind her. Karl Shapiro, a man of medium height and with a black curly beard trimmed short, was the chief of Directorate of Operations. Melania stood up.

Karl held his hand out. "Great job."

They shook hands.

He said, "You heard of the message, right?"

"Yes. But what does it mean?"

Karl shook his head. "That's the problem. Jihadi networks are wiser now. They don't even use codes for the event. We can crack them, and they know it. Someone must know, somewhere."

"I agree. I need clearance, sir, to tap into NSA."

"Attagirl," Karl said. They exchanged a smile. Karl Shapiro had been a friend of Benjamin Wiblin, Melania's adoptive father. He had known Melania from when she was a child.

Karl sat down at Melania's desk and typed a sequence of numbers from memory. There was a series of beeps, then a green-colored portal with the letters NSID began to glow. Karl removed a badge from the lanyard around his neck and pressed it to the screen. After another series of beeps, he was in.

"Thanks," Melania said.

"I got something else for you," Karl said. "A ship that was bought by funds from one of Terambutov's companies. Russian ship, docked in Panama. Human cargo unloaded from one shipping container."

Melania's face tightened. She tapped on her keyboard and located the drone feed that showed the grainy image of the ship and then what looked like matchstick men being loaded into the back of a truck.

Karl said, "The truck moved up through Mexico and now into Texas."

"I need coordinates, sir. This will be a joint task force op, right?"

The CIA and FBI had mingled forces, unusually, to tackle the growing threat of human trafficking into the USA, especially as the networks were often used to import known terrorists into the country.

"Yes. Do you want to hand over to them or do this yourself?"

Melania felt a flutter of resolve inside her. "I can do it."

CHAPTER 12

Melania Stone didn't turn or move the switchblade from Billy's neck as the sirens grew louder still. Doors slammed, the sound muffled by the trees. Flashing blue light glinted in the distance.

She had picked Billy up at a bar in Laredo, pretending to be lost and vulnerable, like the girls that attracted vermin like Billy Cavalli. When he tried to rape her, he got a nasty surprise.

Melania pushed the tip of the knife against Billy's chin again, forcing his head back.

"Right now is a good time, Billy. Where is your truck?"

Billy licked his lips, eyes moving wildly from side to side. "You're an FBI agent," he said in a hoarse voice. "You can't pull a stunt like this. I can complain. I have rights."

"Does attempted rape sound like a right to you, asshole?"

"My word against yours."

"With your previous two felonies of violent sexual assault, who do you think the judge will believe?"

Billy was silent. He had almost given up, so Melania went in for the kill.

"We have all the surveillance evidence against you, going back three months. This time, we picked you up on a drone feed ten miles outside Laredo. A joint task force of CIA Human Trafficking and Policia Federal of Panama tracked you getting into a Panama port and coming out with a truck full of women and children. You want me to carry on?"

Billy squeezed his eyes shut and swore.

Melania eased the knife slightly. She said, "You want a deal with the prosecutor, Billy? I suggest you cooperate. This can get you locked up for a very, very long time." She tried not to smile. "And do you know what happens to child abusers in prison?"

Fear flickered across Billy's face.

Footsteps sounded behind them. Melania was still astride Billy's chest. "Where is the truck?"

Billy closed his eyes and opened them. "There's a J.C. Penney that shut down last year. Near the highway."

Melania stood as two men in suits ran up to them, with three patrol officers in tow. The men in suits were her colleagues in the CIA Human Trafficking task force. Melania filled them in quickly. They sprinted back to the car and drove out.

Melania checked her weapon of choice, a Glock 22, as the agents drove. She didn't know what they were going to find at the truck, but there was every chance they would meet resistance. She rolled the window down, and humid, warm air, streaked with gasoline smell, brushed on her face, cooling her sweaty forehead. They went past empty streets with closed storefronts.

"There." Melania pointed, stretching her hand out the window. The darkened, giant hulk of a department store was dimly visible on her right. It was next to a large parking lot, and the yellow lights of the highway were strung out like a garland behind it.

She bounced her head against the roof of the car as they swung into the parking lot. The driver had killed the lights already. Melania slipped out, her weapon raised and ready.

"This way," she whispered. She had seen the vehicle even before the car had skidded to a halt. This was her sixth bust, and the pattern never changed. A twenty-foot-by-ten-foot shipping container stood on the back of a truck, facing away from them. Lights were off in the truck cabin. But that didn't mean it was unguarded.

Melania gestured in silence, and the two agents spread out to either side of her. Holding the Glock with her elbow ramrod straight, she approached the vehicle. The moon was lost in clouds, but there was a hazy glow from the highway. Her eyes were getting used to the dark, so she moved slowly. The cabin was still black, silent. She got to the back wheels and checked under the truck. It was empty. She wanted to take out her flashlight, but first, she needed to neutralize the truck cabin. She knew the two agents would monitor the shipping container.

She flattened herself against the container and put her ear against it. After several seconds, there was a muffled sound like a cough. Her jaw hardened, a pain slicing across her chest. Three months ago, a similar container had been opened to reveal rotting corpses. It was not an experience she wanted to repeat. She gestured to the agents, and they moved in closer. Melania peeked out the side. The large side mirror in the cabin meant the driver, if he was present, could see her. He could be waiting with a weapon.

She lifted her wrist to her lips and spoke into the microphone embedded in her watch.

"Approach cabin from passenger side. I need a distraction."

"Roger that," a male voice answered.

Melania gave him ten seconds to get into position. Then she counted down another five.

"Four Mississippi, five Mississippi," she whispered to herself and ran full tilt to the cabin. Within three seconds, she was scrambling up the driver's step, gun pointed at the cabin window. The glass remained rolled up. She flashed a light inside and saw her fellow agent doing the same on the other side. Momentarily, she was blinded. The twin lights swept the empty cabin. She yanked at the door. It was locked.

"Clear on the outside," her comms earphone chirped. That was her colleague checking out the perimeter of the parking lot. He must have called the patrol car as well, as she could hear faint sirens.

"Call 911. We need an ambulance," Melania said. She ran back to the container and, shoving the gun into her waistband, climbed up to work the levers. Her colleague, Watkins, helped. As the doors creaked open, she crinkled her nose at the terrible smell of sweat and urine. Human beings were corralled like animals in a pen. She shined her light inside, followed by Watkins.

It was a sorry sight. A mass of barely identifiable human forms lay heaped on the floor of the container. A few people had raised their heads to identify the source of the light. But most were so traumatized they had given up. Melania pulled surgical masks out of her pocket and handed one to Watkins. They both pulled on gloves.

"Stevens called the ambulance. Fifteen minutes ETA," Watkins said.

"Make sure it's more than one, preferably three," Melania said. "We'll take some in our car." She nodded at him. She knew she was going to see the very worst examples of how human beings could treat each other. She also knew there was no getting around it. Long ago, she had stopped wondering what made some men so evil. Poverty alone couldn't be the answer. She just had to accept it and move on. This part of the operation, the bust, was the most disturbing. It was far better to get it over and done with. She could consider her own feelings later. No, it didn't get any easier, no matter how many times she did it.

She went inside, feeling dizzy with the overpowering stench. Watkins and Stevens knew better than to try to help her. Melania always insisted on doing this part herself.

She spoke in Spanish. "You are in the United States of America. I am Special Agent Melania Stone of the CIA. We will look after you."

No one looked at her, save a row of teenagers at the back. Most had dirty, grimy, thin faces. They couldn't be any more than fourteen, she thought as a knife drew across her heart slowly. Most of the children looked like girls, and they either hugged or simply lay over each other. The smell of excrement and urine made her gag despite the mask. Fighting the revulsion and horror, Melania picked her way over the moaning bodies. If they could make sounds, it meant they were alive. That was something.

She squatted in front of one of the girls and took her pulse. It was fast, more than one hundred beats per minute. The basic first aid she knew meant this child was dehydrated. Her forehead was hot to the touch. Her large brown eyes were drooping, but she managed to look back at Melania. A row of headlights appeared as the patrol cars swung into the parking lot.

"What's your name?" Melania asked.

Her lips moved without a sound. Her eyes dropped again, and she licked her dry, cracked lips. Melania leaned in, smelling the odor of waste and misery rise around her like a shroud. She allowed herself to be smothered in it. She draped her arms around the girl's stick-thin shoulders and lifted her. The girl resisted, but she was weak.

"Shh, honey, it's OK," Melania whispered. "I got you."

The bony shoulder blades protruded into her arms. She picked her way to the entrance then squatted. Two of the patrol officers reached out and took the girl from her then lowered her onto a gurney.

Melania turned her flashlight on the remaining teenagers, the beam moving from one face to the other. Then she moved to the bodies on the floor.

From the ground, Stevens and Watkins watched her. Stevens whispered, "Why does she do this each time?"

Watkins shrugged. "Beats me."

Stevens shook his head. "It's like she's looking for someone."

CHAPTER 13

MELANIA – THEN

Eleven-year-old Marinochka shivered as she stood in the breadline. Her *shapka*, or hat, had twisted to one side, so she straightened it with a gloved hand. The snow was coming down in pelts again. Mother had taught her to spit in the cold. If the spit crackled, it meant it was cold enough not to go out at night. Winter in Tver seemed to last for the whole year. Marinochka didn't mind. When the snow was piled up everywhere, school was shut down early. The river, the Volga, became a solid sheet of ice, like a white playground. She could skate on it with her friends, as long as the men had done it first and put down red flags where they said it was safe.

Her mother, Aloyna, had slapped her the first time she went to skate on the river without asking her. Then, Marinochka hadn't known about the red flags. Aloyna had dragged her to the riverside, with her infant sister in the baby carriage. She had pointed out the flags and made Marinochka promise she would never go to the river without knowing where the red flags were. That had been two years ago. Marinochka now knew better.

Which was why she was getting impatient in the line. Flakes of snow brushed against her eyelashes, and she swiped at them irritably. Misha and the rest of the crew were waiting by the river, and they wanted to start a game of soccer. Marinochka was one of the best in her year at school, and she often played with the boys.

The wizened *babushka* in front of her shuffled forward painfully. Marinochka followed as the whole line moved up. After what seemed like an impossible wait, she got to the counter. Two red-faced bakers were pulling trays out of a wooden oven and arranging the bread loaves according to size and color. Marinochka preferred the *chorni khleb*, or black bread. It had a slightly tangy taste but was moister, like a cake that wasn't sweet. She wanted to buy a loaf of white bread as well, but Aloyna had only given her money for one and permission to buy Marinochka's favorite. She knew her mother didn't like it that much but ate it in silence because they didn't have money for two loaves of bread. She also knew Mama put a quarter of the loaf away to feed her baby sister. One and a half loaves of bread had to last the whole week. That, with potato and onion soup, was their lunch and dinner. Breakfast was leftovers from the night before—a few crumbs of bread and cold soup.

Marinochka clutched her mother's cold hand as she bent her head and said prayers before eating. Each prayer Marinochka whispered was for more food. Some of her friends had reindeer meat, pork, and sausage every night. Every night! Marinochka had lost count of the days since she'd had meat. It must be more than three months. When she told Aloyna, she got scolded. Apparently, God didn't want to hear about her food cravings. Marinochka had grimaced. What on earth did God want to hear about, then?

"What do you want, kid?" the burly baker asked. Rudolph had a prominent nose with lots of red veins on it. The name Rudolph the Red-Nosed Baker had stuck. Marinochka suppressed a giggle.

"One *chorni khleb*."

Marinochka got the milk as well from the store next door and walked longingly past the butcher's shop, eyeing the meat hanging from hooks. She saw a man leaning against the yellow wall of the shop. He was picking at his teeth with a hand red from the cold. Marinochka found it odd that he would stand outside and do this, as she had once seen Aloyna do after a meal. The man had chubby red cheeks and blond whiskers that sprouted wildly on his face. She didn't like his eyes. They were very light colored, so pale they almost didn't have any color in them. The man stared back her, and she looked away, remembering what Mama had said about looking at men on the street.

She walked up the hill, puffing, with the bag hanging from her hand. Neighbors had spread grit on the ice, and without it, walking up would be impossible. She reached their house and knocked on the door.

"Where have you been?" Aloyna stood in the doorway, hands on her hips, a frown on her face. "Little Michka is hungry, and I have nothing to give her but water."

Marinochka was scared when mama was like this, but she was also offended. It wasn't her fault the line at the bakers' had been so long.

Before she could explain, Aloyna had grabbed the bag from her hand. She disappeared inside the tiny apartment. "Shut the door," she ordered without looking back.

Marinochka closed the door and pouted. She couldn't hear little Michka crying. *Bet you mama said that to make me feel guilty.*

It was dark inside, the only light coming from the candle in the kitchen. That was the warmest room in the frigid one-bedroom apartment, and luckily the bedroom was next to the kitchen.

Marinochka stood by the kitchen door and watched as Aloyna boiled some milk then tore some bread and mixed it in a pot. Michka was barely two years old. She was strapped in a high chair, waving her hands in excitement as Aloyna brought a spoon to her lips. She ate greedily.

"Can I go and play?" Marinochka asked. She noticed her mother stiffen then relax.

"It's getting late. No more than two hours of daylight left. Do you know how cold it's going to be tonight?"

"I'll only be an hour, Mama. I promise," Marinochka whined.

Aloyna fed Michka one more time then turned around. Candlelight flickered on her face, showing the sunken, starved cheeks, the jutting, thin chin. But the eyes, dark and drawn into their sockets, were kind. Mama was strict, but she was her mama, and Marinochka knew how much she loved her.

"It'll take you fifteen minutes to walk to the river and another fifteen back. You cannot play any more than thirty minutes." Aloyna glanced at the clock next to the stove. "It's four thirty. You must be back in one hour. I cannot come looking for you, Marinochka. You know I can't leave the baby alone."

Marinochka shook her head vigorously. "Don't worry, Mama. One of the boys wears a wristwatch. I will ask him the time."

CHAPTER 14

MELANIA – THEN

The Volga was a curling snake of white, with black, yellow, and red dots on it. The colorful dots moved around, some skating, others kicking a ball around. Some just stood and watched. Marinochka ran as fast as she could, having taken her time to get down the hill. The screams and shouts of the children grew louder in her ears as she came up to the stairs that led down to the frozen river. Breath curling around her face, she stepped off the grass verge and jumped onto the hard ice. It felt as solid as the road but slippery. Her boots were good for ice, but falling on ice was almost customary. It made everyone laugh, if nothing else.

She saw the knot of boys in one corner, and Misha, taller than the rest, turned around and saw her. She waved and walked over. Her school buddies, Natalya and Irena, were there as well. She told Misha, who wore a watch, that she had to leave in half an hour. The match started without delay. There was light in the sky still, but Marinochka knew by six p.m., it would be getting dark. After six thirty, the roads were deserted in their small town. On a cold night like this, even the taverns were shut. Some lit fires outside their houses, and others joined them for sliced sausage and vodka.

Marinochka ran around energetically, sliding and tackling the boys when they got away from her. She liked sports but was too thin to be good at it. She made up for it with enthusiasm. Time passed quickly, and she bumped into Misha when he grabbed her arm.

"You told me to remind you of the time," he gasped, cheeks and nose bright crimson.

"What time is it?"

"Almost five thirty."

Her heart sank. She would be late, and Mama would be angry. "Misha, I have to go."

"But the game is still going on."

"Never mind. You guys carry on. I'll see you later." She whistled at Natalya and Irena, and they came running. She caught Misha looking at her. He was older than her by a year and taller. Floppy brown hair fell over his eyes, and he brushed it away.

"I can walk you home," he said, not meeting her eyes. Misha didn't know what to say. It was the first time a boy had asked to walk her home. It would be nice, but if Mama saw... not worth it.

"Thank you, Misha. But the girls are here. I'll walk home with them now. Maybe next time?"

Misha looked at her wistfully as her friends appeared. "Sure." He turned around and went back to the game.

The three girls climbed onto the grass verge and clambered their way to the steps, stomping over the softer snow. Irena made a snowball and threw it at Marinochka, who ran away, giggling. At the steps, she saw a man leaning against the stone, staring at them. The man caught her eyes because he was standing so still. Lack of movement on a cold day like this was unusual. Feet turned numb quickly. As she got closer, her heart skipped a beat. It was the same man she had seen outside the butcher's shop earlier. He wore the same long black coat and a velvety blue *shapka*. Their eyes met once again, and a shiver passed down Marinochka's spine.

She looked at her friends and settled on walking between them. They passed within an arm's length of the man, and she could feel his eyes on her. She didn't dare look.

When Marinochka knocked on the door, she expected the worst. She must be at least twenty minutes late. The door flung open, spilling meager warmth outside. Aloyna grabbed her shoulders and folded her into a hug. Marinochka hugged her back, surprised.

"You had me scared, *lapochka*. Why are you late?" Aloyna's voice was soft, like the candlelight moving their shadows on the wall. She closed the door firmly and locked it.

"I'm sorry, Mama."

"Come and eat."

They sat at the table in the kitchen and ate from dull steel plates. Marinochka wolfed down her share of the bread, dipping it in the onion soup. She noticed at the end that more than half the bread was gone. She blamed her appetite. She also noticed mama only nibbled at her bread, not eating much.

"Aren't you hungry?" Marinochka asked.

"I had some already," Mama said. Marinochka knew when her mother was lying. Aloyna worked as a seamstress in the local cloth factory, sewing coats for the army. One of their neighbors, a buxom lady called Rustova, looked after little Michka the four days Aloyna worked. The other three days, Aloyna looked after Rustova's baby son. Marinochka knew her mother couldn't work more, as her sister was so little. That gave her an idea.

"Mama, maybe I should leave school and look for work."

Aloyna looked up sharply from her soup bowl. "What are you talking about?"

"Well, if I worked after school or on the weekend…"

"After school, you have homework, and on the weekend, you help me with Michka. Have you forgotten that?"

"No, but…"

"No buts, Marinochka. Education is the most important thing for you. Look at all the girls who work in the factories. They have no future. It's a dead-end job. You want to do that for the rest of your life?"

They'd had this conversation before. Marinochka wanted to work, and Aloyna insisted on school and college. She knew why, but it seemed unfair for Mama to work so hard for so little. It reminded her of the rent due in two weeks' time. She swirled the spoon in her soup and thought about asking the question to which she never received an answer.

Why can't you ask our father?

When she was younger, Mama had told her their father was dead. When she asked her now, Marinochka never got an answer. She had never seen her father and had come to accept that she never would.

Mama got up and put her bowl in the sink with a thud. She only did that when she was annoyed, Marinochka knew. She finished her food then untied the hair band in her ponytail. It was red with a green dragon on it. It was made in China and, like many Chinese items, popular in Russia. She put the band on her wrist.

"We need bread for tomorrow," she said as Aloyna walked past her.

"I'll get it. Now do your homework."

Marinochka stole into the bedroom to retrieve her schoolbag. Michka was snoring in her crib. Marinochka leaned over and kissed her sister's chubby cheeks. She loved their softness. Michka stirred, and Marinochka moved away quickly. It took a while to put Michka to sleep, and waking her would incur Mama's wrath again.

Marinochka sat down at the kitchen table. As she put her books on the table, she could see Aloyna counting money and putting it in her gown pocket. Marinochka knew there wasn't enough money to buy bread tomorrow. That money would go for the rent. She made her mind up. What Mama didn't know wouldn't make her angry. Marinochka needed to find a job.

CHAPTER 15

Hanlon Park
Baltimore
PRESENT DAY

Dias Dashev watched the three young men from the office window on the second floor of the mosque. They parked the car on the street opposite the mosque and got out of the car slowly. They stretched, which was reasonable given they had just made a long journey from Jacksonville, Florida. Dias doubted it was a signal of any kind. He spoke on the radio to a car that had picked up the teenagers' vehicle as it came off the ramp from the interstate south of Baltimore. That car, which had followed the teenagers all the way to Hanlon Park, was now parked three blocks away.

"They're here."

"What do you want me to do?" asked Rashid, the driver.

"Did anyone follow you or them?"

"No."

Dias hung up. He watched the street carefully. A GMC Yukon was parked opposite the halal butcher shop, and a Ford cargo van was loading materials into a shop front. Both had been there for a while. He couldn't see a van that looked as if it had an FBI listening lab built inside it. He had seen the GMC Yukon before and checked out its Maryland license plate. It belonged to a family who lived close by. It was clean. But his mind remained murky, disturbed. His main organizer, Terambutov, had been arrested in New York in an undercover sting operation. The fool had a taste for women, and he couldn't keep his dick inside his pants. Now he was heading for Gitmo, and that meant the whole operation had to be brought forward to... right now.

He spoke on the phone again. "Come closer, but stay outside the mosque. Are you armed?"

"Yes, Sheikh."

"Monitor closely. Call me on this number if you see anything unusual. OK?"

"Yes."

Dias lowered the satellite phone slowly as he watched the three teenagers cross the street and enter the mosque. The one in front was blond, freckly, with the gangly arms and slouched posture of a nineteen-year-old. That would be Matthew, the youngest. The other two were similarly built, wearing baggy clothes, perfectly ordinary young adults at whom no one would cast a second look on the street.

Dias went down the corridor and into the office next to the staircase. He could hear the three young men being ushered in. He opened the office door and walked in. The chubby cheeks of Mullah Shahab Barakat glistened with sweat despite the air-conditioning. His plump body rested easily on the armchair, his fat gut propped up against the table.

"They're here," Dias said.

The mullah, or teacher, leaned forward with a grunt and retrieved the glasses from the glass-top table. The office was small and cramped. Shelves stacked with books on sharia or Islamic law leaned against the wall. Framed photos of Mecca, with engravings of holy scriptures from the Quran, adorned the wall. Shahab put his glasses on which promptly slid down to the middle of his sweaty nose.

The knock came, and Shahab said in a high-pitched voice, "Come in."

The three men entered. Matthew was their leader, a small goatee on his face. James and Ahmed were the other two. All three were American, born and bred. They went to the same high school in a suburb of Jacksonville, and Matthew and James had converted to Islam, unbeknownst to their parents. The two men now prayed in the same mosque as Ahmed. It was Matthew, and not Ahmed, who had found Mulla Shahab's Salafist teaching first on Facebook. All three had quickly become his disciples.

James, the first one in, looked at Shahab reverentially then whispered, "*Aysalaam Aleykoum.*"

"*Aleykoum Aysalaam,*" Shahab intoned. He didn't stand up. He knew his

45

height was disappointing, and while on the chair, his girth was more obvious.

"*Aleykoum Salaam,*" James whispered.

Dias said nothing. He stood in the corner behind the door quietly, face impassive. His pale, expressionless eyes observed the faces of the new recruits closely. These men would carry out the largest attack against the western world, to date. He needed to be sure of them. Normally, Dias would have hand-picked such men himself, and he would have preferred them to be from his native land, Dagestan. But his master, Aliev Daurov, had been insistent. The mullah had also been vocal, claiming how he had radicalized the boys over months, and their chosen path in life was of a Salafist.

The three men embraced their teacher, emotion writ large on their faces.

"Have a seat," Shahab said, wiping his forehead with his handkerchief. He glanced at Dias, who ignored him.

Shahab said to Matthew, "Your new name is Mortaza al-Amriki." He smiled slightly. "Do you like it?"

Matthew nodded, a nervous smile on his lips.

"*Bismillah Rahman-i-rahim,*" Shahab said, pleased.

Dias watched the men fidget for a while then asked his first question.

"Are you ready for what faces you?"

Matthew, the long-limbed one, nodded. He was the one who looked the most composed, which was a good sign, thought Dias.

"Yes, we are," Matthew said.

"Then tell me what you have to do."

Matthew seemed to be the de facto spokesman for the group. He went through the outline of the plan. Dias listened without interrupting. He was aware that Shahab was watching him anxiously. As the chief radicalizer, Shahab had a lot to prove. His supply chain of young jihadis had been faltering of late. If these three men went on to become martyrs, money and influence would be heaped at Shahab's door. If not, he needed to find a new job.

Dias fixed his eyes on each one of the young men. They held his eyes, but it wasn't easy holding Dias's gaze. Anyone looking at him felt as if they were looking right through him. One by one, they dropped their gazes to the floor.

Dias approached Ahmed and stood in front of him. He pulled a Glock out of his pocket, flicked the safety off, and handed him the weapon butt first. Ahmed looked up at him, mouth open, eyes wide. His brown eyes searched Dias's face.

"Go on," Dias said. "Take it."

Ahmed swallowed and took the gun in his right hand. His two friends looked at him, gaping. Dias could hear Shahab breathing heavily behind him.

Dias asked the men, "Are you all ready for the path of the jihadist Salafist?"

The men looked at each other then at Dias. All of them nodded.

Dias looked at Ahmed, his strange eyes blank and devoid of all the emotion that was suddenly evident in his voice.

"Ahmed, will you do anything to fulfil your destiny?" Dias said, his voice rising.

"Brother Dias, I think..." Shahab interrupted.

"Be quiet." Dias said, cutting him off without looking back. His eyes were focused on Ahmed. "Are you ready, my brother?"

"Yes, I am," Ahmed said eagerly, breathing fast and heavy.

Dias pointed a finger at James, who sat next to Ahmed. "Then shoot him."

Dias might as well have slapped Ahmed across the face. The young man's jaw dropped, and his lips trembled. His eyes were like saucers as he stared at his friend. Then both men turned their necks slowly to look at Dias.

"I said shoot him!" Dias shouted. As his voice faded, there was silence in the room, punctuated by noisy breathing.

Ahmed looked at the gun in his hand and lifted it. His hand shook as he pointed it at James. Ahmed's face was red, contorted, sweat pouring down his forehead. Then his head hung forward, and the gun slumped down.

Dias snarled in rage. "You fool! Call yourself a jihadi and can't fulfil a single order?" He reached forward and took the weapon from Ahmed's limp hand. He pointed the gun at James and pulled the trigger. The men cried out and cowered on the sofa.

The hammer clicked on the empty chamber. Seven times. Dias threw the gun on the floor.

"It was empty, you idiots! Living in America has made you soft. You cowards."

The three recruits stared in disbelief at the gun on the floor. Dias reached inside his coat and pulled out a new Glock 19 from his shoulder holster. Patiently, he took a suppressor out of his pocket and threaded it into the gun.

Shahab spoke from behind him. He scraped his chair back and stood up. "Brother Dias, these boys need more training."

Dias turned around and shot Shahab twice in the chest. The fat man slumped back on the chair, a red patch spreading on his white garment. Dias swivelled quickly and pulled the trigger three times, hitting each of the men in the face. All three slumped on the sofa, Matthew at the edge, rolling to the floor, dead before he hit the carpet.

CHAPTER 16

Dias Dashev picked up his sat phone and called Rashid. "Come up to the mullah's office now. Do you still have the body bags in the trunk?"

"Yes."

"Bring five of them. Get the SUV out of the parking lot. Be quick."

Dias hung up and frisked the men quickly. He took their wallets and, from Matthew, the car keys. He searched Shahab and found the roll of fifty-dollar bills Dias had given him the night before. Then he opened the drawers of the desk and put papers into a backpack. He also took the laptop from the desk. His phone beeped. He checked the number and answered immediately.

"It's me," Dias said.

Aliev Daurov's voice was heavy, raspy from too many cheap cigarettes. "How are the new recruits?"

"They were useless. Couldn't carry out a direct order."

There was silence. Daurov said, "Have you taken care of them?"

"Yes, including Shahab. He will not bother us anymore."

"Good. No loose strings on this operation."

"I know."

After another pause, Daurov said, "You will have to do it yourself now, Dias."

"I never saw any other way. No one can be trusted with a task this important."

Daurov grunted. "On your way, come back to Sardinia. I need to see you before you leave."

"Of course."

"Remember, no loose ends."

Dias hung up. There was a knock on the door. He drew his gun and put his ear to the wood.

"Who is it?" he asked.

"Rashid."

Dias opened the door a fraction, gun hidden from sight. Rashid was alone, the body bags folded under his right arm.

Dias opened the door wider, and Rashid stepped in. He took in the macabre sight inside and breathed in sharply. He looked at Dias and nodded. Dias locked the door while Rashid got busy with the bags.

Dias asked, "How many people are downstairs in the mosque?"

"Slowly filling up for afternoon prayers. But we can use the side entrance. I came up that way."

They worked quickly, packing the bodies. The three young men were heavy but manageable. Shahab's figure was much heavier, and it took both of them, resting frequently, to take him down to the SUV in the rear parking lot.

"Safe house?" Rashid said as he turned the ignition keys.

Dias looked at him. "Not with the bodies. Hit the dump on the way."

"Sorry," Rashid said.

The dump was a half-hour drive, and traffic was heavy. It took them an hour to get there and to drive to a secluded spot. They repeated the process backwards, throwing the bags down a rolling hill of garbage.

They were both soaked with sweat by the time they finished. Rashid scratched his head. "What's the fifth bag for?"

Dias pulled out his Glock and pointed it at Rashid. "You." He shot the middle-aged man three times in the chest, sending him tumbling backwards into the rubbish heap.

CHAPTER 17

Father Peter Deakins was having a busy day. He had two weddings planned at St Mary's Church, his own parish. One after the other. Joyous events though they were, it was stifling hot in Owings Mills, a few miles northeast of Baltimore. Owings Mills was a slice of suburbia, scattered with two-story single-family homes with green front and back lawns, and three well-reputed high schools.

It was where Father Deakins had grown up. He had felt the calling from a young age, but with advancing years, the epiphanies had shown him the path. His life would be one of service to God. Like his local church, he was staunchly Roman Catholic.

Everything changed last year when Bishop Recker died suddenly at the age of sixty-five. He had been the bishop at Four Springs, a larger diocese near Owings Mills. A vacancy was created, and Father Deakins felt it calling to him, just as he had heard the calling of God as a teenager. Now God was calling him from a higher place—the Vatican, the ultimate destination of any Catholic priest.

Deakins spoke Italian fluently, having taken classes at college and then a sabbatical year to work as a secretary for one of the Roman Curia Cardinals at the Vatican.

He was quietly confident now, as the bishops in Maryland, Washington, and New Jersey met to select bishop nominees from the local pool of priests. He was on the list, as he had figured. The list was sent to the Apostolic Nuncio, the USA's ambassador to the Vatican.

Unknown to Father Deakins and out of sheer luck or divine Providence, some would say, the cardinal at the head of the Congress of Bishops this year was the same cardinal under whom young Deakins had served as a part-time secretary all those years ago. Deakins's name was *numero uno* on the list sent to the Supreme Pontiff, the Holy See—the pope himself.

The pope received thousands of bishop applications every month, from all over the world. In reality, his team of cardinals at the Curia made a list for him, and he glanced over it to give his final word. The Holy See's eyes were drawn to one line the head cardinal had written—Peter Deakins was the only candidate this year who knew the internal workings of the Curia already. The decision was an easy one.

Today, as Father Deakins, soon to be Bishop Deakins, busied himself with his many duties, he couldn't help but smile at the secret pride he felt within. His father had been right. He would make the Deakins name proud, and in his own way. After the weddings, he had to attend the local council of bishops for a congratulatory lunch. As bishops were only appointed by the pope, it was a time of great importance for any clergyman.

Deakins headed home in his Ford Taurus, humming along to Beethoven's *Moonlight Sonata* as he drove. He parked his car at his one-story bungalow-style residence located within Baltimore, in a neighborhood where crime was high and break-ins frequent. His house had never been broken into, and his simple, pious lifestyle had not gone unnoticed by the council of bishops.

Still humming the tune, Deakins opened the door to his bungalow and stepped inside. He didn't expect, or see, the hand that clamped over his mouth. He heard the door shut as someone kicked it. Then he was thrown forward. Deakins was a reasonably well-built man, five feet eleven and one hundred seventy pounds. But he was no match for the man who shoved him on the floor then stood over him.

The man switched a light on, and his face became visible. Fear stricken and breathing heavily, Deakins balanced himself with one hand on the floor and raised the other entreatingly.

"Please, I am a man of God. Take my material possessions if you must. But leave me in peace."

Deakins noticed the man was very fair, with blond hair. Even his eyes were colorless, blank. Deakins shivered as he realized he could barely look at the man's eyes. They didn't seem to exist, and he had the impression he was looking right through him. The man smiled. Then he became serious, closed his eyes, and started to mutter something in a foreign tongue.

The man opened his strange eyes. They seemed to glow in the light from the ceiling. Fear coiled inside Deakins's gut like a serpent, fangs bared.

The man spoke. "My name is Dias Dashev. Remember that in the afterlife."

For some reason, the man looked familiar to Deakins. Then he realized. His eyes widened. "But you are…"

The man nodded. "Yes, you are right."

Deakins's throat was parched. "Wh-who are you?" he managed to stutter.

A black object appeared in the man's hand, and for the first time in his life, Peter Deakins found himself staring at the muzzle of a gun. It was only for a few seconds. Two bullets spat out from the weapon, cannoning into the chest of Father Deakins. Pain exploded inside him, and his vision dimmed to black. His head crashed into the floor.

CHAPTER 18

Sardinia
CIA Black Ops Site

A sudden, sharp pain like a sting awoke the Scorpion. Darkness rolled across her eyes, and her body jolted as if it were being tossed in a storm at sea. The sting came again, and she moaned with pain. There was warmth on her face, and distant voices floated to her ears. Her eyelids remained stubbornly shut. With effort, she tried to blink. Light sent daggers of pain searing into her skull. A rough hand yanked her head up by pulling on her hair.

"Drink this," a voice said in English.

A glass was held to her lips, and she tasted water. Nausea lurched inside her, and she moved her head and vomited. Gray-green, saline fluid came out of her mouth. She was strapped to a chair, and her head rolled forward. The warmth returned to her face, and she realized someone was holding her face up.

"Can you hear me?" the same voice asked. It came from a distance, and she couldn't see much. Natasha blinked, but her vision swam, going out of focus.

"Hey!" a closer voice barked. Natasha winced as the sound sent waves crashing through her head.

"He asked you a question," the voice repeated from close quarters.

She lifted her head and opened her eyes despite the pain. She was in a room with gray concrete walls. The only light came in through a grill window at the top. A flash of memory appeared in her mind. She remembered getting hit, falling into the sea... and now this. The pain in her left shoulder was sharp, and she felt it increase when she tried to move her hands. Her arms, like her body and legs, were tied by thick nylon rope to the chair. She flexed her fingers to get some blood flowing.

Her clothes were dry. A quick glance told her she still wore the same black tights and vest as before. She couldn't tell what state her shoulder was in, but it wasn't bleeding. A bandage was plastered over it. She opened her eyes wider and focused. Two men in brown uniforms stood on either side of the room. In front of her and to the rear of the room, a man perched on a bare desk and observed her curiously. The legs of the metal desk were screwed to the floor. The man wore a black shirt and dark slacks. She couldn't make out his features clearly—her eyes were still hazy.

"Give her some more water," the man said.

The guard standing behind Natasha brought the glass to her lips again. She glanced up at his face. Flat, deep-set black eyes stared back at her without emotion. She looked at the glass then bent her neck to drink from it. The nausea was playing up still, but she was thirsty. This time she managed to keep some down. Her chin dropped to her chest, exhaustion suddenly overcoming her.

"Hope you feel better now," the man opposite her said. Natasha didn't have the strength to raise her face to him. Her mind was blank. She didn't know what to say. Like a flashlight moving in a dark room, spots of memory appeared and vanished: The boy's face, his curly brown hair, and astonished blue eyes. The needle, stabbing into the man's neck. Killing the security guards. But she recalled nothing before that. It was as if her memory fell off a cliff, disappearing into a stomach-churning, vacant depth where her mind couldn't reach. She couldn't remember a thing.

Her eyes opened, and she stared down at her tied body. This was insane. She had just brutally killed a man. She had gotten into the yacht... the marina restaurant. She worked there. Her name... What was her name? Natasha. Yes, that was what it was. Natasha.

"Natasha," she murmured to herself. "I am Natasha."

"What did you say?" the man spoke sharply. She winced in pain as the guard yanked on her hair, which was a frizzled mess, falling around her shoulders.

Her eyes could focus more. The man was in his fifties, with a weather-beaten, craggy face. His cheeks were sunken, and his eyes glittered as they remained fixed on her.

"What is your name?"

Natasha swallowed the bile rising in her throat. These men were going to kill her. She felt sure of it. They were associated with the man she had killed on the yacht. They had brought her here for a reason, to pump her for information. But she had nothing to give them. The thought made her panic. She had to buy some time, find out more.

She cleared her throat. "Who... who are you?"

"I ask the questions," the man said in a steely voice. "What is your name?"

She had to give them something to keep the charade going. "Natasha."

"OK, Natasha. You know what you did, right?" She recognized the accent as being European but not British. English was not his mother tongue.

She remained silent. The man said, "You killed Mr. Andreyev then two men of our security detail." He gestured to the other three men in the room. Three that she could see, anyway. There could be more behind her.

"Men who were like brothers to these guys. They are angry, Natasha."

She was quiet but noticed the two tall, beefy guards in front stare with undisguised hostility.

"They want answers. So do I. We can do this the easy way. You tell us what we need to know."

"Then you kill me," she said. Her own accent was American. It made sense to think she was American. But apart from her name and country and the recent events, she couldn't remember anything else.

"Whether we kill you or not is not your choice anymore. It is our decision. But you can choose how you die. If you give us more information, I promise a quick, painless death."

"Thanks." She raised her eyebrows. "Is that all I get?"

"Think about your situation. What more do you expect?"

She narrowed her eyes. She wanted to ask them why they were protecting a Russian businessman. But the question didn't seem appropriate now. She needed to find out more about who Andreyev was. She knew the answer. It was hidden somewhere in the recesses of her mind.

But first things first. If she didn't escape from here, even if her memory did come back, it would be of no help.

CHAPTER 19

The blow came suddenly, blinding her with an explosion of pain. The man behind her grabbed her hair and pulled her head back. Her breath came in harsh gasps, and for a few seconds, she couldn't see again.

"Speak," the order came. The man opposite her had come forward now, and she saw him with his hands on his hips, feet spread apart.

A sharp, cool object slid down her neck, lifting up her chin. She knew it was a knife. It forced her to look the leader in the eyes.

"Who sent you?" he asked.

She shook her head, and he reached out suddenly and grabbed her chin. His thick fingers pressed on her cheeks.

His voice was soft yet menacing. "You really want to do this?"

She didn't reply. He let go of her face and slapped her twice in quick succession. A trickle of blood appeared at the corner of her left lip. She stared at him, jaw clenched. Unexpectedly, she smiled. There was warmth inside her, suffusing her guts, spreading into the tips of her limbs. The pain gripping her head and the sting from the slaps reduced as the wave of heat flared inside her like a thousand candles being lit all at once. She recognized this feeling. She knew it as she felt the blood in her veins.

It was anger. Rage was burning inside her, and she would make these men pay.

The leader smiled at her. His dark eyes remained cold and glittering. A few strands of his blond hair fell over his forehead.

"You're a badass, huh?" His accent had slipped, and he sounded American. He changed quickly, back to the heavy, guttural south European accent, but the damage had been done.

"Are you British intelligence? Mossad? Who sent you?" he repeated.

Natasha said, "This is getting a bit boring, isn't it?"

He straightened slowly. "OK. Have it your way." He turned to his men.

"String her up." With that cryptic command, he turned and left the room. Natasha was hauled to her feet. A knife slashed the ropes tying her legs, and she was marched out of the room. The guards filed out in front, and the man behind her pushed her along. The corridor was the same drab gray concrete walls, unpainted. This was no official prison cell. No government would claim this. She wondered where she was.

She was pushed into a larger room on the left. The floor was slick with water. She saw two hose pipes emerge from taps on the walls on either side. The men took up positions alongside them. A horizontal bar traversed the room, high enough to tie and hang a human being from. A sense of unease was spreading inside her. But she hadn't expected anything else.

The guard behind her stepped in front. He gave her a shit-eating grin then showed her the knife. The blade was long and hooked, and her eyes focused on the serrated edge. Something about the knife sparked a memory inside her. She frowned, trying to remember.

The guard seemed to read her mind. "Yeah, this is yours, bitch." He turned the kukri knife around in his fingers. "One hell of a knife, I gotta say."

Like meteors colliding, images and sounds exploded in her brain. Thoughts and words tripped against each other like switches on a circuit board. Sparks of electricity jolted her mind.

The Red Chamber. Her training as an assassin. The pale face of her first victim, looking up at her with a hole in his forehead. How distant, dispassionate she felt as she looked at the dead man. Like an avalanche, more memories cascaded upon her.

Dan Roy—the man who wielded the flashing blade as if it were an extension of his hand. She stared at the shining tip of the knife, remembering everything all at once. She closed her eyes and gasped.

She was the Scorpion.

Her hands were tied behind her back, but she felt the fingers tighten into fists. Her eyes flew open.

The guard had lost his smile and was regarding her with a frown. He shook his head and used the kukri to slice down her vest. The knife glided down it, not puncturing the slash-resistant material. He renewed his efforts, grimacing.

With one hand, he pulled the black material, lifting it off her body. With the other, he tried to cut down it.

Natasha said, "It's made of magnetized ions."

The man gaped at her.

She said, "They oppose almost all metallic surfaces, like the opposite poles of a magnet."

"Say what?"

He was dumb, that much was obvious. She decided to take a chance. "I can take this off. I need to anyway because I need to pee." She did her best pleading expression. "Please. I need the bathroom."

He shook his head and turned away. He called to the other two men in the room. Both came forward and stood on either side of her.

"String her up," he said.

In a flash, she understood. They would tie her to the horizontal bar and leave her hanging. The original aim must have been to have her naked and jet spray her with cold water. But it wasn't easy to take her black one-piece off. It was like a wet suit, molded to her body. They would unzip the back, but to do that, they would have to free her arms first.

She felt the plastic cuffs coming off her wrists. She rotated them, letting blood circulate. The two men had grabbed her arms in viselike grips. The guard with the knife now had a gun in his left hand, pointed at her.

He gave a sick grin. "Undress her, boys."

She heard the guard to her right snicker, then she felt his hand roaming on her back. Her hands were free. So were her legs. It was a schoolboy error on the part of her captors.

Her right leg shot up, the foot catching the wrist that held the gun. The movement was a blur, and the guard saw it coming, but she knew his orders were not to shoot her. At this close range, a shot would be fatal, and her secrets would die with her. Even if he did shoot, she had hedged her bets.

Before her foot hit the gun, she crouched and in the same movement bent her elbows and crossed her arms powerfully. The guards on either side, holding on to her arms, stumbled forward. Their grip on her slipped. She caught the man on her right, her hand snaking into his belt holster and withdrawing his weapon. It felt light, like a Glock.

Using the man's body as a shield, she fired. The bullet caught the guard in the chest, sending him flying backwards. The sound of the suppressed weapon was sharp but light. The kukri fell from his hands. She shoved the man she was holding then kicked him in the back. He tumbled onto his friend, and both collapsed in a heap. She shot twice, aiming for the midsection, then surged forward and finished the kill with two head shots. Both bodies shook once and then stilled.

Natasha crouched and looked around. The door was shut, and she had gotten lucky with the suppressed weapon. A loud bang would have given her away. In any case, her trouble had just begun. She knew nothing about this place and had to find her way out.

She picked the kukri up and stuck it in her belt at her back. She took all three handguns and checked their mags. All were Glock 22s.

The knock on the door was soft at first. Then it was louder.

She worked quickly. She grabbed the bodies and dumped them behind the door. She put her ear against the door, trying to control her breathing.

Then she saw the handle turning.

CHAPTER 20

Natasha flattened herself against the wall, bringing the gun up to face level. As the door opened, she slowly stretched her arm out. She had a dilemma. She couldn't kick the door shut—it would slam. The sound would alert someone at the end of the corridor. She imagined there would be someone on duty at every corner. Or there might be a desk.

In which case, she had to let the person enter the room and kill them on first sight.

"Hello?" It was a female voice. Natasha blanched. The blue uniform of a nurse appeared, and a blond ponytail. She was pushing a steel cart with medicine and syringes in front. Her head moved from side to side, taking in the empty room.

Natasha put the gun barrel against her temple and whispered urgently. "Don't say a word if you want to live. Understand?"

The nurse stopped in her tracks. Natasha repeated her question. The nurse nodded rapidly. Natasha wasn't taking any chances. Just because this woman wore a nurse's uniform didn't mean she wasn't a lethal operator. In fact, tricks like that were precisely what Natasha used herself to fool people. Men, especially.

"Step inside," Natasha ordered. She shut the door with her foot, not removing the gun from the woman's head. "Feet apart. Hands on your head. Now."

The nurse did as she was told. Her body was trembling, which was a good sign. She wasn't faking her fear. Natasha moved the gun down her back as she squatted and searched the woman thoroughly. Then she pushed her forward. The nurse stood there with her back to Natasha.

"Turn around," Natasha said. She lifted the gun to point it at the woman's chest.

The nurse turned around. "*Dios mio,*" she gasped when she saw the weapon aimed at her. Her wide eyes went from the gun to Natasha.

Her skin was very tanned, and her brown hair was swept back in a ponytail. Her uniform came down to her knees, and she had white pumps on her feet. Natasha could tell this woman wasn't an operator. Either that, or she was an extremely good actress.

"Who are you?" Natasha asked, not moving the gun.

"I... I am the nurse," she said unnecessarily. Her eyes fell to the floor, behind Natasha. She gasped again, and her hand flew to her mouth.

Natasha lowered the gun a fraction and moved closer swiftly. "Look, I'm not going to hurt you. But these people were about to start torturing me. What is this place?"

The woman was still breathing heavily. Natasha lowered her gun completely but kept her finger on the trigger.

"What's your name?" she asked in a softer voice.

"Roberta."

"OK, Roberta. Look at me."

Their eyes met.

"I'm not going to hurt you. But if I stay here, these people will kill me. I need to get out of here. Do you understand?"

Roberta shook her head. She stepped back and crossed herself. "Who are you?"

"I will explain everything to you. I promise. First, show me how to get out of here." Natasha hoped her cajoling would work. If it didn't, she would have to go in harder, but she could tell Roberta was brittle. She didn't want the nurse to snap. She had to remind herself again that the woman could be acting. Oscar worthy, but acting nevertheless.

Roberta said, "There are guards everywhere. Cameras as well."

Once again, Natasha tried hard to place the accent. "Where are you from?"

"Here. The island."

Light dawned in Natasha's mind. Of course. She had been sent to the island of Sardinia for the beginning of her mission. "Sardinia."

Roberta nodded. "Si, Sardegna."

Natasha stepped closer. "Why are you working for these guys?"

"There was an advertisement in the local newspaper. They're looking for English-speaking nurses. The money was good, so I took the job. But…"

"But what?"

"It's strange here. Like a prison. They say they work for Sardinian Army, but no one speaks Italian. Most of them are American. They speak English."

Natasha nodded. "That's what I think as well."

Roberta lips quivered. "Look, I'm a single mom. I need to put my son through school and college. This job is all I have."

Natasha indicated the three men lying in a heap. "If I hadn't stopped them, these men would've tortured and then killed me. You want to work for them?"

Roberta was silent.

Natasha said, "Do you know anything else about them?"

"They hire other nurses from nearby towns. I don't know any of them. I just do my job and go home."

Natasha narrowed her eyes. "Is there a doctor here?"

"Yes." Roberta hesitated.

"You need to tell me. It could be important."

Roberta shook her head. "I don't even know who you are. I could get into bad trouble for this…" Her voice trailed off.

"I can help you. If it's money you need, then I can get that. First you need to tell me what you know."

"Why should I trust you?"

"Would you rather trust these men?" Natasha put the gun in her belt. "Look, we can't waste time anymore. I need to get out, with or without you."

Roberta's face was conflicted.

Natasha said, "Is there a guard at the end of the corridor?"

"Yes."

She had thought as much. "You said there are other nurses here. Do they have a changing room?"

"Yes."

"Where?"

"On the third, and top, floor. There's an elevator."

"Which floor are we on?"

"Ground level."

From Roberta, Natasha gleaned the layout of the place—a large compound with high walls, watchtowers in four corners, and electrified barbed wire. It sounded like one of two things: a training camp or a secret prison. The men here were protecting Andreyev, a Russian billionaire. Yet the men spoke in American accents. Russian and American interests diverged sharply, especially when it came to Europe. It made no sense that Americans would protect—then she remembered. Her brain was still cloudy, and thoughts, words, poked out suddenly like a figure appearing out of a dense fog.

She had been sent to silence Andreyev. He was close to the Russian premier but had sold out to the Americans. How exactly, Natasha didn't know. It wasn't her job to know. Andreyev had information that could hurt the Russians. So she had done her job. Now the Americans were after her.

She indicated the phone on the wall. "Can you use this to call the guard? Is there only one in the corridor?"

"Only one close by, yes."

"But he will see us as soon as we step out. Right, I want you to call him up here. Say the prisoner is sick and you need to take her up to the doctor's room. Make it sound urgent, like it's a life-or-death situation. Can you do that, Roberta?" Natasha took the gun from her belt and pointed it at the floor.

Roberta looked at the gun. "I don't have much of a choice, do I?"

"What do you think is the better choice? Staying here or leaving with me?"

"My son…"

"I will protect your son. You have my word."

She held Roberta's eyes. The woman's chest was heaving, and perspiration flowed down her forehead.

Natasha nodded towards the phone. "Do it now."

CHAPTER 21

Roberta swallowed hard and walked to the intercom on the wall, next to the door. She took the receiver in her hand. Natasha walked closer and put the muzzle of the gun against the nurse's head.

"I don't want to do this, Roberta, so don't make me."

The woman nodded, eyes as wide as saucers. She punched digits then pressed the receiver against her ear.

"Quick," she said in a high-pitched voice. "The patient has fainted. I need to take her to the doctor. I need help." She hung up without elaborating any further.

"Good work," Natasha said. "Now go and hide behind the door."

Natasha took up position opposite the door, staying under cover. The door opened, and the guard came in, mystified by the empty room. His boots stepped on the wet floor, and he stopped. Natasha kicked the door this time, slamming it shut.

"Don't do it," she said, weapon pointed at the man's chest.

He didn't have time to aim his rifle. He was of two minds. His eyes flicked from the dead bodies on the floor, to Natasha, then to the nurse behind her. He tightened his grip on the butt of his rifle.

"You can live or die. It's up to you," Natasha said.

The man hesitated then bent his knees, keeping his eyes on her. He put the gun down on the floor then stood with his hands raised.

"Take off your belt," Natasha said.

The man did as he was told. She stepped behind him. Before she picked up the belt, she hit him hard on the back of his scalp with the butt of the gun. The Glock's lightness meant she had to do it three times before his knees buckled and he collapsed. She worked quickly with the belt, tying his hands behind his back then pulling the belt down to attach it to his leg. She had to pull hard, bending his back. It was a stiff, uncomfortable position and a

65

difficult one to get out of. But at least he was alive. She used the kukri to rip out a section of his shirt and tied it around his mouth as a gag.

She kept an eye on Roberta, but the nurse simply watched her with fascination. Natasha finished and stood. She pointed at the medicine tray.

"What's in the syringe?"

"Sodium pentothal," Roberta said.

Natasha smiled. The chemical was used to induce sleep and confusion in subjects, in the hope they would speak the truth when interrogated. She picked up the syringe, made sure the cover was secure on the needle, and put it in her pants pocket.

She asked Roberta, "Are you sure there is no one else in the corridor?"

"Yes."

"OK. You go first, and I'll be right behind you. We head for the elevators and then to the nurses' changing room."

In her mind, Natasha calculated the risks. In order to minimize their chances of meeting anyone, they would have to move fast and rely on luck. She leaned out and checked the corridor on both sides. It was empty. The guard's empty chair at the end had still gone unnoticed. But it wouldn't be for long.

"Go," she whispered.

Roberta walked out, and Natasha crouched, stepping behind her. She made sure the door was firmly shut. They turned the corner and stopped in front of the elevator shaft. Roberta pressed the button and waited for the elevator to descend. Natasha flattened herself against the wall beside it. The kukri was in her left hand, Glock in the other. The elevator pinged, and the doors opened slowly. She let out a long, slow breath. It was empty. They got in, and Roberta pressed the button for the third floor.

Roberta said, "It should be OK up there. It's the living quarters for the nurses and doctor. Most of the soldiers live on the second floor."

"We do exactly the same as we did downstairs," Natasha said, her mind focused.

The corridor was empty when the elevator doors opened, as Roberta had promised. As they walked out, another nurse appeared from the other end.

She spotted them, and Natasha saw the quizzical look on the woman's face.

"Hi," the nurse said.

"Hi," Roberta replied. "This is my sister. Carola."

The nurse nodded, her face unsmiling and wary. Natasha read the name badge. It read Angie. Natasha was of two minds. Her fingers had closed around the syringe. She couldn't afford for Angie to go down and report something unusual. Her chances of escape from the third floor were much lower. She could grab Angie by the neck and inject her in the same movement. She looked behind her. Angie had gone, and so had the chance of keeping her quiet. Natasha nudged Roberta to make her walk faster.

In the changing room, Roberta found her a dress, and she got changed quickly, putting the uniform on top of her black outfit. She glanced at the mirror. From one of the uniforms hanging on hooks, she found a pair of reading glasses. She stuck them on her face. It wasn't much of a disguise, but it would do. The only problem was her vision—objects took on a weird, long shape.

Roberta opened her mouth to say something, but it was drowned out by the sound of a blaring alarm.

CHAPTER 22

Natasha sprang into action. She was at the door and about to yank it open when she heard the sound of running footsteps. She clenched her jaw, took out the Glock, and crouched opposite the door. Whoever opened that door would be the first to die.

The footsteps ran past the changing room. She opened the door a crack. Several nurses and a figure in a white coat ran to a door and went through it. Must be a staircase, she thought.

She stepped out, not expecting Roberta to follow. She turned to Roberta. "You don't have to come with me."

"It's too late. They make us sign a sheet before delivering the drugs. When they find out I'm not in the room, the game's up."

Natasha nodded. She preferred to work alone, but Roberta had helped her.

"OK. We take the stairs down to the ground floor. You lead, and I'll follow behind." She glanced at the name badge on her lapel. She was Debbie Archer, RGN.

As they ran down the stairs, they joined a group of soldiers who came out of the second floor. The alarm was still clanging loudly. The two women stood in one corner as the soldiers rushed down, faces flushed. Natasha kept her face lowered and only glanced up when the men had gone through the lower landing door.

They ran down to find the main reception in pandemonium. Heavily armed soldiers rushed in every direction. Natasha recognized the man standing in the center, barking out orders. His wide forehead and weather-beaten face were covered in sweat. She kept her head low and followed Roberta out through the sliding double doors.

"Stop!" a voice rang out.

Two soldiers approached them, weapons pointed. Natasha kept her hands loose at her sides. She could see the parking lot opposite, and the roughly six-and-a half-feet-high concrete fence with barbed wire on top. To her left lay the main entrance, guarded by a sentry post and car barrier. Beyond that, a dirt road moved down a hill, and she could see the blue waves of the Tyrrhenian Sea in the distance. If she could get down to the harbor, she might get her bearings, if they hadn't moved her too far inland.

"Where are you going?" the first soldier asked Roberta.

"I need to get something from my car."

"Everyone must remain indoors. Haven't you heard the alarm?" It was hard not to. The incessant rings were still assaulting their ears.

Natasha said, "My sister has my inhaler in the car, and I'm having an asthma attack."

She put her hands on her chest, thrusting her bosom out. The soldier's eyes moved to her chest. Natasha moved closer to him and arched her body towards him. She lowered her eyelashes and pouted with her full lips. She knew the effect it had on men, with or without makeup on.

She noticed the soldier had an American accent, and she feigned one herself. "Please, Mr. Officer?"

The soldier's mouth slackened slightly. He licked his lips and swallowed. His eyes moved from her chest, rising up and down rapidly, to her name badge.

"Debbie, right?"

He didn't have a name tag, so she smiled sweetly. "Yes, that's right, Officer." Then she wore a pained look on her face. "Please, we'll be back in a minute."

He adjusted the cap on his head and looked back at his colleague. "Well, I can't see it doing any harm if it's just your inhaler."

His colleague turned hard eyes towards Natasha and then glanced at her chest. He shrugged.

Natasha put on a dazzling smile then grimaced, making a wheezing sound. "Thank you so much."

They walked fast towards Roberta's car.

Natasha whispered, "Give me the keys."

The car was a beaten-up Fiat Salon. Not ideal, but the best they had in the circumstances.

Natasha got in the driver's seat, and she told Roberta to sit in the back. She glanced towards the soldiers. Their gaze was directed to the inside of the building. She turned the ignition on and moved the car out of the parking lot. Her fingers encircled the steering wheel.

"Now hold on tight," she said to Roberta.

CHAPTER 23

Natasha revved the engine a couple of times. "Put your head down," she said to Roberta. She took out both the Glocks and placed them on the seat, between her legs.

She floored the gas. With a squeal of rubber, the Fiat took off, hurtling for the entrance. The sentries turned around as they heard the car. One of them shouted and bent down on one knee, holding his rifle up. Natasha ducked below the dashboard, keeping her hands on the steering wheel. There was a loud crack, and a spider's web appeared on the windshield. She didn't move her foot from the pedal, and within seconds, the car was at the gate.

Natasha raised her head slightly. There was a roaring sound and a brief flash of a human body. She wrenched the steering wheel hard to the left to avoid hitting the hut. The guard's body slammed on the windshield, depressing it, then the body rolled over the car. She ducked again as she made out a figure in her peripheral vision. The gun was out in her right hand, and she fired even as the car hit the lowered bar at forty-five miles an hour. Bullets slammed against the Fiat's body, wrenching the steel and punching holes in it. The bar snapped in two, one part flying high over and beyond the car. A chatter of automatic fire echoed in her ears. The back window smashed into fragments, showering glass over the cowering figure of Roberta. Then the car was through, hurtling down the hillside. Smoke and dust poured in through the open window. Her hair was swept back in the wind's fury.

"Roberta!" she screamed.

There was no response. She shouted the name again, fearing the worst. Miraculously, she was unhurt. A head appeared in the rearview, and Roberta lurched forward.

"Are you OK?"

Before the nurse could answer, Natasha saw movement in the mirror. Two Humvees had lumbered out of the entrance and were speeding in her direction. Dust distorted a lot of her vision, and she couldn't be sure if a third vehicle was also behind the Humvees.

"Roberta, which way?"

The nurse seemed to have woken up from her dizziness. She shook her head. Her ponytail had come undone, brown hair falling over her face.

"Keep going till you come to a T junction. Then take a left and head towards the sea."

"That leads to Porto Cervo yacht harbor?"

"*Si.*"

Natasha closed her mouth in a tight line just as an explosion rocked the path. The car was thrown off course, smoke billowing in a great burst from its wheels. Desperately, Natasha wrenched the wheel to get back on track. Any farther out to the left, and she would roll down the hill. Green cypress and pine trees carpeted the slopes. Another explosion sounded almost immediately after. This one was farther off and hit the road ahead of them. Small rocks and debris smashed into what remained of the windshield, shattering it further. It was almost useless to look out of now.

"Get down!" Natasha screamed. She unhooked her right leg and slid down on the seat then kicked the windshield as hard as she could. After her third kick, the window separated from the edges.

To her left, there was a clean fall. She would drop almost forty feet, easily, she thought as she glanced. Then the trees began. Chances of survival were slim. But she had no choice. She moved the steering wheel from side to side, mouth set in a tight line. If she didn't weave around on the road, she was a sitting target. As it was, she doubted they would make the safety of the main road. Something had to be done, and fast.

"*What are those?*" Roberta shouted.

"Rocket-propelled grenades," Natasha shouted back. "They're reloading. Sooner or later, we're going to get hit. Is there any other way down this hill?"

A bend in the road appeared, and she was forced to slow down. Dust choked her mouth and face, almost blinding her. The roar of the Humvees grew louder.

Roberta yelled in her ears. "There is another path. But you have to leave the car. It's not wide enough."

"Will it take us down to the harbor?"

"Yes."

"How long does it take?"

"Couple of hours. Maybe three."

Natasha thought quickly. The Humvees were still around the corner, not in sight. The corner was a tight one, and the bigger vehicles had to turn slowly.

"How far is it?"

Roberta pointed ahead and up. "Over there."

Natasha jerked to a stop. She threw the gear into reverse and shot back just as the first Humvee arrived around the bend. Then she speeded forward and reversed again. The cloud of dust this generated was cover for the two figures who burst out of the car and sprinted down the road.

The Humvees screeched to a halt, and doors slammed as soldiers got out. Roberta turned out to be fitter than Natasha had expected, which was a relief.

"This way," the nurse panted.

They left the road and dived into the green bushes. Soon, they were within dense undergrowth, trees looming large above their head. Natasha could still hear voices from the road.

"How do you know this route?" Natasha asked.

"My great-grandfather was a bandit. Sardinia is famous for them."

"Really?"

"Yes. The bandits hid in the hills and robbed rich and corrupt politicians. They gave the Nazis hell as well during the war. For this reason, local people have supported them. This is an old smuggling route."

The silence was deepening now, with the sound of birds floating down from the trees. The forest was dense around them, and the path was stretching upward into the hills.

"We go up before we head down," Roberta panted. She had barely finished her sentence when a bullet exploded above her head.

CHAPTER 24

Roberta cried out as bark from the tree spit into her face. She collapsed, and Natasha scrambled to her. There was no injury in the scalp. She gripped Roberta's face in her hands and found no trace of blood. She was only shaken, but her shout would have given away their position.

"Quick," Natasha whispered in her ear, "you need to move."

Roberta looked around fearfully. This time she understood and kept her voice low. "What about you?"

"I need to hold them back. Now go up in a straight line. The higher up we are, the harder it will be for them to find us."

Roberta made tracks as Natasha hunkered down in the bushes. Years of bush training in the Primorsky Krai rainforests of far eastern Russia took over. She removed the kukri from her belt and held it in her hand. She stayed very still and waited. The snapping of a twig jolted her senses. It came from her twelve o'clock. Precisely the angle the bullet had come from. She heard another sound, a body shifting in the undergrowth, commando style. So there were at least two people. With more behind them. She could kill both of these, but the others would catch up with her.

She turned around very slowly and took off her boots. She tied them around her neck with the laces holding them together. With her naked feet as silent as a leopard's, she flitted from tree to tree, her black outline merging with the green of the forest. She ran, stopped, listened, and ran again, staying low. She could feel herself climbing. When she looked down, the valley stretched down below her, all the way to the road that snaked down to meet a blacktop two-lane highway, a yellow ribbon running down its middle. That must've been the road Roberta wanted to catch.

She couldn't see the men but knew they were heading up slowly. But climbing with all their gear was harder. Natasha turned and headed up. The summit of the flat-topped hill wasn't far away. It was made of rock, the black granite shining in the sunshine. Somehow, she had to get through that. There had to be a path, and she hoped it would lead down the hill.

Natasha stopped and leaned against a tree, winded. She knelt, her mouth parched. She needed water and rest. She had time for neither and also seemed to have lost her guide.

"Psst," a whisper came from above her.

Natasha dived to the left behind a tree as soon as she heard the sound.

"It's me," Roberta whispered.

Natasha scrambled up the slope, and they started climbing again. The path was steeper now and the vegetation sparser. Despite her tiredness, Natasha knew this was dangerous, as soon they would be bereft of cover from the forest.

"Don't worry," Roberta said. "We're not far off."

Natasha heard a buzzing sound. It was faint, but her senses were razor sharp. She stopped and listened.

"Up there." Roberta pointed.

Natasha shielded her eyes against the sun and followed her direction. It was a four-winged object, a squat machine with four green legs. It hovered in the air behind them, above trees.

"A drone," Natasha whispered. "How far are we from the summit?"

"Another ten minutes."

She took out the Glock, wishing she had a heavier weapon. The drone was about one hundred and sixty feet up, she calculated. The Glock would fire that far, but a heavier weapon, preferably a Dragunov rifle, would have been more accurate. She aimed, holding the gun wrist with her other hand. If the drone tracked them in the open, they had no protection. She imagined the drone was weaponized with small explosives, and if they dropped...

Natasha took a deep breath then exhaled slowly. At the mid-point of her exhalation, she pulled the trigger slowly. The first shot missed. The second one clipped one of the wings, and the drone went into free fall. She didn't wait to see any further. They ran up the hill, legs pumping, breath bursting from their open mouths. There was no cover here at all, and the sun burned Natasha's back. Her black outfit didn't help with the heat, but she was glad to be alive.

She followed Roberta into a shallow culvert that burrowed between the granite at the summit. It was cooler in the shade of the rocks. Gasping and panting, they came out on the other side, and they stood with their hands against a stony outcrop, looking out at the majestic view that stretched out in front of them. The cobalt blue of the Tyrrhenian Sea became opal green as it unfurled to the horizon and the distant landmass of Italy. At the slopes of the hill, below them, lay the sprawling harbor of Porto Cervo, the jewel in the coast, or Costa Smeralda. It was a playground for billionaire yacht owners, and the smattering of two-hundred-foot hulking yachts proved the point.

As Natasha looked at the white yachts, her memory jerked. The marina was clearly visible, a row of jetties sticking out into the blue water.

She wiped her sweaty brow and ran her hand through her sticky hair. She had been sent to kill Andreyev, but that was merely the beginning. Far more important and dangerous tasks lay ahead.

"Ready?" Roberta asked her. Natasha nodded.

CHAPTER 25

Montrose, Virginia

Dan took himself down to the shooting range. As a rule, he didn't visit the range if he had drunk alcohol, but he'd had one splash of bourbon and a burrito afterwards. He checked into the range, got the Sig out, and put his noise-cancelling earmuffs on. There were fifteen carrels in all, and he took the farthest one. He pressed the button at the side of the carrel and moved the target a hundred yards back. He slapped a mag of .45-caliber slugs into the Sig, aimed, and fired rapidly. He felt the thrum in his muscles with each press of the trigger, the recoil of the heavy weapon absorbed into his hand as though the gun were made for it.

He dragged the target closer and frowned at the result. Four of the seven rounds had gone above the head, only three in the middle. He pushed the button and tried again. Then he moved the target back to two hundred yards and kept up the rapid firing. He shot fifty rounds with his right hand and fifty with his left.

Shooting allowed him to focus. His mind flew along the bullet's trajectory. He never underestimated the value of practice, but after fifty shots, he could tell when he was going to miss the target. Almost never.

When he finished, he got back into the car and slumped on the seat. His fingers drummed on the steering wheel. The truth was, he was *trying* to make himself relaxed. Trying a bit too hard. Which meant he was achieving the opposite. He was getting restless. What was this craving in his bones? An endless yearning to get out and do… what? What he had always done. The way of the warrior. What else was there for him? He angled the rearview mirror on himself. Large brown eyes, square jaw, full, embarrassingly sensitive lips. Skin tanned to brown. A face that had many admirers of the opposite sex. But a face and a life that filled him with unspoken regrets. He turned the mirror away and closed his eyes.

This life doesn't last too long. Damn you, McBride, he thought. *Damn you for being right.*

He sighed and picked up the phone. McBride picked up on the first ring.

Dan said, "Don't talk. Just listen. I need creds to check out the prison. The CIA guys will try to stop me. I have to find out exactly what happened there. I need contacts inside the AISE in Rome. Or whichever Italian city is easier."

AISE, or *Agenzia Informazioni e Sicurezza Esterna,* was the Italian equivalent of the CIA.

"I need weapons—HK416 with all the add-ons, two Sig P320s chambered for 0.45, with fifty extra mags each, radio, flash bangs, frag grenades, GPS beacon if it all goes to shit, evacuation zones. Oh, and don't forget a kukri knife."

*****

The next day, from twenty thousand feet up, Dan looked down at the glimmer of emerald-green and turquoise-blue water of the north Sardinian coast. The island lay to the left of Italy and right below another island called Corsica.

The Grumman G-111 Albatross seaplane that had carried him from Milan was coasting smoothly in a blue sky. As he scanned the rugged coastline and the beautiful multicolored sea, he imagined the name *Costa Smeralda.* The Emerald Coast. Very apt. Porto Cervo in the north of the island was his destination. The port was set up in the 1960s by Prince Aga Khan, one of the richest men in the world at the time. It was designed to be a playground for billionaires and their yachts. It remained that, but the south of the island had opened up to normal tourist traffic and the school vacation crowd.

The plane zoomed to a lower altitude. White antennas raised needlelike fingers from barren brown peaks of mountains. Dan wished he had packed his binoculars. Scoping out the infrastructure came naturally to him. Destroying key nodes of communication came in handy when trying to outwit the enemy.

The plane banked heavily and prepared to land. A speaker above his head turned on, telling all crew to fasten seat belts. Dan looked around him. Two other CIA guys had accompanied him from Milan's Malpensa Airport. They spoke little, but he had caught their stares when they sized him up. They didn't look like Special Operations Group, the CIA's paramilitary wing, composed from ex-Special Forces personnel. To Dan's eye, they were more case officers, or internal ops, as the CIA called them. Agents who were fluent in the country's language and customs and well-adjusted to its culture. The fact that they came from the CIA's Rome office was further evidence of that.

His eyes caught those of one of the agents. Jack Rumsfeld, his name was. He was in his thirties, Dan guessed, a few years younger than him. By now, he should have enough field experience to handle himself, but Dan knew not to trust their skills in a combat zone. The other guy, Charlie Hassock, continued to watch outside the window.

Dan nodded at Jack, who twitched his lips. Apart from a handshake and name exchange, neither of them knew much about each other. Dan only knew what McBride had included in his mission folder. The rest, he was guessing. He wondered what they knew about him.

The plane glided into the sea, roughly ten miles out from Porto Cervo. The RIB came up to the plane, bobbing up and down on the gentle waves. Two US Navy warrant officers manned the black rubber boat, and a boatswain helped the three passengers aboard. The pilot waved at them and waited while the RIB's powerful twin motors at the back lowered into the sea. The nose of the boat lifted up as it surged towards the coast.

As they walked down the concrete road on the harbor, Jack Rumsfeld caught up with Dan.

"I hear you have clearance to come with us," the younger man said.

"Guess you heard right," Dan said.

"You know we are heading to a top-secret location."

Dan glanced at Jack and shook his head slightly. This guy had a way with words. Aloud, Dan said, "It's a black site. I know."

"Right." Jack wiped sweat from his forehead, the fire dimming in his eyes somewhat. "So," he asked, "which department are you from?"

"DOD."

"Which part?"

This was one aspect of Dan's cover. "The part that handles DOD issues abroad. Consular operations."

Jack frowned. "Never heard of that department."

They had approached a low-roofed building with a series of glass windows on its side. The two warrant officers entered, and they followed.

"It's a small office," Dan said. "And brand-new."

"I see," Jack said. His face expressed that he didn't see at all.

Dan looked around him warily. They were in a lobby, and two armed men in black fatigues stood at the far corner. Another set of doors led away from the room. There was a reception desk in one corner, now unused, and another armed man leaned against it, watching them carefully. Charlie Hassock, the other agent, was striding forward. Dan saw one of the guards stiffen and increase the pressure on his trigger finger. Dan frowned, his right hand slipping to his waistband out of reflex.

He didn't have his weapon on him.

CHAPTER 26

Jack was next to him, and Dan reached out to him. The younger agent stumbled as his chest hit Dan's outstretched arm. He looked up in surprise, eyes widening further as Dan yanked on the collar of his windbreaker, dragging him back. If these guys started firing, there would be no escape. They were caught in a crossfire.

"Hey!" the shout rang out from behind Dan. It was a woman's voice. He whirled around to find himself staring at a dark-haired, attractive woman wearing blue slacks and a matching blue vest. The bulge of her shoulder holster was visible beneath the light black summer jacket. Her right arm was bent at the elbow, reaching inside for the weapon. But she didn't draw it.

"Take it easy. There's no danger here," she said.

Dan flicked his eyes left and right. Behind the woman, the doors to the harbor remained shut. Air-conditioning hummed in his ears.

He jerked a thumb behind him and asked, "Is that why there's a gun pointed at me?"

The woman didn't answer. Neither did she change her position. Dan knew her fingers were seconds away from drawing her weapon.

He said, "If there's no danger, then leave your gun alone. Tell them to put theirs down."

The woman stared back at Dan. Any other time, he would appreciate the luster in those sea-green eyes, matching the sparkle of the waves outside. Her small nose contrasted with the sharp, strong chin. The lips were red and full. He let his eyes roam over her face and watched her blink.

"You must be Dan Roy," she said.

"Am I?"

"If you're not, then get the hell out," she shot back.

Dan shrugged and headed for the door. She stepped in his way. Her head was at the level of his chest, and his two-hundred-thirty-pound frame was easily double hers. But the fire in her eyes and the upward thrust of her chin was unmistakable.

"Stand down, or I'll make you." The weapon had appeared in her right hand, and she pointed it to the floor. It was a Glock 22. A light gun. Dam smiled at her.

"If I can disarm you by the time you aim that thing at me, do I still have to stand down?"

She looked daggers at him and whipped the gun at his chest. She came forward till she was less than two feet away.

"Go ahead and try," she said in a tight, clipped voice. She chambered a round. The room was deathly quiet. All sounds from outside seemed to have been sucked into the silence, centered on Dan and the woman.

Dan crossed the gap between them till the barrel of the gun was brushing his chest. He pressed himself into it. Her large green eyes were enormous now, and his face was inches away. She smelled of lavender, an old smell from his childhood. Something else too, flowery. They stared at each other without blinking.

"Before you shoot me," Dan said, "please do me the courtesy of telling me your name."

"Melania Stone, CIA."

"CIA is a weird last name, Melania Stone."

"You think this is funny?" Her tone was hard, but her voice faltered. Dan was leaning his thick pectoral muscles into the barrel, but he could feel her wrist slackening. The safety was still off, and her finger remained on the trigger.

"Nothing funny about dying, Miss Stone. I'd rather it be a painless one and you shoot me in the head, in fact." He looked down at the gun then at her.

Melania frowned. "So what the hell is your name?"

"Just like my file said. Dan Roy."

Slowly, she withdrew the gun, eyebrows still knitted together. She curled her full lips upward.

"Are you always an asshole, Mr. Roy?"

"Only when someone points a gun at me."

Melania shook her head, and her nostrils flared. She holstered her weapon. Tension seemed to go out of the room, like a balloon popping. She strode away to the double doors at the far end of the room, around the metal detector that stood in her way.

"Get them inside," she snapped at the men.

Three AR-15 rifle barrels pointed at Dan. Jack Rumsfeld was looking at Dan with a mixture of revulsion and fascination on his face. Dan shrugged, and they all stepped towards the door.

Jack asked, "Would you really have let her shoot you?"

"I can think of worse ways to die," Dan said.

CHAPTER 27

Jack Rumsfeld and Charlie Hassock walked down a corridor, followed by Dan. One of the armed men walked ahead of them, and the other two behind. Another door opened into a wide open-plan space. Desks lined the interior, with screens and keyboards. Heads were hunched over computers. The room was dark, lit only by the light of monitors and a larger roll-down screen at the end of the room. A map of Southern Europe and North Africa was shown on the screen, with red thermal images lined in areas of Algeria, Libya, and farther south. A command and control room, Dan guessed. They walked through it and into an office. The door shut behind his back, and he realized he was alone, apart from one of the armed men behind him. The room had a screen on the wall showing the same map, and at a desk, behind a computer, sat Melania Stone.

"Sit," she said.

Dan did as he was told. She flicked her eyes towards the man behind Dan. "Leave us," she said.

The man hesitated for a second then turned and left. As the door shut behind him, Dan looked at the camera above him then at the bank of CCTV screens on the opposite wall. Images flickered from one room to the other and also the exterior, including the sea.

"It might not be obvious," Melania said, "but we have patrols everywhere. This place is secure."

"Guess you have to be."

"What does that mean?"

Dan checked his response, aiming to keep her in the dark. He doubted that was possible, as McBride had probably briefed them on what he knew.

"Means what I said. Best not to take chances."

She narrowed her eyes then looked away briefly. She clicked on her keyboard and stared at the screen then at Dan. She nodded.

"So let me get this straight. Your handler at Intercept was vague. Do you know the agent who breached the black site?"

Dan kept his face impassive. "That depends."

"On what?"

"On who the agent was."

Melania sighed and clicked again. Then she turned the screen around to Dan. He saw the image of a female form clad in black nylon-like material. She was strapped to a chair. Melania zoomed the image in. The face was still blurry, so she switched to a new image where a hand had stabilized the unconscious woman's face. The left side of the face was swollen and bruised. Both eyes were shut, but Dan would have recognized that face anywhere. He felt a tightening in his chest and, with effort, kept his face impassive. He averted his eyes from the screen and focused on Melania.

She was watching him very closely. "You know her, right?"

"I didn't say that."

"You wanna play hardball on this, Mr. Roy, go right the fuck ahead. But do it with someone else, as I don't have the time."

"Call me Dan."

She ignored him. "I'll ask you one last time. Do you know her?"

"All those hours of interrogation training at the Farm. Questioned while hanging upside down from a tree. Doesn't match a woman's intuition, does it?"

She stared at him in stony silence.

Dan sighed. "OK, I've seen her once. Protecting an SVR colonel in Turkey."

"So she's a Russian agent?"

"Yes."

"Anything else?"

Dan kept his face blank. "She got me into a tough spot, and I crawled out of it. Never saw her again. That's it."

"That's it?"

"You asked me, and I told you."

Melania sat back in her chair. She pursed her lips and stared at Dan for a while. "Let me tell you what she did, Mr.... I mean Dan. She killed one of the best assets we have on the Kremlin's finances. An oligarch who was close to the premier himself, till he found out his daughter was killed by one of the premier's cronies."

Dan shifted in his chair. "How did she know?"

Melania clenched her jaw. "We're looking into it. But finding her would help one hell of a lot."

"You have a leak who told the Russians he was selling them out."

"Maybe. Or it could be his time was up in any case." Melania paused and then continued. "Then this woman killed three of our men before she was captured."

Dan raised an eyebrow. "And then she managed to escape from the black site, too, right?"

"She had inside help. One of our nurses, called Roberta. We checked her house. It's empty. No one knows where Roberta is. She has a son who's vanished as well."

"It's a small island. Can't be that hard to track them down."

"Roberta's cell phone is dead. We tracked the signal to the black site. She left it there. She could be dead, killed by"—Melania pointed at the screen—"this agent."

Dan kept his thoughts to himself. He knew the Scorpion would put distance between herself and her attackers as quickly as she could. Chances were, she had vanished somewhere into Italy or farther abroad already.

Melania said softly, "Roberta might be dead, but I'm worried about the boy."

Dan appraised her. It was unusual for a seasoned agent to have such concerns, but he appreciated it. He wanted to tell her Natasha, the Scorpion, wouldn't kill the boy. Not the Natasha he knew. But once again, he kept his own counsel.

"Let's check out the site," Dan said.

CHAPTER 28

Dan observed the glitzy bars and shining yachts as the Jeep rolled out of the harbor. Porto Cervo definitely lived up to its reputation. They drove past a night club called Billion. Dan noticed the armed guards outside the night club.

Tanned skin, smooth limbs, and lithe young women in skimpy dresses were on parade everywhere. Trendy designer bouquets rubbed shoulders with well-known fashion labels.

"Like what you see?" Melania asked, her voice dripping with sarcasm.

"I can see, but touching is a different story."

"Got that right."

They left the harbor for the rolling hills of North Sardinia. Sun-bleached vegetation covered the slopes. Goat herders stopped at the roadside and stared at the Jeep as they passed. At the site, they were allowed in after the customary checks, despite Melania's credentials. She did the tour and explained to Dan how the Scorpion had escaped.

"She was wearing a nurse's uniform, right? With a name badge that said Debbie?"

Melania nodded. They drove out again, to the hilltop where the Scorpion was last seen. As they climbed, Melania wiped away her sweat and asked, "What's her real name?"

Dan shrugged. "I didn't know her identity. She was a threat. That's all."

Melania stopped climbing. "Your handler at Intercept said the same thing, once he'd seen the photo. Why don't I believe you?"

Dan paused, his throat parched. Neither of them had a drink. He started to climb again and spoke over his shoulder. "You can believe what you like."

She trudged after him, and he could feel the frustration radiating from her.

When they reached the peak, Dan led her through the granite stones massed at the flat summit. He looked down at the land below and the sea that followed it. On either side, brown-and-green hills rose to a blue sky. The land formed a gentle crescent-shaped bay that cradled the blue sea till it unfurled itself into the Adriatic.

Dan looked below and saw human habitation. White houses with pastel-colored tiled roofs. They looked like small villages, situated well behind the glamour of the harbor, houses of the men and women who serviced the billionaires' playground.

Melania said, "That's where we looked." She pointed at a crop of houses surrounding a lake. A black road snaked through it, ending up in the harbor. "Roberta lived in that village called San Cristo."

"You still remember the location?" Dan asked.

"If I'm on the ground, I will." Melania turned back.

Dan called after her. "I want to go down the hill. This path must carry on, right?" He pointed at the dirt line that carried into the trees. "She went this way. It's better to retrace her steps."

Melania grumbled then agreed. She switched on her radio and called for support to meet her at the village. Dan felt for his Sig then looked at the hills and forest stretched out below him. He glanced at Melania.

"Sure you can handle this? We need to hike for couple of hours."

She gave him a frosty glare then walked past him. Dan watched her go then took the Sig out. He followed her at a brisk pace.

By the time they reached the bottom of the hill, both were panting. Going downhill was harder on the joints, and they did it slowly. Dan didn't find any clues. He wasn't sure what he was looking for, but a sixth sense was tingling softly inside him. Natasha had been here. She was an expert at tracking and surveillance. Maybe he was being paranoid, but for some reason, he felt eyes on him. Much to Melania's irritation, he had yanked her back to hide behind a tree on several occasions. So far, any threat had been nonexistent.

An armored Jeep met them at the road on the base of the hill. Both drank thirstily from cooled water bottles. The stone-walled white houses cast cool shadows as they walked into the village. A few children were playing in the street. They stopped and gaped at Dan as he walked past them. Melania led him to Roberta's simple single-story stone cottage. The windows, shutters, and doors were of rough brown wood. All were shut.

"We put a lock on the door ourselves," Melania said, taking the key out of her pocket.

Dan looked around him. The children had gone in, and the cobbled street was suddenly deserted. Melania went up the four steps that led to a landing and the front door. She used her key to open it.

"Wait," Dan called out. Melania turned, eyebrows raised.

Dan said, "When did you last visit?"

"Four days ago. But we have the place on lockdown and twenty-four-hour drone surveillance. The drone feed is examined every day. Plus we have a two-man crew patrolling the street every day, dressed as farmers. Trust me—if this were a trap, I would know."

Dan had placed the Sig back at his waist when he entered the village, but now his fingers encircled the butt.

"Me first, if you don't mind," he said.

Melania shook her head. "Don't start that tough-guy act."

Dan grinned. "You're not gonna try to shoot me again, are you?"

"Don't tempt me."

She opened the door and was about to step in when Dan grabbed her shoulder.

"What?" she hissed.

"Standard procedure. Expect the threat, make yourself a smaller target."

She rolled her eyes, but when she looked forward, her knees were bent, and her gun arm was straight at the elbow. She went in first, followed by Dan.

The interior was dusty, as if it hadn't been touched for days. It was a living room, with sofas around a fireplace. Two doors led from the back of the room. Dan pointed to the right, and Melania gave him a thumbs-up. Before Dan got to the door on the right, he tackled the window opposite the front door. He sank to his knees then lifted his head to peer through the cracks. An overgrown garden met his gaze, bordered by a low, crumbling stone fence at the rear. Beyond that lay the brackish water of the lake. Hills rose in the distance.

Melania had already opened the door and stepped into the room on the left. Dan watched as she scanned the room then cleared it. He listened outside the door on the right then kicked it open without stepping inside. The Sig searched up and down and from side to side, then he lowered the weapon.

It was a bedroom. A single bed was laid at the corner and next to it, in an L shape, a smaller, child's bed. Both were empty. Dan searched under the beds and found nothing.

Dan turned as Melania came into the room. Rays of light from the closed window striped across her body.

"Did you remove anything from the rooms?" he asked.

"There wasn't much. A couple of old clothes for the boy. Nothing useful. The other bedroom and bathroom are empty as well."

Dan nodded. He stood up. Then he saw the red dot dancing on Melania's chest.

CHAPTER 29

There was no time to think. Dan hurled himself at her full tilt. His arm circled around her waist, and they crashed into the wall behind them. There was a whine then a fracturing sound as the shutters of the window splintered under the force of bullets. Dan felt the burn of hot metal as a round singed his back, then he was on the floor, body over Melania's as the rounds pumped in, pockmarking holes in the wall. Plaster crumbled under the impact and fell on Dan's body.

Dan counted six suppressed rounds, then there was silence. He rolled off Melania and edged towards the door, into the living room, the Sig pointing up and ahead as he crawled on the floor. He could hear Melania barking orders into her radio. Moments later, there was a screech of tires up front then fast footsteps.

Dan sensed then saw Melania come alongside him on the floor. Her hair was plastered over her forehead, and her breath came in gasps. "Don't shoot. They're our guys."

"Whatever you do, don't stand up," Dan said between gritted teeth. "The shooter's still there. Tell your guys that as well."

"Down, down!" Melania shouted as the door burst open. Dan hollered as well, raising his voice above hers, and the two agents who had rushed inside finally got the message. They fell to the floor, weapons pointed at Dan.

"Hold your fire!" Melania screamed. For a split second, Dan was worried. The interior of the hut was dark due to the closed windows. If the men opened fire, then both he and Melania were dead. His trigger finger tightened involuntarily.

Luckily, both the CIA men recognized Melania on the ground.

"We need to get out of here," Dan said. "Is there anyone in the car?"

Everyone looked at each other.

Dan could have groaned. "Move it, now!" he shouted. Shooting out the tires of the getaway vehicle was the best way to ensure the targets remained within firing range. He couldn't believe the CIA agents hadn't thought of that. Obviously not SOG men, he thought bitterly.

Dan was the first one out, sliding down the steps. He noticed every angle, shape, and corner between the houses, and the shadows on the alleys. The Sig moved around as he scanned, and he wished he had his reliable Heckler rifle with him. He opened the passenger door, and Melania jumped in and scooted over to the driver's side. The keys were in the ignition, and she started the engine as the remaining men rushed inside the car. They got into the back, and Dan rode shotgun, pointing his weapon out the window. The shutter of every window remained closed. The streets were deserted.

Tires screeched and blew up black smoke as the car hurtled down the cobblestone road. They bounced up the ramp into the asphalt road, and the Jeep swerved as Melania swung the steering wheel, then they were speeding down.

"What the hell happened there?" one of the agents asked.

The voice sounded familiar, and Dan turned to see Jack Rumsfeld. His face was ruddy, and sweat poured down his forehead.

"We got shot at by a sniper. She's probably around still, so keep your head down." He grinned as Jack and Charlie ducked immediately. His grin faded as he looked at the hills rising in both directions. Theirs was the only car on the road. If they were in range, despite the moving vehicle, it was possible they could be hit again.

"Speed up!" he shouted as the wind blew his words away.

"I am," Melania said, shoulders hunched over the steering wheel.

Dan watched the speedometer climb past seventy-five miles per hour. He continued to look for threats, like sunlight glinting off a gun barrel. Any trained sniper would cover their weapon with a black cloth. And snipers worked in teams of two. Dan was surprised they hadn't been shot at again. His real concern was another team. With the Jeep accelerating, he was pretty sure the last sniper was now out of range.

After a half hour of tense driving, they reached the harbor. Dan breathed easier as the Jeep swung inside the compound. They got out of the car and convened inside the reception area.

"You OK?" Dan asked Melania. She nodded and walked behind him.

"You're bleeding," she said. Dan winced as he felt her touch his back. There was a rip in his blue shirt. He had barely felt it till now.

"It's not much. I can stitch that up with some local anesthetic." Melania caught Dan's eyes. "Yes, I used to be team medic, so don't worry." Her eyes softened. "Thank you for that."

Dan shrugged. "The window shutters saved you. The shooter could see shapes but didn't have a clear sight. And she was to one side, not face on."

"She?"

Dan nodded. "This had to be…" He broke off before he said the name. "The agent who escaped. She's letting us know that she's on to us."

"That takes balls."

"She's got big brass cojones. Trust me. But she also has backup. She's as hard as nails but not stupid. She had to get the weapon from somewhere, and I have a funny feeling we might be outnumbered."

"Why do you think that?"

"This was blatant. But…" Dan trailed off as he frowned.

"But what?"

Dan didn't speak. An odd thought was forming in his head. The Scorpion never missed a fixed target. Had she seen him?

Melania said, "We'd better stitch your back up. It's not much of a laceration, but don't want it to get infected."

She took him to the clinical room, where Dan sat on a hospital gurney as she rummaged round in a drawer.

"Lie down," she instructed. Dan removed his shirt. He took a small rectangular object from his pocket and examined it.

Melania glanced over as she filled a syringe with Marcaine for the anesthetic. "What's that?"

"A matchbox." Dan examined it closely. White letters stood out on a black surface. "From a place called Billion." His memory triggered as he said the name. "Wait. Isn't that one of the night clubs on the harbor?"

"Yes," Melania said, coming closer. "Where did you get that from?"

"The living room floor of the hut." He looked at Melania then at the syringe in her hand. "Stitch me up," he said. "Then it's time for some dancing."

CHAPTER 30

Melania and Dan were sat on the outdoor seats of a bar opposite the Billion nightclub. In this stretch of Porto Cervo, they had to look the part in order to mingle with the distinctly upper-class masses. Dan was wearing a brown button-down shirt stretched tight across his chest and biceps, with matching brown linen pants. Melania had wanted him to wear a suit, but he had demurred. Instead, he had a dark cotton summer jacket, which was draped across the back of the chair. It was Melania who looked stunning in a black dress that came down to just above her knees. Her fake diamond necklace glowed when it caught the sun. Dan tried not to stare at it or at the suggestion of her cleavage.

Evening had arrived, but that meant longer shadows only. It didn't get dark till after nine p.m. The Billion had open doors, but the people filtering in and out were workers and security. Dan saw a woman with a clipboard come out of the entrance, touch her right ear, and speak softly. His eyes were drawn to the discreet, almost invisible receiver on her coat lapel. A white van came and stopped a few paces outside the entrance, and a man got out to open the rear doors. The delivery guy unloaded a crate, and two men came out the main entrance of the club to receive it. A younger woman came with them, and from her clothes, Dan could tell she was a cleaner. He glanced at Melania and nodded.

Melania got up and walked slowly across to the club entrance. The van drove off. Dan watched Melania speak to the woman. She frowned and then appeared lost in thought. Melania pressed something into the woman's hands. She looked at it and nodded.

Leisurely, Melania strolled away from the club. Dan paid for his drink and followed. They caught up a block down the road, outside a Rolex shop.

"Well?" Dan asked.

"Roberta worked there. The woman recognized her photo. But she can't remember the last time Roberta was there."

"Why did she leave?"

Melania shrugged. "She worked two jobs, obviously, to make ends meet. Maybe it got too much for her."

"Maybe. But there's something else that doesn't fit."

"What?"

Dan fixed his eyes on her. "Your guys did a sweep of the hut, right? You said apart from some old clothes, they found nothing."

Melania frowned at him. "Where are you going with this?"

"How come I found this matchbox on the floor when I walked in? It was below the window at the back. Your guys should have spotted something obvious like it."

She pursed her lips. "What are you saying?"

Someone left it there for me to find.

He said, "I don't know. But it seems weird. Either your guys missed it, or someone went there after you guys left."

"Possible, but we had the place under surveillance."

Dan smiled. If the Scorpion wanted to breach a location, she would know how to avoid detection.

He said, "Let's see if we can get inside. You first."

Their reservation had already been made, as Mr. and Mrs. Papadopoulos, heirs to a Greek shipping magnate. The identity was one of several used by the CIA station in Rome.

The Billion club had no lines. Guests remained seated inside their limousines till their turn came. Dan noticed the heavyset guards, all a similar height to his six three, turn to stare at him as he walked up. The bulges of their shoulder holsters were obvious, and from their swarthy, thick-boned features, he identified them as Russians. They took their time to search Dan, patting him down carefully. When they stepped aside to let him through, Dan could feel their eyes on his back. He waited in the lobby for Melania to appear from the cubicle where she was being searched along with the contents of her handbag.

A liveried doorman opened a huge set of black doors to reveal deep-red-carpeted stairs ascending into a space where house music thrummed gently and laughter trickled downstairs.

"Be on your best behavior," Melania whispered.

"I'll try. Did Andreyev come here?"

"Yes."

They went to the bar, which was lit up by the ceiling-height mirror behind it. After Dan ordered a bourbon for himself and a Diet Coke for Melania, he leaned against the marble bar and observed. A few guests had arrived, and all were seated on plush red sofas and armchairs. A live band was tuning up on the circular stage to the left, after which another set of doors had one half open to reveal a dance floor where a DJ was mixing house tunes. The women looked like young models, with a scattering of trust-fund chicks. The men were on the older side, with larger bellies and heavy jowls. Dan hadn't seen too many billionaires in his life, but if this was anything to go by, he wondered if a slim billionaire was a rare species.

He turned his attention back to Melania. "Tell me about Andreyev."

"His father was a Politburo member. He got a chunk of the oil and gas assets when the Soviet Union broke down. Typical Russian oligarch."

"I guessed that already. I want to know what brought him here." He glanced at her. "And who betrayed him."

"Like I said, we're still looking into it. He was here because it's easier to meet here in person than in Russia, and he hardly ever visits the USA. He'd been an asset for us the last two years, since he had found out about his daughter's death."

"Whatever he had to say was important enough for him to be silenced," Dan mused.

A flicker of movement caught his eyes. A curtain twitched in the far-right corner of the room, next to the doors to the dance hall. A woman's face appeared briefly, then a pair of hands gripped her neck and pulled her inside. It was the woman who had spoken to Melania outside. Dan got up.

"Stay here. If we get separated, don't look for me. I'll meet you at the station."

Before Melania could speak, Dan had walked across the room. He parted the curtains of what was a service entrance. There was a small landing with shelves on either side. Stands for champagne bottles stood to the right, and a flight of stairs led straight down. A pair of legs in tights and a black skirt appeared briefly, struggling against someone. Then they were pulled away. Dan glanced behind him. Apart from Melania, he saw no one staring in his direction. He went down the steps rapidly. He paused on the last step. The hallway in front was clearly a service alley for goods and workers. Two men in blue overalls walked past Dan, chatting. He flattened himself against the wall. He gave them ten seconds then stepped out into the well-lit hallway. He turned right, the direction in which the woman had been dragged. A golf cart was parked to the left of the wide corridor. Fluorescent lights ahead bathed the place in a white glow. Dan couldn't see any doors, so he guessed the woman had been taken in one of the golf carts. He looked behind him and saw no one. He broke into a jog. A hallway branched off to the right. Up ahead, he could see the parked golf cart and doors to offices. He glanced straight down and saw more doors. He had to take a chance. He turned right and stopped at the golf cart. It was parked opposite an office door. Dan looked up and down. So far, he hadn't been spotted, but his luck would run out soon.

He pressed his ear to the door and heard voices. A woman's voice was louder, and she was crying. Dan knocked on the door. The room went silent, apart from the woman's voice.

"What is it?" a gruff voice asked in Russian.

"The boss has called on the phone," Dan replied. His Russian was broken and rusty from lack of use, but he could hold a basic conversation. He took three steps back. A bolt was slid back, and the door opened a fraction.

Dan rushed in, kicking the door so hard with his right leg the screws splintered from the doorframe. He bent low and crashed in, grabbing hold of a man, who stumbled back. He hooked his arms around the man's midriff and used him as a shield to hit the table in the middle of the room. A chair crashed behind him, and he heard a shout. He hoped he hadn't hit the woman, but he needed this fast entrance.

As soon the guy's back hit the table, Dan punched him hard with an uppercut, lifting his chin. He wanted to feel for his weapon inside his coat, but he had no time to withdraw it. The man standing up behind the table was his more immediate concern. He saw the guy's hand dive inside his jacket, and Dan wasted no time. Using the other man's body for leverage, he catapulted himself over the table like a pole-vaulter. He smashed into the man's body just as his arms were getting free. He heard a suppressed round explode in the air behind him, but it went whistling above him.

The man Dan had slammed into slid down to the floor, Dan on top. He grabbed hold of the gun hand and, drawing his neck back, hit his broad forehead into the guy's face. The nose ruptured with a sickening sound, spurting blood. Dan head-butted him again, and the man tried to fight back. Dan brought his right fist down fast and punched the man in the side of his face, rocking his head to the left. The gun came loose in his hand, and he cocked back the hammer, pointing it under the table. He could see the woman's feet, clenched together. A man was on the floor, trying to get up. Dan shot him twice, hitting his kneecap then the upper body as the man screamed then sprawled on the floor. Behind him, there was another man. He was hiding behind a sofa at the back, but he chose this moment to stand up and aim.

Big mistake. Dan lifted his head slightly and immediately felt a round splatter into the wood, chipping fragments into his face. He ducked and rolled to the side. He came up shooting, pointing at the midpoint of the shadow behind the sofa. His first two shots missed, but the third shot got lucky. The man grunted and fell forward. Dan aimed and shot him in the head. He felt a hand clawing at his feet, and he turned quickly. The man on the floor was trying to get up. Dan double-tapped him in the face, and red bone fragments flew in the air as the man slumped down once again.

He jerked the weapon, which felt like a Makarov semi-automatic, around. The room was empty apart from the woman, who was cowering on the floor now.

He slid the magazine out and counted two rounds left in the seven-clip mag. He slapped it back in. There was no time anymore to question the woman. Someone could've heard the door crashing in. He knelt and got closer to the woman.

"Do you know the way out of here?" Dan whispered urgently. The woman was in shock. She kept her face averted and shrank away.

"Hey," Dan touched her arm as she moved away again. "I'm not here to hurt you. I came to help. You knew Roberta, right? Remember the woman in the black dress you met on the street? She's my friend."

Slowly, the woman lifted her face. Her tear-streaked features were plain. Makeup had washed out of her eyes, and her hair was wild.

"Who... who you are?" she asked in broken English with an Italian accent.

"A friend. You just have to trust me on that. Do you know the way out of here?"

The woman nodded. Both their heads turned as they heard voices, muffled and low at first then louder as someone shouted.

CHAPTER 31

Dan frisked the fallen man nearest to him. He found a wallet, which he took, and another Makarov with a spare mag. He stuck the other gun in his belt and, holding the new weapon in his hand, ran to the door. He leaned out to see two men running down the corridor. Dan sank down to one knee as they saw him. They drew their weapons as they saw him aim, but Dan was faster. He fired twice and hit the guy in front. The man behind was aiming when two 9mm rounds found his chest and neck. He sprawled in a heap over his friend.

"Let's go!" Dan shouted. This time, the woman needed no encouragement. Dan pushed her out of the door and followed as she ran down the corridor. An alarm bell started to blare, an ear-splitting claxon that shook the walls. The woman had stopped and was pressing a button. It was a service elevator. Dan looked behind him to see another three figures appear at the other end, ahead of the woman.

"Get down!" he screamed. He fired almost immediately. His shots went wild, hitting the floor and walls, but it had the desired effect of making the men flatten on the floor. The woman crawled inside the elevator. Dan ran full tilt, weapon trained forward. He couldn't run and aim, and he didn't want to waste bullets. But the men started to rise. They sensed their advantage. All three guns were drawn. Dan fired before they could aim and dived for the floor as he reached the elevator shaft.

The woman was holding the door open. Dan jumped inside as a hail of bullets clattered against the metallic surface. The woman was pressing the button repeatedly as Dan heard running footsteps.

"Stand back," he said.

He aimed straight forward. He couldn't lean out the doors, as they wouldn't shut. A figure appeared in front and skidded to a halt. Dan fired before he could, and he hit the man's leg. The man fired as well, screaming in agony, but the elevator doors closed just as bullets thudded into them.

Suddenly, it was quiet as the elevator hummed up the shaft.

Dan checked the mag, threw it away, and slapped the new one inside. He drew the hammer back, chambering a round. Locked, cocked, and ready. He glanced at the woman. Her face was as white as a sheet, and she was on her tiptoes, back braced against the wall.

"What's your name?" Dan asked.

"Carola."

"OK, Carola. You're gonna have to help me out here. Reckon you can do that?" She didn't say anything.

Dan asked, "Are there fire sprinklers in this place?"

"Yes."

"From the ceiling, right?"

Carola nodded.

"Where is the nearest fire alarm?"

"There's one outside each elevator door, built into the wall."

"Is there a fire extinguisher nearby?"

"Yes, just outside the elevator as well."

Dan nodded. His first priority was getting out of the elevator alive. He reached up into the roof of the elevator and lifted the panels. He indicated to Carola. "Get on my shoulders, and get on the roof."

Carola lifted her left forearm. She had a cut that was bleeding. She said, "*Ho un'idea migliore.*"

"What does that mean?"

"I have a better idea."

*****

Dan looked through the crack of the panels in the elevator roof. The muzzle of his gun fit snugly into it, and it pointed at the floor of the elevator. Dan held the gun with both hands, his knees bent, feet on either side for balance. He had less than five seconds, he guessed. His vision of the elevator was limited but at an angle where he had just enough leverage to see outside the doors.

The elevator pinged and lurched to a stop. The doors slid open. Voices whispered outside, then the first feet appeared. The thug had a gun pointed at Carola's figure on the floor. She lay face down and facing away from them, blood smeared around her brown hair. Another pair of feet appeared.

One more. The first thug started to kneel. *Too late,* Dan thought with bared teeth. He fired twice in rapid succession then tilted the gun and fired at the other guy. Both figures crumpled to the floor. Dan kicked the panels with both legs viciously, and he dropped just as Carola rolled to one side, making herself into a tight ball. Dan heard a suppressed round and flinched then flung himself over Carola. But no bullet hit him or ricocheted off the elevator walls. He opened his eyes to see Melania standing outside, legs spread, gun held in both hands. A dead man in a dark suit lay at her feet near the elevator.

"Next time," she said to Dan, "just ask me for help."

Dan grinned as he helped Carola to her feet. He found the fire alarm on the wall and punched it. The alarm that had been blazing downstairs suddenly ripped over the throbbing house music on the floor. The music played on, but sprinklers opened up in the ceiling. Shrieks and screams rang out from the fashionistas on the dance floor.

"Let's move!" Dan shouted. From the corner of his eyes, he saw the curtains of the service entrance twitch. He aimed his weapon at them, seeking cover against the wall adjacent to the elevator.

"Take the girl. I'll hold them as long as I can."

Melania was pointing her weapon at the opposite end of the room. Men and women were running out of the bar and dance floor.

"You sure?" she shouted.

"There's no point in both of us dying, is there?" Dan shouted back.

She gave him a glance, which Dan missed as the curtains twitched again, and the dark muzzle of a gun appeared between them. Dan fired immediately, and the gun fell. The alarm was blaring in his ears. Melania had grabbed Carola and was rushing towards the entrance.

Dan kept his gun pointed up with one hand, and with the other, he frisked the dead man at his feet. He picked up two Makarovs and extra mags. The curtains parted, and two burly figures burst out. Dan was ready. He dropped them both with shots in the chest and finished with slugs in the brain. He had to move, but more figures poured out of the service entrance. The elevator was trying to move as well, but he had already jammed the doors with a dead body. The doors kept slamming on the prostrate figure, but the elevator didn't budge.

Dan fired rapidly, holding a Makarov in each hand, blazing fire as he emptied the magazines of both. He stepped back as he fired then threw the weapons on the wet floor. He had one gun left in his belt at his back and took it out and slapped a new mag in.

There was pandemonium at the entrance. He jumped down the stairs to the people gathered at the double doors that led outside. Two security guards were waving everyone through, and Dan couldn't see Melania or Carola. He hoped they had gone through. One of the guards looked up as Dan rushed down the stairs, and put his right hand to his ear. The people blocking Dan's way were made of money, thin and waiflike. There was no time for subtlety or manners. He barged into them. Men grunted and tried to grab him, but their soft, flabby hands might as well have tried to hold on to a bucking steed. Women screamed as some toppled over, tottering on their heels.

Dan used the confusion to get close to the security men, staying low. They saw him coming but couldn't fire. Dan straightened just as they reached him. They came from either side, fists swinging. Dan took a blow to the left shoulder, ducking his head. The other man spun on his heel for a roundhouse kick. Dan moved inside his space and grabbed the leg as it came around. It surprised the man. The quickness of Dan's movements surprised a lot of men, who didn't expect a man his size to be so supple. Holding the leg in a lock, Dan bent over and lifted the man over his shoulder. He threw him over his friend, and they both fell in a heap. Dan pointed the gun, but there were too many people around, many of whom screamed again at the sight of a weapon.

The door burst open, and three of the thugs ran out and skidded to a halt as they took in the chaotic scene before them. Dan turned around, crouched, and ran outside. Bullets pinged off the wall, but billionaires didn't pay their security to shoot at them, so most of the rounds were aimed high and went wild.

A crowd had gathered outside the club. Dan came to a stop, panting, sweat pouring down his head. There was a cut on his forehead, and a trickle of blood fell over his left eye. He brushed it off as he watched people shrink away from him in fear. Desperately, he looked around for an armored Jeep or any car that looked as if it had CIA agents inside. There was a shout behind him, and he glanced back to see his friends appear in the street, brandishing their weapons at him. They screamed at him, and Dan broke into a run. He turned a corner quickly, the glinting sea now facing him. He had only just arrived in Porto Cervo, and he didn't have his bearings. If he headed for the water, however, he could try to steal a boat. He fished his cell phone out. Two missed calls from Melania. He heard an engine roar and flinched then pressed his back against a shop window.

The black Jeep roared to a stop next to him, and the passenger door was flung open. Jake was in the driver's seat. Dan could see the outline of two more people in the back. He jumped in, and the Jeep took off in a blaze of black smoke. There was a smacking sound at the rear of the vehicle.

"They're shooting at us," Melania barked from the back seat.

Dan saw Carola crouching with her hands over her head. The car sped up smoothly, leaving the chaos behind.

Dan said, "You can get up now, Carola."

She didn't, and Melania had to help her back to the seat. Her wild eyes glanced around feverishly.

"We should be safe now," Dan said. "You're a brave woman. Not many would have the guts to do what you did."

Carola didn't say anything. Dan looked behind them to see if they were being followed. It didn't seem like it. They got to the compound quickly and ran inside the building.

When they were inside Melania's office, they sank into the chairs, exhausted.

"Drink, Jake. Water, anything." Dan said.

Jake nodded and moved out.

"What the hell happened in there?" Melania asked.

Dan explained to her then asked, "Where did you get the gun from?"

"There was a guard at the bar. I knocked him out with a bottle."

Dan nodded. "Thank you. Never easy busting out of a guarded building."

Melania turned her attention to Carola. "They saw me talking to you, right? I'm sorry."

Carola shook her head. "They're animals. One of them touches me up, and the others do nothing about it, just watch."

"What did they do to Roberta?"

"Same as the rest of us. They tried to have sex with us then pimp us out. To their masters and others who came to the club. Roberta realized and left."

"Why didn't you?" Dan asked.

She looked down. "I have a sick mother. She's on a breathing machine in Cagliari, our capital. I need the money, which is better here than anywhere else." She looked up, and her eyes were wet. "But there's a price to pay."

Dan asked, "Roberta had a boy, right?"

"Yes. She used to leave him with her aunt when she came to work."

Melania frowned. "What aunt? That didn't turn up in our inquiries." She turned to her keyboard and clicked then stared at the file that popped up on the screen.

Carola said, "Well, your place was kind of…"

"Scary?" Dan said.

She nodded. "This is a small island. No one likes what's happening here."

"Like what?"

"Rich people have always come here, but now the rich come with their private armies. They're different, more rough and demanding."

Melania asked, "Do you know where we can find this aunt of Roberta's?"

CHAPTER 32

Grozny, North Caucasus
Chechnya
ONE MONTH AGO

Natasha, the Scorpion, watched as the armored vehicles stopped at the checkpoint before the compound. Papers were checked, then the barrier lifted, and the vehicles rolled in. She walked slowly on the other side of the road. Chechnya was a mainly Muslim country, and she wore a hijab over her head and large sunglasses to hide her face, looking like any other Chechen woman out for an evening walk with her baby. The carriage she pushed didn't have a baby in it. It had a very lifelike baby doll's face peering over a blanket. Underneath the blanket and within easy reach was a fully loaded Dragunov SVD-63 semi-automatic rifle. Inside her baggy gown, she had two Makarov handguns, one strapped to her right thigh, the other on the left belt line. Around her waist, she had her most trusted weapons, the sharp needles of various sizes, each with a small handle at the end. They were handmade for her by the armorer who supplied the Spetsnaz. On her belt at her back, she had four fragmentation grenades.

She was hoping none of the weapons would be necessary. But if she was attacked, the only way out of this place was to unleash hell. Chechnya was a war-torn country, a hive of criminals and Islamists. Grozny, the capital, had a reputation for kidnappings and violence that made it one of the most dangerous places on earth, a place where the Scorpion's skills were ideally suited. But she wasn't here for that. She wouldn't shirk away if it happened, but like all men or women of violence, she unleashed her sting of death when there was no other option. Only fools opened up their guns and blasted away.

Her style was much more nuanced. Far subtler. Her victims only felt her presence before they died from multiple rapid stab wounds.

No, she was here because the leader of the Chechen Army, the de facto leader of the country, had requested her presence. His name was Aliev Daurov. To get her attention, Daurov had gone through at least three different individuals. Each of them was embedded deep in the SVR intelligence machinery. The third and final link in the chain was Colonel Borislov, one of her trainers at the Red Chamber, the elite, secret school of female operatives of the Spetsnaz.

Natasha was a lone operator now. She remained attached to the Spetsnaz but only in name, not in allegiance. She had no ideology. Nothing to prove or die for. She was trained to kill, and that was all she knew. When the message arrived on her encrypted app, she had stared at it for a long time.

Daurov was a slippery beast. He had not disclosed what he wanted, and she would have to be careful around him.

The compound opposite belonged to Daurov. She strolled past the entrance, noting the sentries on the watchtowers at each of the four corners. Machine-gun barrels poked out from behind sand bags. The guards were alert, with binoculars hung from their necks, which they used to scan the distance. The Scorpion took a right and stopped at the traffic lights. She moved down the road, circling the compound. Anti-aircraft gun installations caught her attention, rearing up from other watchtowers. The compound walls fell onto the Sunzha River, which wound its way through Grozny. The compound was a virtual fortress.

She walked down three more blocks, picking up her pace. From a pay phone, she called the number. A man answered in a thickset, heavy voice.

"*Shto yest?*" What is it?

"The Scorpion," she said simply.

There was a pause, then the voice returned.

"Our meeting is in ten minutes. Come inside the Oblast compound in the center of Grozny."

"No. We meet by the river, at a location I specify. In half an hour, not now. I will call when I am in position."

Another pause. "You don't trust me?"

"I trust no one."

"I own the whole of Grozny, *darogi debushka*." Dear lady. "If you don't trust me, you are not safe anywhere in Chechnya."

Natasha's hackles rose as she recognized the sexist jab in the comment. Her teeth clenched, but she kept her voice even.

"I have killed warlords with bigger armies than yours, asshole. It's *you* who's not safe while I am in Grozny. Got that?"

"Talk is cheap."

She smiled. "That sounds like an invitation. I accept."

Another pause, then Daurov sighed. "Borislov said you were a hard nut. OK, where do you want to meet?"

She told him the spot where the river bent to the left, on its way out of the capital. She put the phone down. She had left her car parked near the pay-phone booth. She got into the three-liter Zil car and gunned it to the location. She didn't have to wait long. Evening had arrived, and the last light of the summer day was being snuffed out by a bank of dark clouds. A procession of headlights appeared down the only road that led to the riverbank.

The hijab was off the Scorpion's head. The Dragunov was out of the carriage and strapped to her chest. Her waterproof, skintight black outfit lay beneath the baggy robe. She discarded the robe, slipped on the mask, and crawled into the reeds at the river's edge. A breeze ruffled the water, moving the reeds as she slipped through them. Three cars came to a halt on the road above her. She took her phone out.

"Only you. Go to the bridge and walk down to the middle." The bridge leading out of Grozny lay to her right. There were no lights, as the bridge had been heavily bombed during the second Chechen war. It managed to remain upright somehow and work, despite the lack of repairs. "When you reach the middle, stop. I will meet you there. If anyone comes with you or you have snipers in place, you die."

CHAPTER 33

The Scorpion watched as Daurov spoke to his men. One car drove off down the road. She watched it go over the bridge, and its taillights vanished from sight. A man stepped out from the second car. His height and size were the same as Daurov's. He wore the same green desert camouflage uniform Daurov wore. If she hadn't seen Daurov first, it would have been easy to mistake one for the other. Daurov leaned over and whispered in the man's ears. The man turned and walked slowly towards the bridge.

In a flash, she understood. The man was a body double, a trick used often by Middle East dictators and not unknown in Russia. Daurov watched his double go, standing by his car. The other car moved off as well, leaving only Daurov with his car and three bodyguards—three that she could see. There was a driver as well and maybe three more inside.

The guards were looking around, but Daurov's attention was on the bridge. It was a few minutes' walk for the double to get there. The Scorpion knew she had not been spotted. The river was a dark ribbon now. They were expecting snipers. Ideally, Daurov should be inside the car, but she knew the man was stubborn. No one would expect a threat from the ground up.

The water rippled gently as she parted the reeds and slid onto the bank. The grass verge led up about ten feet to the lip of the road. She stayed still for a while. No one looked down at the darkness of the riverbank. But she knew they would soon, and with flashlights. She had to move fast. Silently, she took out her longest needle and put it between her teeth. One of the Makarovs came into her hand, and she screwed a silencer on. She moved rapidly in the shadows, as stealthy as a jaguar.

The three guards formed a loose semicircle around Daurov. She stopped roughly five feet away and stretched her gun arm out. The first shot hit the man closest to her in the temple. Bone fragments exploded from his skull as the bullet erupted through the brain matter and smashed out from the other

110

side. The Scorpion had aimed already and fired before the first bullet made contact. All three bodies collapsed on the ground. She leaped out onto the road and rolled over to make herself a smaller target. She threw one leg out, catching Daurov as he flung himself back to the open door of the car. He stumbled and fell, and she was on his back in a flash.

She grabbed his hair and pulled his neck back. The needle was in her right hand now, the razor-sharp edge pushing into the soft of his neck. Two men tumbled out from the car, rifle muzzles pointed at them.

"Stop!" Daurov cried out hoarsely.

"Good call," the Scorpion said. "Tell them to throw their guns into the river. Do it. Now!"

Daurov nodded the best he could while she tugged back on his hair. She heard the rifles splash into the water below.

"Now tell them to lie face down with their hands folded on their heads. Right where I can see them."

They did as she ordered. She transferred her attention to Daurov. "Who's in danger now?"

He puffed for a while, face crimson. To his credit, he wasn't showing fear, but she knew he was feeling it.

"OK, you win."

"This isn't a game, Daurov," she growled. "Why did you call me?"

He didn't answer for a while. She pushed the needle in but stopped before drawing blood.

"Talk," she ordered.

"You need to take out a high-profile target."

"Who?"

When she heard the name, the needle slackened in her hand. She breathed heavily, looking at the guards but not really seeing them. Her mind was blank. Was Daurov bluffing?

She said, "You must be joking."

"No. And I have a very good incentive for you."

"Money?"

"Something more important."

This time, she lowered the needle all the way. Daurov coughed and spluttered. She kept a hold on his hair.

"I can kill you in a heartbeat," she said. "Are you lying?"

"No. And when you hear what it is, you will believe me. *Natasha.*"

He said her name with emphasis. Her breath froze in her chest. Her fingertips went cold, and she gripped Daurov's hair harder. Borislov wouldn't have leaked her name. No one knew her identity.

"How do you know my name?"

"If you let me stand up, I can tell you. Is this any way to conduct a business meeting?"

"It's my way," she breathed.

But she got off his back and jerked him upright. The needle went back into position at the side of his neck. She glanced at the guards. They hadn't moved, but she could see them looking upwards, following her movements.

"Put your hands up. Tell your dogs to lie still. Otherwise, you're dead."

Daurov barked at his guards in Chechen, a language the Scorpion understood.

"Now tell me," she said.

"I need to get an envelope out of my pocket."

"Try another one."

"Look, I am impressed with you already. You're certainly living up to your reputation. But believe me, I can still have you killed, any time. But now is not the time. We have business to conduct. I need to show you the details of the order, and it's not going to kill you."

She didn't trust him an inch but knew it was a good argument. She did need to see the documents. It would contain the blueprint of any building she would have to infiltrate and background on the target.

"You can take the envelope out, remove the documents, and put them on the ground." She pressed the needle harder, pricking the skin. She felt him stiffen.

"Then I want you to lie down right here, like your guards are. Got that?"

"Yes."

She took out her flashlight with her left hand as the papers dropped to the ground. Daurov lay down as she picked the documents up. She sat down cross-legged and went through them one by one.

When she was finished, the color had drained from her face. She folded the documents and tucked them into her vest. She said nothing as Daurov sat up. She stood as he did.

Daurov said, "Do you believe me now?"

Her eyes flashed in the moonlight that emerged from behind clouds. "How do I know it's true?"

"You don't. But can you take the chance?"

She remained silent, her jaw clenched tight. "When this is over, you are a dead man, Daurov."

He smiled. "You won't be the first person to tell me that."

CHAPTER 34

Daurov watched the Scorpion vanish into the shadows. Seconds later, he heard the car. One of his men stepped forward, and Daurov put his hand up.

"No. Let her go."

He had given the Scorpion fifty thousand US dollars in cash, two new passports, a social security number, and details of a job interview at the Bimini Resort in the Bahamas. That was where the operation would begin. She also had papers from him that granted her safe passage out of Grozny, on a flight to Sheremetyevo Airport in Moscow.

He picked up his cell phone and dialled the encrypted line that led to an office inside Lubyanka Square in Moscow.

Colonel Borislov answered on the first ring. "I'm listening."

"She almost killed me. You could have given me some warning."

"I did. I told you not to invite her to your palace. To her, it sends out the wrong signal."

"She just killed three of my men."

"You're lucky she didn't kill all of you."

They were both silent for a few seconds. Borislov was old KGB, a wily operator. He had served in the military wing called the GRU. His rank was higher now, and he had the ear of the premier himself. He was in the SVR, the First Directorate of Russian intelligence, the department that conducted overseas spying.

Borislov asked, "Did you show her everything?"

"Yes. She took the bait, like you said she would."

"Don't for a moment think she won't cross-check and find out the truth."

"Will she deliver?"

Borislov paused. "She has never failed before."

"If this goes all the way, you know what's going to happen, right?"

"Yes. We have it covered. Don't worry. Think about yourself now. Are you ready?"

Daurov's voice hardened. "Remember you are speaking to the head of the Chechen Army, Borislov. I'll go when I think I need to."

"No. You go now. That's the whole point. We are not sending Russian federal agents on this. No SVR or FSB personnel can be there when it happens."

"That's right. You want to blame the Chechens as the fall guys. Like you always have. Nothing changes about you Russkies."

"Whatever you say," Borislov commented mildly. "But start preparations."

"And if I don't go?"

"Then your army loses the funding from us. You also have no protection from the Islamists or ISIS." Despite Chechnya being a predominantly Muslim nation, Islamic terrorists hadn't created a strong foothold in the region. The allegiance between the Chechen Army and the various offshoots of Al-Qaeda had been thwarted with incentives from the Russians, who were no friends of the Islamists.

"Sure, we lose your funding. Then we get it from the Middle East, right? You want the Wahhabis down here, firing up our youth?"

Borislov said, "Have you forgotten the second Chechnya war?" Russia had fought two wars against Chechnya, the most recent being the second war in 1992. Losses on both sides had been considerable, but the smaller country had suffered the most.

Daurov hardened his voice. "Our boys are fighting for you in Syria. We are your secret weapon. How dare you threaten me with a war?"

"I am not. We do appreciate your help in Syria. And I hope our partnership continues. But this operation takes precedence. You know what's at stake."

Daurov breathed heavily, still incensed. He didn't trust Borislov, but the support his army received from the Russian state was huge. Chechens had always endured a love-hate relationship with their giant northern neighbor. For the sake of his people, Daurov knew he had to keep up appearances.

"Very well. But I need my men to have access to the latest equipment the Spetsnaz have."

"You will, no problem. When you get there, I will have new contacts for you."

Daurov said, "You know this can start a war?"

"There's a war going on already, Aliev. It's time you joined it."

CHAPTER 35

Sardinia

PRESENT DAY

The Scorpion lay the cold muzzle of the Dragunov rifle against her chin and pondered. She was leaning against a rocky outcropping on the hill overlooking Roberta's village. Seeing Dan Roy again had been a shock. When she found him on the viewfinder, her heart had jolted. It wasn't possible, but it was. As clear as daylight, as tough as granite, the man who had once been her lover. Here, in Sardinia. She didn't believe in coincidences. Dan being here was for a specific reason—to hunt her down. When he entered Roberta's hut, it reinforced her belief.

A grim smile came across her features. In a way, she was glad she left the matchbox on the floor of the hut. She had done it after the CIA had done their sweep. She wanted them to know what was happening inside the Billion club. Now that Dan was involved, she was sure he would pursue that clue. What had happened last night at the club was concrete proof of that.

The Scorpion's jaw tightened, and her eyes narrowed. Dan Roy… no man had ever aroused such conflicting emotions in her. A supremely agile fighter and a gentle, patient lover. He had almost killed her then taken her to the throes of ecstasy she hadn't felt before. As she stared at the village way below her, keeping her eye on Roberta's hut, she breathed out a sigh.

She couldn't let Dan get in the way of her mission. She wouldn't falter when it came to killing him. Her fingers circled the butt of the rifle tightly. There were higher things than Dan at stake here.

A buzz sounded in her pocket. She glanced around her. Nothing but empty countryside. She took out the cell phone and peered at it. A scowl came over her face.

"What is it?"

Daurov had mirth in his voice. "Is this how you greet your employer?"

She gritted her teeth and kept silent.

Daurov said, "You did well to escape from that CIA place. Congratulations on killing Andreyev."

Still, she said nothing.

He asked, "Where are you now?"

"On the island."

"I want you to see me. I will let you know the time and place. Plans have changed."

"Changed? How?"

He told her briefly, and she listened. The frown deepened on her face. Daurov was holding back, she could tell. But she knew better than to push him.

She said, "Once this is over, you have to keep your side of the bargain."

Daurov gave a cackling laugh that sounded like a hyena's. The Scorpion felt hairs rise on her neck.

His voice became stern. "Don't worry about what I'll do, *darogi debushka.*"

"Stop calling me that, asshole," she hissed. "We had a deal."

"It's still there. Just make sure you fulfil your end. We need to meet soon." The line went dead.

Breathing heavily, she stared at the screen, wanting to smash the cell phone on the rocks. The bastard had her over a barrel, and he knew it. She looked up at the blue skies of the windswept island. Somehow, she had to get out of this mess.

She monitored the hut from her vantage point for a few more minutes then got up and walked off. Roberta had shown her the smuggling routes that the old *banditos* used in the hills. After almost an hour of fast walking, she was at the village where Roberta was hiding with her aunt.

The Scorpion stiffened when she saw three running figures emerge from the outskirts of the village. She hid behind a tree. Three women, and the one in front was Roberta. The Scorpion stepped out.

Roberta saw her. Sweat was pouring down her face, and her eyes were red with tears. "It's Paolo!" she wailed. He was her eight-year-old son. "I can't find him anywhere."

CHAPTER 36

Dan headed over to the drink machine and got himself a plastic cup. He drained it and went back to Melania's office. She was alone, staring at the screen, chin in hand. Dan went to say something, but she lifted a finger, not taking her eyes of the screen. Then she got up, took out her phone and went out. Dan saw her going out the front doors then speaking on the phone out in the courtyard. By the gesturing of her hands, Dan could tell it was an intense conversation.

When she swept back in, he said, "Busy day at the office?"

She pulled a face. "Federal government crap. What do you want?"

"Where's my duffel bag?" The bag had been waiting for Dan in a locker at Malpensa Airport. He had boarded the seaplane from there and wasn't subject to further checks.

Melania gave him the key to a locker, and Jake took him down a corridor to the changing rooms. Dan was stiff from sleeping on the sofa the night before. He had a room reserved at a beachfront hotel under an alias, but he didn't have a car, and it was going to be later today till he got one. Melania and the others had sleeping quarters on-site.

He took out his duffel bag, unlocked the padlock with the key in his pocket, and examined the contents inside. His trusted Heckler and Koch 416 with all the mod cons and an HK MP submachine gun as well. That took up most of the space inside the bag. In a side pocket, he had two Ka-Bar kukri knives, and he put the one with black tape wound around the butt on his belt at his back. The black tape provided a better grip when his palm was sweaty. He racked the slide of his old Sig P226 and put a round in the chamber. The handgun went into a shoulder holster.

He patted the eleven-inch kukri knife on his belt line and stood, turning around. Melania was standing there, leaning against the doorframe.

"What's that?" She pointed at the knife.

"A kukri knife. Used by the Gurkhas, a mountain tribe in Nepal."

She stretched her hand out. Dan hesitated for a while. Their eyes met, and she shrugged.

"I'm not that good with a knife. Don't worry."

Dan grinned and unhooked the kukri. Melania turned it around in her hands. "One hell of a curve on it. Looks badass."

"It *is* badass," Dan said. "Most of my Delta buddies use one now." He put the knife back in his belt. "We ready to rock?"

She pointed at the duffel bag, which was still unzipped. "You've got quite the arsenal there."

Dan knelt, zipped up the duffel, and locked it. Then he stuffed it back in the locker. He had the key from Jake.

Melania said, "You don't like talking much, do you?"

Dan shrugged. Melania stared at him for a while. "I called DOD. Asked about Consular Operations. No one's heard of it."

"Not my problem."

"But your creds are authentic. And for some reason, you have clearance at the highest level of the CIA."

Dan said, "I'm just an employee."

She raised an eyebrow. "I don't think so. Who are you, really?"

"We're on the same side, Melania. Nothing else matters."

She shook her head and walked back to her office. Dan followed. Carola was waiting in the Jeep with Jake and Charlie. Melania took the front passenger seat, while Dan rode in the back. Roberta's aunt's village was deeper into North Sardinia. The road twisted and turned like a black asphalt ribbon through sun-dried yellow-and-brown hills. The blue-green Tyrrhenian Sea sparkled in the distance. At any other time, Dan would have enjoyed the ride, but his mind was filled with a sense of foreboding.

The Jeep dropped them off a third of a mile away from the village. A mistral wind, warm and humid, blew off the hills, ruffling the brush in a field as they crossed. Sardinia was known as the windy island, where the climate of northwest Africa and south Europe combined.

Dan did a three-hundred-sixty-degree sitrep as he walked, the trusted Sig in his hand. He kept glancing at the hills. He couldn't shake the feeling he was being watched. Melania and the other agents had their weapons out but not visible to casual sight. They moved in formation, surrounding Carola. The brush came up to waist height for Dan. The others concealed themselves with some effort, moving fast, bent at the waist. Dan held the rear, moving slower, eyes roving. If there was a sniper in the hills, he wanted to see the muzzle flash of the first shot.

Ten minutes away from the village entrance, they went to ground. Carola walked on her own. She had a cell phone with an alarm button at the top. She had to press it twice for help. Her instructions were simple—find Roberta's aunt and her son. If she found nothing, all she had to do was come back.

Twenty minutes passed. Melania stood up. "I'm going in," she said. She was dressed in a coarse cotton blouse and pants, similar to what the Sardinian peasant women wore.

"No," Dan said. "Despite your outfit, you're still a stranger."

"Carola should've called by now," Melania said.

"I know. Give her another ten. She might be asking around. We don't even know if the aunt still lives here, never mind the son. Try calling her."

"I have, twice. She's not answering."

Dan thought. If Carola was in trouble, those missed calls would warn the enemy. But Carola not answering was an ominous sign. He felt bad. The woman was brave. He should have gone in with her, despite his presence acting against the mission.

"OK," Dan said. "I go in first…"

"No, you don't," Melania said forcefully. "There are rules. We can't go in there and start shooting."

"Rules? When you got shot by a sniper, where were the rules?"

"Minimum collateral damage, Dan. Don't forget I work for the US government."

Dan opened his mouth then shut it. There was no point in arguing. This was precisely the reason why his time working for the army was over. Rule books and bureaucracy were made to serve those who made the rules. There was little justice for people like Roberta and her son. Dan believed in a more direct form of justice. If it was due, he wouldn't flinch from delivering it.

"Fine," he said. "You go ahead. But I have to be on comms with you. Hook me up."

Jake gave Dan a receiver and an earphone, and they did their comms check.

"Your call sign is Alpha 4," Melania said.

He winked at Jake, who smiled back nervously. Dan watched them go, sighing in frustration. They were like three sitting ducks in a row. He looked at the hills again then set off himself. He moved deeper into the brush, keeping the village to his right. This was quiet country, but the village should show some signs of life, but it was eerily quiet, like the last village they had visited—where the sniper was waiting for them.

Dan remembered the cartridge case he had picked up from the room. It was not from a sniper rifle he was familiar with, which pretty much ruled out anything used by the US forces. He focused on the task ahead. As the village approached, he slowed down. Gun scanning around the brush, he got close to the stone wall of one hut that backed into the jungle.

"Base, this is Alpha 4," Dan whispered. Dry grass crunched behind him. He rolled on the ground just as the boot aimed for his head hit the wall. Dan lurched backwards and slammed into the man who was trying to hit him. He grunted but barely budged. Dan came off him. The guy was massive, wide and thick in the shoulders. He lifted his gun, but Dan kicked his fist hard, and the suppressed shot zipped into the sky. In the same movement, Dan closed the gap, bent his elbow, and crunched it against the man's temple. He stumbled back, shaking his head, but the gun was still in his hand. Before he could aim it, Dan pulled his Sig out and shot the man in his center of mass. The heavy slug tore into his chest, and the man collapsed.

Dan crouched and glanced around.

His earbud chirped. "Alpha 4, sitrep?"

"Where are you?" Dan asked, vaulting over the stone wall, and moved towards the hut.

"Keep walking for one minute. It's the first hut by the pond, on the left."

"I just killed a sentry. Keep a look out."

"Roger that."

Dan walked fast. The quietness of the village was unnerving, but it wasn't deserted. The wooden shutters of a window opened in front of him suddenly. Dan reached for his weapon but relaxed when he saw an old woman staring at him. The face of a child appeared next to her. He hurried along till he saw a pond where the road bent to the right. The cluster of cream-and-pastel-roofed huts was thicker here. A figure popped out from the hut on the left, and Dan lifted his weapon. It was Melania. He followed her inside. The hut was similar to Roberta's, but Dan could smell something else. A rotting, putrid smell. It reminded him of kill houses the terrorists had in Iraq.

He saw the feet before the body. Jake and Charlie stood on either side. The flesh was decomposing, and the body was at least two days old. It was an old woman. One side of her face was caved in. Dan looked past them to the other room, where Melania had entered. She was crouched on the ground, over another body. Blood was still seeping out of the bullet wound to the head.

Dan gritted his teeth. It was Carola. He took two paces, knelt, and put two fingers to the carotid artery at the neck. The pulse was absent. He looked at Melania, her face as white as a sheet. Dan fought to quell the rage that was rising inside his chest like a black tsunami. His voice was harsh when he spoke. "Move. We got company."

CHAPTER 37

This time, Dan took the lead role. He figured they were surrounded, or at least the sentry he had killed had fired off a warning before attacking him. He stepped outside and stayed in the shadow of the roof. His gun arm scanned left and right, up and down. Across the dirt road, the door to a hut opened. A teenage girl stepped out, no more than fourteen or fifteen, Dan guessed. He lowered his weapon. If the gangsters were hiding around here, this was the worst possible scenario. Civilians were still here, women and children. A firefight was not an option.

His head jerked as the roar of an engine registered. From behind an alley, an SUV roared out. It had black-tinted windows that were lowering as they got abreast of where he was standing.

"Get down!" Dan yelled.

He turned and grabbed Jake, who was standing right behind him. He flung himself towards the doorstep, crashing the door open as he did so. They fell to the floor as the first bullets sprayed the doorway, shaking the windows as the wooden shutters felt the impact of the rounds. It was a sustained burst, set on automatic mode. Dan saw Melania crouched by the window, returning fire. She stopped when the car passed.

Dan sat up, panting. Melania was on the mic already, calling the Jeep. When Dan told her about the teenager across the road, she and he jogged over. Dan kept watch while Melania knocked on the door several times. Finally, an older woman answered. Melania spoke in Italian.

"Who were those men?"

The woman tried to shut the door in Melania's face, but she jammed her foot in the door.

"We can help you. One of my friends has just been killed by those animals. Carola. Did you know her?"

That stopped the woman. "Carola? Yes, I knew her. What happened?"

Melania told her, and the woman put a hand to her face. Melania asked her if she knew Roberta and her aunt.

"Yes. Roberta's boy, Paolo, was abducted yesterday. Someone snatched him while he was playing. It's these same bastards." She spat on the ground.

Dan said, "They are Chechens, right?"

"I don't know," the woman said. "But they speak in a funny language. Someone said it's Russian. They're crawling all over our island. Women and children are going missing from our villages. They have descended on us like a curse."

Dan said, "Do you know where that car went?"

"No."

The Jeep screeched to a halt behind them. Jake leaned out from the back window. "We passed the SUV on the way. Getting a drone fix on them right now."

Dan and Melania jumped in, and the Jeep did a three-point turn, raising a cloud of dust. Jake was in the rear, holding a tablet that had the drone feed on its screen. The software calculated the GPS location and displayed it on a box in the right corner.

"Where we headed?" Dan asked.

"Back towards the sea," Jake replied. Then his face creased in a frown. "What the..." He picked up the tablet and shook it. Then he took out his cell phone. "Damn display's gone."

"Uh-oh," Dan said.

There was a crashing sound behind them, and a fireball roared past Dan's window and erupted in a blaze of orange and yellow in front of them. Dirt exploded from the road onto the windshield, and the impact shook the car. The driver swerved the car to the left. The tires screeched in protest as the car tipped, forsaking the asphalt road. But the driver managed to retain control, and the car swung back on the road. It drove through the crackles of a yellow flame on the road.

An engine roared, and Dan saw a black SUV in the rearview. He could see the snouts of guns pointing out the window. The driver pressed on the gas, and the Jeep, a smaller car than the SUV behind them, shot forward.

"I need a gun," Dan said.

"What for?" Melania asked.

Dan checked that the magazine on his Sig was full then wound the window down. Wind howled in through the gap. He checked the SUV—it was catching up fast.

"What are you doing?" Melania asked.

Dan didn't answer. Jake handed Dan his Glock. Dan checked the mag again, racked the slide, and held a weapon in each hand. He waited till the SUV was within range. His Sig could shoot longer distances, but for the Glock, he wanted the car to be within one hundred feet.

He twisted, putting a foot against the seat, and leaned out of the window. Wind whipped at his face. The SUV was in range now, and the muzzles of rifles were raised in his direction. He didn't waste time. If those rifles started firing, he had no chance. He jammed his waist against the corner of the window and pressed both triggers hard and fast, the sound a dull roar in his ears, mixing with the noise of the car as it hurtled down the road.

He aimed for the tires first, trying to get a hit. It was impossible with both cars moving at speed. But he did hit the front left tire and watched as the round pinged off—armored tires.

Dan emptied both mags then ducked back in. He wound the window up fast. Everybody had their heads down. The bullets streaked in, smashing into the car. The armored glass of the rear windshield was dinged repeatedly with a sound like a baseball hitting a bat. Dan watched as the SUV tried to swing out in front, but the Jeep covered its path. It tried the other way with the same result. On either side, there was tall grass strewn with rocks and boulders. The car then came forward, its fender bouncing the Jeep's rear.

"I can't go any faster!" the driver shouted.

The SUV withdrew then smashed in harder, its fender twisting with a metallic scream as the Jeep's rear bumper caved in.

"He's trying to push us off the road!" Dan shouted.

The shove came again, and Dan's hand shot out to steady the steering wheel. He gripped it and pulled it towards him, but there was another massive blow, pushing him against the dashboard. The back of the Jeep swerved then fishtailed out into the road. The car spun out of control, tires blowing black smoke, then came off the road. Dan saw a boulder in front of them, getting bigger by the second. It was the size of the car but not as wide.

"Watch out!" he screamed, pulling the driver down with him. The driver had braked as hard as he could, and it had slowed the car down. They hit the boulder side on, glass smashing into the rear seats. The airbags blew out in front, pressing Dan's face against a taut white surface. Over the airbags, he saw the SUV zoom past them without stopping.

The silence inside the car was deafening.

Dan kicked his door open and fell out the car. Steam rose from the twisted hood of the Jeep. He tried to open the rear door, but it was locked. He got back inside the car and unlocked it. Melania was unconscious, her head lolling over her neck.

CHAPTER 38

There was a sound, as if someone sunk inside a well were shouting. Melania listened hard, but she couldn't make out the words, muffled and distant. There was a dimness in her mind, but some light was spreading around the edges. Slowly, the light got tighter, stronger at the center. The sound became louder too.

"Melania!"

Her eyes flew open. She saw blue sky and a man's face. Tanned, square jawed, nice looking. Dark-brown eyes stared at her intensely. Her mind fumbled for a few seconds then found it. Dan Roy. The mysterious black-ops guy who had joined her team.

She put her palms on the ground and sat up. Her head felt heavy. With effort, she got up, still kneeling.

"Easy," Dan said.

She ignored him. Her head swung from side to side, and she felt sick. She coughed, then bile trickled out of her mouth. A tissue was held out to her, and she accepted it gratefully. Then she sat down on her butt. A warm wind blew in her face. She looked around her. Dan Roy was on the phone. Jake and Charlie, her two colleagues, reclined against the Jeep.

"You guys OK?" she managed to croak.

"Yeah," Jake replied.

Dan came back and handed a cell phone to her. "I borrowed yours to call base."

She took the phone from him.

He sat down on his haunches. "They took out the drone. That's why we lost the feed. They wanted to blow us off track."

"Who the hell are they?"

Dan rubbed his cheeks. "Chechens and Russians."

"How do you know?"

"Done multiple ops against them in Belarus and Europe. I speak the language too. Chechens are tough guys. A lot of the Russian mafia hit men are ex-Chechen Army."

Melania nodded. "So what the hell are they doing here?"

Dan shrugged. "Why was your asset Andreyev here?"

Melania sighed. She tried to stand up again, took Dan's extended hand, hauled herself up, and steadied herself with it.

"Maybe you should sit back down," Dan said.

"No." She took a few deep breaths, feeling the clean air invigorate her lungs. She checked her phone then looked up at Dan. "If we find them, chances are we find Roberta and her son. From there, we get the agent who escaped our site."

"It's a stretch, but potentially, yes. This agent, you have to be careful of her."

Melania flapped her hands at her side. "You've hardly told me anything about her."

Dan folded his arms across his chest. She tried not to watch, but her eyes were drawn to the rippling muscles of his forearms.

He said, "Her name is Scorpion. She's a graduate of the Red Chamber, an elite training camp the Spetsnaz run. For female assassins only."

Melania narrowed her eyes. "I might have heard of the Red Chamber. Some say it's a myth."

"The Scorpion's not a myth. I have the scars to prove it."

"What did she do to you?"

Dan ignored her question. He said, "I have a feeling the sniper who shot us was none but her. I can't be sure, but the whole setup had her fingerprints all over it."

Melania was silent, thoughtful for a while. Then she asked, "Where do you think that SUV went?"

"I don't know. But checking the drone feed before it went kaput is a good idea."

The replacement vehicle pulled up shortly, and they left. Back in the compound, Melania made a beeline for Jake's desk in the open-plan analysts' office. Jake sat down and got the feed up on his screen. They peered over his shoulders. The drone had been above their heads from the beginning of the operation. It was a handheld drone, but the camera on it was strong enough to record images with startling clarity.

Minutes before the drive-by shooting, they saw movement in an alley around the corner. It was the SUV, and men were piling into it.

"Stop," Melania said. The frame focused on the men. "Zoom in."

When the zoom was close to the face of the man getting into the front passenger seat, Melania froze. Her mouth opened, and she felt like a jackhammer had punched her in the gut. She couldn't move.

The man was bald, but those pale, colorless eyes, she would have recognized anywhere.

CHAPTER 39

MELANIA – THEN

The school gates were busy with children and parents kissing goodbye. The snow had relented today, and the skies were a scrubbed, vivid blue. The cold was sharper, if anything. Marinochka always came to school alone. She did enjoy her studies and was a favorite of the teachers, and the stipend she got from the state meant her school meals were free.

The day passed by in a blur, and closing time came quickly.

She was out of the school gates and walking down a side road, lost in her own world. Sadness layered like silt in her heart, and her lips trembled. Why was her life so hard? Her friends lived in bigger apartments and had TVs in their homes, and their parents drove Lada cars. Why couldn't she have some of those things?

As she turned a corner, Marinochka bumped into someone. She shrank back, apologizing. When she looked up, her heart almost stopped when she recognized the face.

It was the man she had seen earlier, by the butcher's shop and at the river. His pale, colorless eyes were scarier closer up. Marinochka stepped backward quickly, her shoes almost slipping on the ice.

The man smiled at her. When he did, the seriousness in his face vanished, and he seemed like a nice person. The eyes still unnerved her. The man leaned forward, as so many grown-ups did when they spoke to children.

"Are you OK?"

Marinochka swallowed, eager to get away. "Yes, I'm fine."

His smile was broader. "Well, you don't look OK." He cocked his head to one side. "In fact, you look a bit sad. Anything happen at school?"

Marinochka was so unused to a man asking about her welfare that for a while, she didn't know what to say. She opened her mouth then realized she was speaking to a stranger. Mama had forbidden her from doing that, and she must have a reason.

"I should go home now," Marinochka said, looking down.

"Sure. Just put a smile on your face, OK?" His lips curved upward, and even his pale eyes were touched by the mirth. Despite herself, Marinochka found herself nodding.

The man reached inside his pocket and, for some reason, looked around him before he took his hands out.

"Here, take this," he said.

Marinochka looked at the gray bank note in the man's hand. It was a fifty-ruble note, more money than Mama earned at the factory in two weeks. She gasped. "I can't take this."

The man, whose name she still didn't know, leaned forward again. "Of course you can. And there's more if you come to work for me."

Marinochka knew she should go home. Talking to strangers wasn't allowed, and taking money from strangers? No way. But her curiosity was piqued. She looked around her. There were other people around, walking in the distance. Surely it was safe here, in broad daylight.

He thrust the money towards her. "Take it."

Marinochka shook her head, squinting up at him. "No, sorry." She thought for a second then asked, "What sort of work do you do?"

"We make engines for cars. We need strong girls like you, who can work hard."

"How much do you pay?" She mentally slapped herself. Did she just ask that?

"Three rubles an hour. Say you work three hours after school. That's nine rubles a day. Think what you could do with that money." He stopped speaking suddenly, and Marinochka wondered what he wanted to say.

But hope flared in her heart like a rainbow after a storm. Wow. What could she do with that money? She could buy the week's groceries, for starters. Go to the butcher's for meat. Tell Mama not to work so hard. The possibilities were endless.

But doubt still raged in her mind. Should she do this? What if Mama found out?

"Can I think about it?" Marinochka asked.

The man gave her a reassuring smile. "Of course. No pressure. It's totally up to you. I'll see you around." He waved then walked off quickly. Marinochka stared at his back, open-mouthed. Then she turned to walk back home, her mind on fire. It was only then she realized that she hadn't asked his name or how she was going to contact him.

CHAPTER 40

MELANIA – THEN

After close of school the next day, Marinochka came out and scanned the road up and down anxiously. Her school friends laughed and chattered, and parents hovered around them. Marinochka couldn't see the man. She left the crowd behind and started walking back home.

She heard footsteps behind her, crunching ice. The man waved at her, and she stopped. He smiled in that engaging way again. Marinochka looked into his strange, washed-out eyes and wondered if she was doing the right thing.

"So did you have time to think?" he asked.

"Yes, I did." She paused. "What's your name?"

He laughed at that. Marinochka wondered why it was so funny.

He said, "Sergei."

His flat eyes bored into her, and she stared back at him.

"Look," Sergei said, "I'll give you the address of where the factory is, and you can come and have a look by yourself. If you don't like it, then no problem."

Marinochka nodded slowly. That made sense to her. "Where is the factory?"

"Five miles away, across the river."

Marinochka's face fell. "That's too far. I'd have to take the bus."

"I have a car. I can take you there and drop you back off here. Or you can wait for the bus."

Marinochka knew the bus was slow. She would be late back home, and Mama would be angry if she didn't know where Marinochka was.

"OK. I'll come in the car with you."

Sergei smiled and raised his hand. As if by magic, the rumble of an engine sounded, and a van rolled up. The only windows were at the front, on the driver and passenger side. Sergei slid the side door open. Inside, Marinochka saw a wooden bench along either side and space in the middle. Like a strange school bus. A man was driving the van. He had a baseball cap pulled over his face, and although he was staring at her, Marinochka couldn't see him well.

"Get in," Sergei said. "It's not a long ride. We'll be there in ten minutes."

Marinochka hesitated one last time. Her mother's sad, worn face floated in front of her. Little Michka crying for milk. Marinochka thought of how hungry she was herself.

She walked forward and stepped inside the van.

The door slammed shut. It was dark inside and cold. Marinochka hugged herself. She could hear voices in the front. The van set off, and she had to hold on to the side as the vehicle lurched. She heard a sound behind her and turned quickly. She couldn't make anything out in the darkness. She wished there were a light here. She drew her knees up to her chin and sat tight as the van rolled on.

The sound came again, closer this time. It was a soft, sliding sound, as if someone was scooting close to her. Her heart thudded, and fear blossomed inside her. She opened her mouth to scream, but a hand wrapped itself around her mouth. The hand jerked her head back, and she felt herself falling. She struggled, but the hand was too strong. She smelled gasoline and sweat. Then a wet cloth was wrapped over her face, and it had a weird, sweet smell. So sweet she had to inhale it. Marinochka kicked out with her legs once, twice, but could feel her body growing feeble. Then her eyes closed, and her world faded to black.

CHAPTER 41

MELANIA – THEN

Marinochka was swaying. Her body felt as if it were being carried by the waves of an invisible sea. But she wasn't wet, and after a while, she realized her eyes were shut. She opened them and looked at the black roof of the van. She tried to sit up, but it felt strange. She fell back immediately, and her back hit the side of the van. Pain spread up and down her spine, and she winced. Her hands wouldn't move, and when she looked, she saw that her wrists were tied. That was why she couldn't balance herself. Her feet were also bound, with coils of nylon rope that bit into her flesh.

It was light outside. She could tell by the rays of sun filtering in through the cracks in the roof. The floor rattled as they went over an uneven road. As her eyes got used to the dark, Marinochka could see more figures on the floor. Opposite her, four more girls were laid out, hands and feet tied. There was a boy too. He seemed younger than the girls. All of them were sleeping.

Fear caught inside her throat. These men were kidnapping them. Sergei's colorless eyes invaded her mind. She shivered. Then she remembered what happened after she got on the van. With a gasp, she swivelled her head from side to side. She muffled a scream when she saw the man. He was sitting on the wooden bench, near the corner close to the driver's seat. His beady black eyes were observing her silently. There was no expression on his face. She noticed the shallow depressions of small pox on his clean-shaven cheeks. He seemed younger than Sergei.

She closed her eyes and swallowed, breathing rapidly. Where were these men taking them? More importantly, why? If it was just to work somewhere, why did they have to be tied up?

Mama's face returned to her mind, and she whimpered. Tears rolled down her cheeks. Why hadn't she listened to Mama? She had always told

Marinochka not to speak to strangers. Now she was paying the price.

She sobbed in silence for a while. Her hands were tied, so she couldn't dry her eyes. She looked at the man, who was still observing her, his face bland.

"Who... who are you?" Marinochka stuttered.

The man didn't say anything.

"I want to go home," Marinochka whimpered. "My mama is waiting for me. Please take me home."

The man said nothing. Marinochka repeated herself, and the man looked away from her.

Marinochka raised her voice. "Please!"

"Shut up!" the man shouted back. His voice was much louder than hers, and it shocked Marinochka into silence.

She leaned back against the van, a vacant, sick feeling spreading inside her. Part of her mind refused to accept what was happening. This must be a bad dream. She would wake from this any minute. She would talk to Sergei, and he would let her out of the van. This was all a bad dream, wasn't it? How could it be real?

She turned back to the man. "I want to speak to Sergei." She tried to speak in a calmer voice.

The man ignored her. She wanted to ask him again but didn't want him to shout back at her.

She bit her lips and tried to fight the nausea churning in her guts. Any minute now, she promised herself, this dreadful nightmare would be over. She would wake up and be in their small bedroom, Mama sleeping next to her, and baby Michka, her little *lapochka*, snoring in the crib next to her.

Why couldn't she just wake up?

She stared down at her hands and saw the red hair band on her wrist. She could see the green dragon painted on it. Mama had a similar one because they had bought matching pairs. The thought made her sob again. She missed Mama so much. She forgave her for all the scolding and harsh words. Marinochka just wanted to see Mama, and she would listen to everything she said.

The van began to slow down. Soon it came to a halt. The man in the corner got up and opened the sliding door of the van. Marinochka craned her neck. She caught a flash of Sergei's face as he came out of the passenger side. She wanted to shout his name, but something told her it would be a mistake.

She looked opposite her and saw the other children stirring. Two of the girls were wide awake and stared back at her. Marinochka observed closely, but she didn't know them. The man with the pockmarked face came back in.

He squatted in front of them, his face as blank as before. This time he spoke. "I will take the rope off your legs so you can walk. Anyone who tries to run or scream will be beaten so hard you will wish you were dead. Do you understand?"

He hooded his eyes and stared at them intently. "Do you understand?"

The children who were awake nodded. Marinochka watched the man with alarm. In his quiet posture and his unnerving calm manner, she detected danger. When he looked at her, her skin burned with revulsion. There was a look in his eyes, a gleaming, funny expression that made her feel like vomiting. She couldn't meet his eyes.

A voice shouted from outside. The man came forward, and Marinochka folded her knees quickly. The man opened the back doors of the van. Daylight had faded. Marinochka saw rusted walls of a warehouse and smokestacks behind it. There was an eerie quiet about the place.

The man came back and leaned by her feet. He cut the rope with a knife then held the blade up. She glanced at it, her eyes wide, then back at him. He was giving her a warning. She nodded quickly, gulping. He did the same with the other two girls who were awake. They waited while the other girl and the remaining boy were carried out. Marinochka saw Sergei when she was outside.

"Sergei," she called out.

He ignored her, walking in front.

"Sergei," she called again.

He stopped then turned. His lips were tight with anger, she could tell. But she didn't care. She had to know what was happening. She opened her mouth to speak, but he slapped her across the face. It rocked her backwards, and she stumbled to keep from falling.

"Shut up, you stupid bitch!" Sergei snarled. "Didn't you hear what he said?

If I hear your voice one more time, I'll bury you underground."

Tears blinded her eyes. She had sunk to her knees, terrified. She felt a blow land on her back, and pain mushroomed inside her. She cried and fell forward. Pockmark Face leaned over her.

"Get up and keep moving." He spat then walked ahead. He stopped to check she was coming.

Marinochka got to her feet, sobbing. She walked towards the group, who were disappearing inside the deserted warehouse.

She wanted to escape, to run as hard as she could. Pockmark Face stepped closer, as if reading her mind. She saw the knife in his hand, pointed straight at her belly.

CHAPTER 42

MELANIA – THEN

Marinochka didn't know what to expect inside the warehouse, but what she saw took her breath away. Hundreds of children either lay on the dirty floor or leaned against the wall. There were some women too. Most of the children were teenage girls, about her age or older. A few men strolled around. All of them had rifles in their hands and their fingers on the triggers. Marinochka had never seen a rifle before, but the way these men held them, she could tell they would fire without hesitation.

Something sharp prodded her in the back, and she moved as fast as she could. Their little group got to a clearing by the wall, and Sergei ordered them to sit down.

Bottles of water were given to them, and Marinochka barely had time to have a mouthful before it was snatched away. A girl next to her was crying, and she looked to be the same age as her.

"What's your name?" Marinochka asked.

The girl didn't answer immediately. Eventually she lifted her red-rimmed eyes. "Mia." Her head dropped back on her chest.

"Don't worry, Mia. Someone will find us."

Mia shook her head. "If there was, they would've found us already."

The last light faded from the sky, and it became colder. There was one fire burning in a corner of the freezing warehouse, and the men were huddled around it. Marinochka lay down on the cold, dusty floor and felt the bodies around her pressing closer for warmth. A foot pressed against her head, and she moved. When she laid her head back, she realized she could use the foot as a pillow. A weight was pressing down on her leg as well, and she guessed it was another body part, everyone sleeping against each other for some warmth.

Sleep didn't come to her. The men had taken the ropes off her hands. Men with guns patrolled by and stood in front of the entrance. There wasn't going to be any escape. She knew that.

There was no remedy for the pain inside her. Her heart ached when she thought of what Mama was going through now. She had probably left Michka with Rustova and was running around the freezing-cold town, begging the police to help. She kept saying Mama's name over and over again till her eyes grew heavy.

*****

The sound of shouting voices burst through her senses. Marinochka woke up quickly and sat upright. The men were shouting orders. One of them was pulling prone figures up by yanking on their collars. A man walked past them with a basket, and he threw a loaf of bread at them. Several hands clawed and fought for it. Marinochka clutched wildly. She was starving. She got a mere handful before it was all gone. She gulped it down while reaching for a bottle of water that was being passed around. Fights erupted inside the warehouse, and men shouted for order.

Marinochka saw a girl being lifted and slapped so hard she sprawled on the floor, unconscious. She saw Sergei walk up to the man. He pointed a finger at the girl and shouted at the man. When he looked away, his eyes landed on Marinochka. She lifted her hand immediately.

"Sergei," she shouted.

He looked away as if he didn't even know her.

Pockmark Face came back, this time with a rifle strapped to his chest. "Get up!" he barked. "Form a line."

The tired bodies shuffled together, and they were paraded out. Marinochka needed the toilet badly, but she dared not ask anyone. When they were outside, Sergei turned to them at the front.

"If anyone needs the bathroom, do it now."

Marinochka looked around her. Everyone was looking at each other confusedly. From the corner of her eye, she saw trucks rolling into view. They had giant rectangular containers on their backs. She counted five trucks, which came inside the compound and rolled to a stop in front of them.

Around her, girls were beginning to squat. Embarrassment reddened her cheeks. She heard the hiss of urine and closed her eyes. But she knew she had to go as well. She didn't have any choice. When she opened her eyes, she noticed some of the men were leering at them. She caught Pockmark Face standing very still. The look on his face scared her. It was the same expression he had worn when he got close to cut the rope from her feet. Nausea rumbled inside her. Marinochka turned around quickly, and with her back to him, she squatted. It was shameful, but she had to do it. The stench of urine hit her nostrils, and she wondered how much worse this would get.

The tailgate of the nearest truck was lowered, and one by one, they entered the container.

CHAPTER 43

MELANIA – THEN

When the truck was full, bodies packed in a sweaty, humid, suffocating mess, the tailgates lifted, and the doors slammed shut. It induced a sudden darkness in the interior of the truck, and several frightened voices gasped. Mia grabbed Marinochka's arm. The truck lurched as it set off down the road.

"Where are we going?" Mia whispered in a fearful voice.

She was younger than her, but Marinochka wasn't sure by how many years. Mia couldn't be more than nine, she thought. She made her think of her baby sister, Michka, and a lump came to her throat.

"I don't know."

"I'm scared."

Marinochka didn't say anything. Fear was ever present inside her, like a river flowing invisibly in her bloodstream. But along with that came a dullness in her senses. She now knew it would be a miracle if she got back home again. Hope, that strange, mystical candle that lit people's souls, was slowly burning out inside her.

These men were well organized and armed. They reminded her of the men who stood outside the Tver *politzia* station with guns in their hands. When the truck had stopped at a checkpoint, no checks were made of the cargo. Marinochka had been waiting and hoping. After all, every car was searched at checkpoints. Only government cars and military trucks were allowed to pass unchecked. Did these people work for the government?

The few rays of sunlight that came in through the truck's roof eventually vanished. It was dark outside as well as inside. They truck shuddered to a stop. Moans for food came from around Marinochka. The tailgates were lowered, and the doors creaked open. It was pitch-black outside. Two powerful flashlights beamed inside. She recognized Sergei's voice.

"Ten of you will be let out at a time. If you try to run, we will kill you then leave you in the field. Understand?"

Hardly anyone spoke.

Sergei shouted, "Understand?"

A smattering of voices agreed.

There was no food, and the hunger was like an ulcer inside Marinochka's stomach, gnawing at her guts. Rough hands forced her down, and the beams guided her to the line of children either standing or squatting. Shame prickled inside her, but she knew she had to do it. This truck wouldn't stop just because she wanted it to. A night breeze hit her face, cooling the sweat. She didn't know how long they had been travelling, but it had clearly been almost a day. It was warmer here than in Tver. She knew that. Tver to Moscow was a two-hour journey by road, and they had been travelling since early morning.

The darkness stretched away in front of her, bereft of any lights. The road they were on had potholes in it, and she could tell it was barely used. Briefly, she thought of running. What would happen if she did? A bullet in the back? She wondered if that would be any worse than the fate that awaited her.

A boy next to her zipped up his pants. She couldn't see his face clearly, but he was taller than her and, she assumed, older. He was breathing heavily. His stance was rigid, and she felt tension radiate from him. The flashlights were at the ends of the line, and she was in the middle. She heard the boy murmur something and recognized it as a prayer. She turned to look at his face, hidden in the dark night. In the distant starlight, his eyes seemed to gleam. He ignored her, but his breathing got heavier.

"Hey," Marinochka whispered.

He ignored her, so she repeated herself. The boy glanced down then looked away again.

"Are you OK?" she asked.

"Shut up," the boy whispered. There was a steely edge in his voice.

She gaped at him. Suddenly, he moved. He ran towards the field, running steps sounding clearly on the dry ground. One of the beams swung around. The light caught his back as his legs pumped.

"Hey you!" Sergei shouted. "Stop!"

But the boy didn't stop. Another voice shouted, and she saw Sergei step forward. The rifle that was strapped to his chest came easily into his hands, and yellow flame shot out from the muzzle. The noise was like a rolling thunderclap, so loud Marinochka had to put her hands over her ears. Several of the children screamed. The boy had almost disappeared from the beam's arc, but she saw the bullets tear into his back. He stumbled, throwing his arms up in the air. Then he fell, twitched once, and was still. Pockmark Face and Sergei rushed towards him, their flashlights bouncing up and down. When they stood over the dead body, Sergei kicked it with his foot.

Marinochka looked away, bile rising in her throat. She kneeled, nausea rising inside her, and vomited. The children were crying, wailing. Another beam trained on them, and their cries became screams of fear.

A man caught a child by the hair and bellowed at him. "Shut up!" He grabbed the child and threw her on the ground. He advanced down the line, pointing his rifle to the sky and shaking his light at them.

"Get on the bus! All of you, now!"

The children scrambled for the truck. Many were crying. Some were sick. Bodies moved in front of Marinochka, and she felt a hand touch her face. It was Mia.

"What... what happened?"

Marinochka folded Mia into her arms. "Nothing. Remember to do as they say and keep quiet."

CHAPTER 44

MELANIA – THEN

The floor of the truck was never clean to begin with, and now it was covered in a thick layer of dust. The truck had stopped in another deserted field, and loaves of bread and bottles of water were thrown inside, causing the usual chaos and fighting. Marinochka got enough for her and Mia, but her heart broke when she saw some of the children not even make the effort to fight for food. Their eyes were flat, lids drooping as they slumped against the side. Marinochka banged the door, as she was close to it. She kept hitting it till she heard voices. It was daylight now, and the miserable sight it showed almost made her long for the dark.

Bolts slid, and the door creaked open. Sergei stood there with a scowl on his face. His startling pale eyes stared without emotion, flicking around. When Marinochka raised her hand, he looked at her. Recognition flared in his face.

"What do you want?" he asked in a rough voice.

"Some of those children at the back... they look sick."

Sergei didn't even look beyond her. A shit-eating, nasty grin came on his face. "When you take fruits to the market, some go rotten. Get used to it."

"But..."

"Shut up, bitch. Remember what happened to the boy?" Sergei glared at her.

Marinochka looked down, a heavy lump weighing down her neck.

The door clanged shut, and the truck started moving again. It was getting hotter now. The sweaty bodies were bunched together, and the only circulating air came through the cracks in the ceiling and doors. The sound of coughing was louder, and so was the occasional moaning.

Day passed into night, and Marinochka had fallen asleep by the time the truck came to a stop. Loud shouts and the beams of flashlights awakened her. The doors were slammed open, and the fresh air was like a benediction on her face. She sighed in relief and stared at the sight in front of her. They were on a road, but it looked out to water. She could see large boats docked at the harbor, and red and yellow lights gleamed from tall cranes that lifted shipping containers into larger boats that were farther out.

Behind their truck, the other three trucks had lined up. She could see the people from one truck trudging slowly up the gangplank of a boat. Their heads were bowed, and they leaned on each other for support. Nearly all of them were children and most of them girls.

Sergei appeared again. The rifle was in his hands, and he pointed it at them menacingly. Marinochka stepped back, heart hammering in her chest.

"Any of you try anything, we just throw you in the water, and you can drown. Got that?"

There was a mumble of tired voices. One by one, they came down, several barely able to stand. Sitting and shuffling or crawling, they formed a line that eventually stretched to another boat. Marinochka saw Pockmark Face leaning against the deck, a toothpick in his mouth, staring at them lazily. He held a gun in plain view. Their eyes met, and she saw the same strange look cross his face, followed by a smile. She looked down quickly.

The breeze blew in strong, carrying a fresh saline smell. Where was she? Mama used to say that when she was younger she went to Odessa, a city by the Black Sea, for vacation. Was that where she was?

A sudden panic gripped Marinochka. A black weight gripped her throat and threatened to burst out of her mouth. If they were being loaded into a boat, were they leaving Russia? Were they going to another country? If so, any faint hope she had of seeing Mama and Michka again was now gone.

No. She couldn't go. As long as she was alive, she would fight to see her mother and sister. But if she left the country, that hope was dead. She didn't speak any other language. How would she survive?

She looked around her wildly. Sergei was at the back, checking the inside of the truck.

"Sergei!" she shouted.

Pockmark Face looked in her direction. She ignored him. She shouted for Sergei again. He had his back to her and turned around slowly. He shook his head, eyes blazing. With quick strides, he crossed the distance between them. Marinochka was near the end of the line of silent, beaten children dragging their exhausted bodies up into the boat.

Before she could say a word, he grabbed her hair and pulled hard. Marinochka screamed. He threw her on the ground then kicked her as she tried to get up. He stood over her as she sobbed.

"What makes you think you can call for me? Huh? Do I look like your servant?" His face was a mask of rage.

"Please... I don't want to leave Russia. I want to see my mama."

He taunted her in a copycat, high-pitched voice. "*Want to see my mama.* You're lucky I haven't gotten rid of you already. Now get back in the line and shut up."

He walked back to the truck. Marinochka gathered herself as she stood up. Her whole body was shaking with indignation but also with the first kindling of anger. It came out of helplessness, and it sparked a fire in her like brimstones rubbing against one another. She dried her eyes and brushed her hair back. From the corner of her eyes, she saw Pockmark Face momentarily distracted as he loaded the first lot of children on the deck. More men stood by, directing the children down a hole in the deck. She shuddered to think what lay in the hold of the boat.

Sergei was busy in the truck cabin, and another man was smoking a cigarette, rifle hanging from his neck, and speaking on a cell phone. All of them were distracted. She seized her chance. Directly opposite, across the tarmac road, lay a virtual city of shipping containers. If she could run between them, maybe even hide inside one... Marinochka was wearing jeans, and her shoes were boots that were good in the snow but could help in running, too.

She sprang to life, running as hard as she could. She had underestimated how weak she was. Her legs flailed and almost gave way as she sprinted. She crossed the road when the shout rang out. It was the man on the cell phone. She heard a gunshot and felt the whine of a bullet as it zipped over her head. More voices joined in, and then she had reached the first container. She ran around it and flattened herself, breath heaving in her chest.

She could hear them coming. She streaked out to the next container. From the shouts behind her, she guessed the men were hard on her heels. She ran desperately, hoping she would bump into a dockworker. She could explain everything to him.

She took a hard left as she heard the shouts to her right. A shadow stepped out from behind the corner. She ran full tilt into it and smacked backwards on the floor. A hard hand reached out and grabbed her by the vest, pulling her up. A slap lashed against her cheek, and she felt herself falling. Her eyes blinded in a flash of light, and she saw stars as her head hit the shipping container. Hot, fetid breath panted against her face.

"I'm going to fix you, *durakh*." Stupid.

It was Pockmark Face. Her vision swam, but when she blinked, the deep scars on his face came into focus. She felt his hands reach out and squeeze her breasts. She fought with him, but the running had exhausted her. She cried out as he pressed her against the container, and his knee forced between her legs.

"Not here," a voice rang out next to her.

Sergei and three other men had arrived. All had guns drawn. Sergei's face was drawn into a snarl. He reached out, grabbed Marinochka, and slapped her once again. Then he put the gun to her forehead.

"Do you want to die? Answer me!"

He pressed the muzzle against her forehead, and it hurt like mad. She began to cry. Sergei didn't ease on the pressure.

"Yes!" she wailed suddenly. "Shoot me. Get it over and done with. Do it now." She cried harder. The muzzle of the gun eased off her forehead. She bent double and sank to the floor.

She heard Sergei spit on the ground. "Put her in the cage. We sail now, before someone starts asking questions."

CHAPTER 45

MELANIA – THEN

The rolling of the boat made Marinochka sick. The boat was big. She could tell by the space in the hold. The children were kept to one side in a barricaded area. She was in a separate cage by herself. Her punishment for the escape attempt was starvation. For two days, she watched as the men came and handed out bread, cheese, and water to the captives. She begged them to throw some to her. The men ignored her. The children ate what they got, and it went so quickly there was never enough for them to throw to her.

The seasickness affected everyone. The stench in the hold grew worse. It was hot, too, and the hold was kept under lockdown unless one of the men came down. By the end of the second day, when she was delirious with hunger, she sensed a man approaching her cage. She could barely see.

"Have you learned your lesson now?" It was Sergei.

She couldn't speak. Her head lolled to one side as she lay on her back in the cage. Sergei opened a grill at the bottom of the cage and pushed forward a plate with a cup of water. Then he walked away. She reached for the food, and the smell of it made her gag for some reason. But after the first bite, she ate ravenously.

That night, after the food round, she heard the trapdoor lift and footsteps coming down. She recognized the figure when he approached her cage— Pockmark Face. She lurched to the back of the cage, remembering what he had done to her at the dock. He came forward and grabbed hold of one of the bars.

"Ready for some action?" he slurred, and she knew he was drunk. His left hand snaked down and undid his belt. She looked away, revolted. He took out a key with his right hand and slipped it into the lock then moved the door to one side.

Marinochka could feel her heart thudding against her ribs. Her breath was stuck in her chest, and sweat poured down her face. She shrank into a corner of the cage. The other children were silent, but she knew they were watching.

"Come on." He reached out a hand.

She shook her head slowly. He took a step forward. The iron bars were digging into her back. She had nowhere else to go.

A voice boomed down the trapdoor. It said something she couldn't understand. The language was related to Russian. She could tell by the accent. But the words were unfamiliar.

Pockmark Face frowned then rocked on his feet. Another figure lumbered down the steps. It was Sergei.

"We need them clean," Sergei said. "Otherwise, no money. Remember that."

Pockmark Face passed a hand over his face. He zipped up his pants, went out of the cage, and slammed the door shut. Sergei locked it up, and they both went upstairs.

*****

The boat rolled on endlessly. They stopped several times, but they were never let out of the hold. At high sea, they were moved from the boat to a larger ship. This was a proper ship, with shipping containers stacked high like giant Lego parts. Marinochka watched the blue waves all around her, white froth whipping from them as they lashed against the ship. She had never seen a vivid blue sea like this, stretching all the way to the horizon. They were taken by a rubber dinghy to the larger ship. The dinghy was full of children, and as the boat slammed up and down on the waves, Marinochka heard a scream. A group of children were pointing at the waves. She stood up to look, and her heart froze. She saw a little head bobbing up and down in the giant waves. A hand appeared, signalling for help. She looked at Sergei and Pockmark Face, who were driving the dinghy.

The child was getting smaller as the ocean currents carried her away. The two men looked at each other and shrugged.

"Sit closer, and away from the edges," Sergei shouted. Marinochka felt empty inside, as if her heart had been ripped out and thrown to the sharks. She looked around her anxiously, trying to find Mia. Could that have been her? Mia wasn't on the boat. Marinochka closed her eyes and prayed as tears rolled down her cheeks. Many children were still waiting in the smaller boat. She whispered feverishly to a God who didn't care to keep Mia in that boat and for her to be safe.

The children were put inside three shipping containers on the deck. As the doors clanged shut, Marinochka wondered, not for the first time, if going to sleep forever was better than staying alive like this.

CHAPTER 46

MELANIA – THEN

It was a voyage in almost perpetual darkness, night without end, across a heaving, endless ocean. The only light they saw was when the container doors opened and food was flung inside. Days passed, and Marinochka didn't know how to keep track of time.

She spent her time praying and hoping she would one day see her mama and little Michka.

She imagined it would be sometime in the future.

Mama would have grown old, her hair white. She would be bent at the waist like a babushka. Maybe she would even have a walking stick. And Michka? Why, Michka would be taller than Marinochka was now, and she might not even recognize her own sister. This became one of her favorite dreams. She would wake up in the tomb-like atmosphere of the container, withering bodies dying around her, and she would see Michka's green eyes shining with happiness. Even as she woke up, the intensity of the dream didn't leave her, and for a few precious seconds, her sister's eyes would be holding her own, sustaining her like the blue waves carrying the ship.

One day, Marinochka woke up to great turmoil. Children were screaming all around her. She sat up then rolled over as the container lurched. She tumbled against several bodies, and they held on to each other, frightened out of their wits. Then the rolling stopped. The bolts squeaked, and the doors opened. Sergei stepped inside. He picked his way down the container. The terrified children were as silent as mice. He stopped in front of Marinochka.

"This one," he said over his shoulder.

Another man entered, and it was Pockmark Face. He reached over and grabbed the top of her vest. Marinochka screamed and fought, but he ignored her. He put her on his shoulder and carried her out. The ship had docked at a berth. She kicked him, but the weeks of living in cramped conditions had wasted her muscles, and her efforts were feeble. Pockmark Face swatted her limbs away with ease. Even her cries were weaker.

She felt strong arms lift her, and briefly, she saw Sergei's face. His colorless eyes showed no emotion. Holding her over his shoulder, he climbed down a rope ladder to a boat. Pockmark Face carried another child down, and they repeated this process twice more. The sunlight and wind on Marinochka's face was refreshing, but she didn't care about that anymore. She looked around her. Above the boat, from a pole, she could see a flag flying. It had red and white stripes, with white stars in a blue box in the top left corner. She had never seen the flag before. Apart from the four of them on that deck and the two men, the boat seemed empty. That was till she saw the two men who emerged from the cabin, smoking.

One of the new men spoke in a tongue that she didn't understand. It sounded softer. The men were the same skin color as Sergei but more tanned.

Sergei spoke back to them in the same language, and there was an argument, which the new man seemed to win.

Sergei shook his head. The new man nodded, his eyes sweeping over the four of them. Marinochka could see they were all girls about her age.

The new man chuckled at something and threw his cigarette in the water. Sergei said something in Russian under his breath. He took them downstairs in a similar hold to the previous boat. But there was no crowd here. Instead, they each had a straw mat in one corner where they could lie down. The mat even had a pillow. After what Marinochka had just been through, this was sheer luxury.

She sat down and rolled the red hairband off her wrist. She kissed the green dragon on it.

"Every time I wear this, Mama, I think of you," she whispered. "And one day, I will find you and my little Michka."

She tied up her hair in a ponytail and lay down on the straw bed.

*****

A sound infiltrated her consciousness. She didn't wake at first, as the sound was muffled. But when it came again, her eyelids flew open. It was louder now, and it had that booming quality that she had learned to associate with gunfire. Voices rang out, and steps pounded the deck above. The sound of gunfire came again in bursts. She heard screams and shouts, and the deck above her head shook. Marinochka looked around. The other three children with her, all girls, had their knees tucked into their chins, rocking. One was crying. Marinochka went up to her and called the other two. They sat in a huddle.

All of a sudden, there was silence upstairs. Footsteps could be heard, but the gunfire had stopped completely. The trapdoor at the corner of the deck lifted. Rays of sunlight burst into the darkness. The girls huddled together. Marinochka could feel fingers digging into her sides. Her own fingers were like claws too. All of them had been through violence and at the mercy of desperate men. There was no reason to think this time would be any different.

A flashlight beam trained down, and a head appeared. It was a man, and he was looking in cautiously, as if he expected to have his head blown off any minute. When the beam fell on them, it stilled. The man gasped and withdrew his head. Then two flashlights fell on them at the same time, and a pair of men craned their necks to look through the trapdoor.

One of the men shouted something, and Marinochka realized he was speaking to them. It was a language she didn't understand, but it sounded familiar. The man asked them something again.

She thought for a second then cried out in Russian.

"It's only us. There's no one else here."

The men at the trapdoor went quiet. They discussed something between themselves in a low voice. She strained her ears but couldn't hear their words. Then one of the men slid the barrel of a gun down the trapdoor. Marinochka's heart thudded against her ribs. The children hugged each other tighter. One foot tested the top rung of the stairs, and the gun lowered, scanning the depths of the hold. Slowly, the two men came down, guns jerking around.

One of them ran over and knelt by the children. Marinochka stared at him. He was clean-shaven and had curly black hair and very dark skin. He stared at them closely, his mouth falling open. He whispered a word she understood.

"Jesus."

The two men spoke rapidly on their cell phones. Marinochka felt frustrated. She still didn't understand a word. The men spoke to each other as well, looking at them all the while. But she could tell these men were not like Sergei or Pockmark Face. They wore nice clothes, for starters. The looks on their faces were of surprise and shock, but Marinochka had learned by now looks could be deceiving. Actions spoke louder, and these men didn't reach out to touch them or grab them roughly like the others. They kept their distance and smiled at them occasionally. She didn't smile back.

Running steps came from above, and two women is green uniforms came rapidly down the trapdoor. God's name was invoked time and again, and soft blankets were handed to them. One of the women in uniform was in tears as she helped them up the trapdoor steps.

This is new, Marinochka thought.

It was a blur after that. A lot of people had lined up on the harbor, staring at them. The same red-and-white-striped flag, with white stars in the top left corner, flew from several flagpoles. White vans with blue and white flashing lights took them down roads that reminded her of Moscow, but these roads were, well, different. The cars looked bigger and nicer. Lots of pictures of happy, smiling women hung from large signboards on the roadside. A green-uniformed woman gave them a can to drink from. She took a sip. It was sweet and tasted of apple. She drank it greedily.

Marinochka was separated from the other three girls at the hospital. She could tell it was a hospital by the sick people waiting and the smell. But it was so much nicer than the hospital in Tver. The lights were brighter, the walls were painted in yellow and pastel colors, and it didn't look like a gloomy old place built a hundred years ago.

They had some tests done at the hospital, and much to Marinochka's relief, a Russian translator arrived. She was a woman in her fifties and explained to Marinochka that she needed to give the doctors permission to take blood from her. Marinochka stared at her, uncomprehending. In Russia, they were told in a rough voice to stretch their arms out. The translator must have seen the confusion in her face.

"This is how they do things in America," she said.

America? What?

"Am I really in America?" she asked, dumbfounded.

The woman smiled. "Yes."

Wow. Marinochka lay back and let the doctors take blood from her arm and swabs from her mouth. She imagined America as a distant, foreboding country. On TV back home, America was shown as a country of rich people, where the poor starved and were ignored. But the older children at school said it was different. And from what she had seen so far, Marinochka had to agree.

She had a proper bath that day in a cramped hospital bathroom. Feeling the warm water against her skin, washing away layers of black dirt, felt like being born again. She emerged from the bath into a warm, fluffy towel. Her eyes closed in wonder as she wrapped it around her. Did such soft towels really exist?

Was this a cruel dream from which she would wake up soon?

Marinochka couldn't believe her luck. She slept soundly that night, and the next morning, the translator arrived again to take her to another building. She sat while a man and a woman dressed in suits asked her questions via the translator. She told them everything, not leaving anything out.

When she was done, she had to ask them. "My mama is called Aloyna Karmen. She lives in Tver. I have the address. She lives there with my baby sister, Michka. Can you tell her I am here? Please?" Her voice broke at the end, and tears rolled down her cheeks.

The translator patted her hand and spoke to the pair opposite. They wrote something down on a piece of paper and nodded to the translator.

"They will look for your mama, darling. Don't worry."

The building had a dormitory where other children were sleeping. All were girls, but Marinochka had preferred the hospital suite, which was for her alone.

Before she lay down on the bed, she took the hairband off her ponytail and kissed the green dragon.

"Every time I wear this, Mama, I think of you," she whispered. "And one day, I will find you and my little Michka."

CHAPTER 47

MELANIA – THEN

The next morning, Marinochka woke up and got dressed to find the translator already downstairs. Her name was Liliana, and she introduced Marinochka to Anna, another lady who was a teacher and fluent in Russian. Marinochka didn't understand why she was being introduced to a teacher till she followed them to an office.

A man was waiting inside, opposite the same two people in suits she had seen yesterday. The man stood up when Marinochka entered. He wore a suit as well, but it looked nicer on him. He was middle-aged, and his hair was dark brown, slicked back with gel. His eyes were the same color as his hair. He was handsome, she couldn't help noticing, and when he smiled, his teeth were perfectly white. He had an engaging, warm smile, but she was wary of men and didn't smile back.

He stuck his hand out to her and said something. Marinochka looked at the outstretched hand in confusion. When she looked up at his face, the smile was still present, but there was something else in his eyes, a softer, kinder look, as if he felt sorry for her. He lowered his hand slowly.

Liliana said, "This is Mr. Benjamin Wiblin. He is going to adopt you."

Marinochka frowned. "Adopt?"

"It means you will live with him while you are in the USA."

"But I want to go back to Tver. To my Mama. I told you." Marinochka's voice was raised. She couldn't help it. A hollow feeling was spreading inside her chest, and the ground seemed to shift beneath her feet.

"Where is my mama?" she said again. "And my sister?" She turned to the couple on the other side of the desk. "I gave you my address yesterday."

Liliana touched her hand. "Do you know how long you have been gone from home?"

157

Marinochka struggled to answer. "No."

"Almost four months."

Her mouth fell open. She searched for words and found none.

Liliana said, "They searched for your mother. No one of that name lives at that address anymore. The place is empty. Whoever did live there hasn't left a forwarding address."

Marinochka's hands balled into fists, and anger burned behind her eyes. "No! It's not possible. My mama and Michka live there. We have always lived there."

Liliana shook her head. "I'm sorry, *lapochka*. We don't know where your mother is."

She trembled, and everything shook before her eyes. The world tilted on its axis, and she felt herself falling. A pair of strong arms supported her and gently lowered her to a chair. It was Mr. Wiblin, and he spoke to her softly.

Liliana translated. "He says you can stay with him while they search for your mother."

Marinochka looked at the handsome man. He held her eyes, and she averted hers quickly. She was afraid of all men, and she had no reason to think this one would be any different.

She glanced up at Liliana. "Will you come with me?"

Liliana smiled. "No. But Anna will come daily. She will teach you English and homeschool you till you come up to US school standards."

Anna, who was younger and blonder, smiled at Marinochka. She said, "Mr. Wiblin is being kind to you. He is an important man. A US congressman."

"What's that?" Marinochka blurted.

"It means lots of people have him speak on their behalf, to the nation's leaders. So in his state, and nationally, he is an important man."

Marinochka sneaked a glance at Mr. Wiblin, wondering what all that meant. He was staring at her intently, and she found his gaze disconcerting. She looked away quickly.

It lasted a while, but in the end, Marinochka knew she didn't have a choice. She said goodbye to Liliana, who promised to call. With Anna, she followed Mr. Wiblin to his car. He had a driver, who opened the door for them. The spacious car smelled of leather. When the windows went up, it was nice and cool inside. She caught Mr. Wiblin looking at her again, and she closed her eyes. A new fear was pressing into a tight, hard knot inside her stomach.

CHAPTER 48

MELANIA – THEN

The Wiblin family home was a sprawling affair. When the massive double wrought-iron gates swung open, the car crunched gravel towards an imposing mansion. Long pillars fronted the portico, with a door in the middle wide enough to let an elephant through. Marinochka couldn't help but stare, wide-eyed and open-mouthed. Houses like these rivalled what the tsars used to have.

Was that what Mr. Wiblin was? Some sort of an American tsar?

They walked inside, Anna translating as Mr. Wiblin explained their surroundings. The place had been in the family for six generations, apparently, including the surrounding four acres of land. Marinochka was silent, drinking it in with her eyes. Her shoes clicked on the marble floor. The large hallway opened out into a giant living room with rooms in both directions. Huge trees were visible outside.

They turned around as they heard footsteps coming down the stairs. A woman descended, dressed in a skirt and flowery vest. She was attractive, blond-haired, but her face was pale and eyes withdrawn, as if she hadn't slept well.

Mr. Wiblin went up to her and introduced Marinochka first then Anna.

Anna said, "This is Mrs. Janice Wiblin. Say hello."

"Privyet," Marinochka said and went red-faced immediately. She really needed to learn some English.

Anna translated for her, and she saw Mr. Wiblin smile, amused. But Mrs. Wiblin wasn't. She remained frosty and tight-lipped, and her eyes stared above Marinochka. Without a word, she walked out the front door. Marinochka stared after her. It was clear that the lady of the house didn't want her living here. Again, a sense of fear clenched inside her gut.

*****

Anna came every morning and stayed till early evening. As obsessed as Marinochka was with thoughts of Mama and Michka, she knew her hopes of finding them were much higher if she spoke English. With the same zeal that had made her a grade A student back home, she plunged into her studies. After four weeks of intensive English lessons, aided by watching TV, she could speak her first sentences in English. She hardly saw Mr. Wiblin except in the evenings on weekends. But when she did, he seemed delighted at her progress.

"Picking things up fast, kiddo," he said one summer evening as birds tweeted outside. She had been in the house for five weeks and was settling in. She had her own room with a bathroom attached.

She stared at him. "What is *kiddo*?"

He stared at her in that way she found weird. She looked away, unable to meet his eyes. The memory of how Pockmark Face and Sergei had looked at her was still too fresh.

"Kiddo means kid. Like a child."

"Thank you, Mr. Wiblin." She stared at her feet, lost for further words.

"Call me Ben," he said, clearing his throat.

She glanced at him and saw that look in his eyes again. It bothered her. He seemed to be in a different world when he had that strange expression in his eyes, as if he were a scientist examining a new species of life.

She took a deep breath. "OK, Ben." After a pause, she asked, "Where is my mama?"

She didn't miss the startled look on his face. For a while, he didn't speak. Then he murmured, "I don't know... Marinochka. But I know we are looking for her."

"I want to find her. I want to go back home." She felt lonely and lost again, that black tidal wave of belonging nowhere rising up like a storm inside her. She trembled. Ben stood up and came towards her. He stood an arm's length away and didn't touch her.

"For now, this is home. Do you understand?"

She sniffed. "Yes. But promise me you will look for her?"

"Of course." His eyes met hers, and for once, she didn't look away.

He said, "Can I suggest something?"

"What does that mean?"

"Means I want to help you. With your name, actually. Your name has to be easier for people to say. How about something like…" He looked up and put both hands on his waist. Then he clicked his fingers. "How about Melania?"

"Melania?"

"Yes. Do you like it?"

She shrugged. From watching countless TV programs, she had learned one phrase American girls used when they agreed with something. "I guess so," Melania said.

CHAPTER 49

MELANIA – NOW
Sardinia

Melania dropped onto a chair, her heart pounding. She couldn't believe what she was seeing. But it was there, in black and white. The face stared up from the screen, as if it were looking at her.

Sergei.

The blank, emotionless stare in those strange eyes, devoid of color. How could she ever forget? Revulsion, anger, and frustration suddenly engulfed her, each conflicting feeling fighting for a place in her heart.

"Give me a second," she said and stalked out of the room. She went outside in the sunlight and leaned against a cement wall. It couldn't be anyone but Sergei, the man who had abducted her and sent her life reeling down an abyss. She screwed her eyes shut to blank out the images and sounds of that part of her life—which lay submerged in her mind like the unseen, immovable part of an iceberg.

She focused her mind back on the present. Why was Sergei here? What was he doing with the Chechen gangsters?

The door slid open, and Dan Roy stepped out. He walked easily, light on his feet, despite his size and bulk. Physically, at least, she had never seen a man like him. He didn't meet her eyes but leaned on the wall next to her. He reached inside his pocket and extracted a cigarette packet and a Zippo lighter. He lit a cigarette and offered the packet to her. Melania hesitated. She had smoked briefly in college but given it up quickly. In the end, the need for *any* relief from the turmoil in her mind won out. She held the cigarette between her lips while Dan lit it for her with the big Zippo flame.

Melania took a deep drag and blew out. The nicotine rush made her a bit dizzy, and it felt different. Almost good.

Dan said, "Do you know what Brits call a cigarette?"

"Smoke?"

"Nope."

She shrugged, smoking.

Dan said, "Fag."

"Fag?"

She turned to look at him. "As in…"

"Not like faggot, no. They just say fag."

Melania took another drag and held the cigarette between her unpolished nails. No makeup either, she thought. One hell of a life, serving her country.

"Just a fag," she said.

"You know that guy on the screen, right?"

She shook her head. "Was it that obvious?"

"Not really. You saw something in that photo that alarmed you. But the man's face was most prominent."

Melania flicked ash.

Dan said, "Who is he?"

She took her time replying. "I need to look into it," she said eventually, appreciating the time Dan gave her. Her hand went to the pendant necklace that Ben Wiblin had given her upon her graduation from CIA University. It had the Wiblin coat of arms on it. Touching the pendant had become a habit for her, and she did it absentmindedly.

She stubbed the cigarette out on the ground. "Thanks for the… fag."

Dan's eyes were invisible behind his shades, but she thought his lips twitched briefly. "Anytime."

"Didn't realize you smoked."

They walked back together.

Dan said, "Didn't realize you did, either."

She grinned. "I don't, till you decided to tempt me."

"I only smoke when stressed. You looked that way, so I figured can't hurt to offer you one."

"Well, thanks."

She walked back to the control room, where Jake and the others were still examining the drone feed.

"We got the license plate," Jake said. "It's an Italian number, registered in Treviso, a town in North Italy."

"Have you tracked it?"

"Waiting to hear back from Italian authorities. Sardinia's police chief wants to speak to you about the incident in the Billion club. It's gonna hit the media, and they want to get their facts straight."

Melania grimaced. The media vultures were to be avoided at all costs. "Tell them we had nothing to do with it. If he argues, ask to see proof."

Jake nodded and got back to work.

Melania said, "We can collect signals from the bay area, right?"

Jake nodded again.

"I want you guys to collect everything you can get hold of—phone calls, VOIP calls, credit card transactions, emails, videos, keystrokes, phone taps, any electronic signals, basically, and send it to me. I'm sending it to the NSA and SID. Something's going down here, big enough for the bad guys to shove us out of the way. Let's find out."

She took a copy of the drone feed and went into her office. She locked the door and sat down at her desk. From a locked drawer in her desk, she took out a cell phone and powered it up. She called line number 1.

After one beep, she said, "Woodville, this is Greystroke. Requesting access."

A metallic, machine voice asked, "What is your status, Greystroke?"

"Alone in the forest, waiting for an epiphany."

"Repeat that, Greystroke."

She did then held on. There was a series of clicks followed by the buzz of static.

Then a human voice said, "Who is this?" It was Karl Shapiro, her boss at the Directorate of Operations.

"Melania."

"Any news on the agent who vanished from the site?"

"Looking for her, sir. I need to access Signals in the NSA."

"You want Chuck's number and password?"

"Precisely."

After another three minutes of secure passwords and voice recognition, she was finally speaking to Chuck Jones.

"I want your analysts to run a face file for me. I have the visual image on a drone feed. Caucasian male, last known name Sergei. Human trafficker."

"I can get the guys to run it on MYSTIC and ID-300. What we looking for?"

"Any hits. We found him here, and I know him from a previous operation. Connected to Chechens as well. "

"Send me the files, and give me half a day."

She thanked Chuck and hung up. The windows in her office had iron bars outside, and she could see the hot Mediterranean sun tilting on its axis, leaving a dull glow and longer shadows. She came out of her office and went into the analyst's office.

Dan Roy was nowhere to be seen. She looked in the gym and the locker space at the back. She guessed he had left. Melania said goodbye to the staff and walked to her accommodation at the rear of the compound. Her thoughts returned to Roberta and her son, Paolo. That much, she had known from Roberta's file. She wondered where that boy was now and if he was safe. When she thought of Roberta as a mother, anxious for her son, Melania's hurt lurched. The deeper she got into this case, the more she dragged up the past.

She opened the fridge in the kitchen of her small one-bedroom apartment and cracked open a beer. As the sun went down and night blacked out the sky, she opened her laptop to check if there were any emails. Nothing.

She dug inside her pocket and took out the red hairband, the green dragon sewn on it now faded with age. But to her, it glowed as bright as the day she had received it. She put the hair band on the table and stroked it gently.

"Guess what, Mama and Michka. Today I saw the man who stole me from you. The one who destroyed our lives. I will find him, and I will make him talk. Then I will find you. I will not rest till I have found you."

Melania picked up the hair band and grazed it against her lips then held it in her fist, against her beating heart.

CHAPTER 50

Dan told the CIA staff he was heading back to his hotel. It was time he checked it out, having spent his first night in the office. But he had other priorities. He made sure he had his weapons with him then walked to the beachfront. It was a short distance from the harbor, and he avoided the main road leading up to the busy, glitzy street. He found an old, unused railway line, weeds growing between the rails. Rusty carriages of old cargo trains hulked in one corner. It was probably used to ferry stuff from the harbor to the beach. Maybe there was an old mine somewhere. From his file on Sardinia, he knew the island was used for tungsten and titanium mining by the Nazis during the Second World War.

The wind ruffled the collar of his blue shirt as he walked. After the day's heat, the evening breeze coming off the sea felt good. His mind went back to the events of the day. He could feel the Scorpion's presence without actually having seen her. It was weird, but Dan had always known to trust his sixth sense.

Carola's death weighed heavily on his mind. She had paid the price of helping them with her life. Melania would track her family down, if she had any. But Dan wanted his own brand of justice for her.

The railway came to an end abruptly. He crossed a few disused yards then jumped over a six-foot fence. He was on the main road now, and it was suddenly very different. Not one, not two, but three Lamborghini Diablos rumbled down the road. Pink, blue, and red, three in a line. The beautiful people on the sidewalk stopped and stared. Glass windows of shop fronts throbbed as the super cars moved slowly down the road.

Dan used the distraction to lower his sunglasses and peek around the street. He couldn't see any suited gangsters keeping an eye on proceedings. He pulled the baseball cap lower over his face and walked on. The Billion club was coming up, and he noticed the traffic getting heavier. Cars were parked in front of the nightclub, which seemed to be open for business again. The security detail was different now. Three men with MP5 submachine guns patrolled the front. When cars pulled into the drive, they were scanned with a handheld metal detector before anyone was allowed out of the car. Dan crossed the road and, staying with the crowd of pedestrians, walked quickly. He took the next right, hooking around the club. He headed for the rear, going past more fashionable boutiques, sun-bronzed long legs, and a smattering of Porsches and Ferraris.

The club had a rear parking lot, as he had suspected. He couldn't avoid the stare of the guard as he walked past, and he noticed the CCTV cameras inside the lot, aimed at the street. But he also saw a black SUV inside, its front fender damaged so badly it was practically hanging off. He couldn't get the license plate number, and when he looked up, the guard was pressing on his right ear, and his lips were moving. Dan didn't speed up—that was the first sign the guard would be looking for. He strolled casually forward then went inside the second shop. It was a clothes boutique, thankfully for men as well as women. He pretended to be interested in a suit while peering at the parking lot.

The guard was looking around with purpose. Weapons bulged from both shoulder holsters. He was speaking to someone through the receiver embedded on his suit. Dan saw movement in the parking lot. Two men got into the banged-up SUV. They revved the engine and rolled out towards the entrance. The bar lifted, and the guard, who was still speaking, waved them through.

A scooter came to a stop in front of the shop. It was a pizza-delivery guy. He took his helmet off and left the engine running. From the box attached to the rear of the scooter, he took out a number of pizza boxes and walked to a shop. The broken SUV drove slowly past the shop where Dan was looking from. He didn't waste any time. He was out the door in a flash and on the scooter. The pizza-delivery guy had left his helmet on the seat. No one stole such things on a small island. Not till now, anyway.

Dan put the helmet on his head and took the scooter off its resting leg. He did a rapid three-point turn, making the cars coming down at him honk loudly in protest. He gunned the small engine, his eyes on the SUV as it trundled down the road. The car took the road heading out of the tourist zone of Porto Cervo. Dan stayed three cars behind, but the traffic soon got lighter. The shops and bars gave way to shacks and walled compounds as the road headed to the island's interior. There was no cover now, and the SUV could clearly see anyone following. Dan decelerated and watched the SUV become smaller but still visible. He would speed up if the car took a turn. He heard a buzzing sound in his ears. Without looking, he knew it came from behind him. The buzz became louder, and in the side mirrors sticking up from the scooter handles, he could see a black motorcycle headed his way. It was a powerful machine. He could tell by the size of engine. The driver was covered from head to toe in a black outfit and black helmet and visor and was bent over the machine.

Dan sped up, and so did the motorcycle. He watched it getting bigger in his mirrors. It wasn't a contest, really, between the 500cc engine and his little scooter. But it was the driver who held his interest more. The person was slim, and his heart skipped a beat as he realized it was a woman.

The Scorpion.

CHAPTER 51

A truck barreled down the road, heading towards Dan. Dust covered him as it went past. He had sped up to the maximum speed of sixty-five miles per hour now, the scooter's engine protesting, its small wheels wobbling as Dan cranked the bike to its maximum power. The motorcycle growled behind him and switched lanes. It came alongside him easily. Dan sneaked a glance, but the driver's features were hidden in the head-to-toe black outfit and the helmet.

The motorcycle pressed closer to Dan, forcing him off the road. He turned the accelerators on the handles, making the engine whine. He braked suddenly, and the motorcycle shot forward. They were on a clear stretch of a straight road, but around them was a dense forest. Dan knew his scooter was useless, and if he had to protect himself, he needed to escape on foot. There were villas dotted around, and he could steal a car from one of them if need be.

The scooter slowed rapidly, and Dan was off it before it came to a stop. He jumped into the undergrowth and rolled over, the branches catching at his body. He protected his face with his forearms and lay flat as he came to a stop. A quick glance told him the motorcycle was also coming to a stop. Just as he had predicted, it was harder to make a machine that size stop quickly. It was way ahead of him, but he saw the driver leave the vehicle, turn, and run towards him in the blink of an eye. Fast and deadly. Only one killer he knew moved that fast, and his earlier assumption had been correct. He watched her reach for a sidearm, and he moved.

He was up and running for the cover of the trees when the first bullet whistled above his head and thwacked into the branch next to his face. Dan increased his pace, but the going was slow. The forest was dense, creeping ivy twisting around his feet. Dan took his kukri out and hacked at the vegetation. He needed to get distance, his main fear being the needles that the Scorpion

170

used so effectively. If she got within range, she wouldn't miss, and he knew some of them were tipped with curare poison. Ancient tribes in the South American jungle used darts tipped with curare. The poison stopped muscles from contracting, and within minutes, a person died, as they couldn't breathe. Dan had no intention of dying that way. He crashed on, boots trampling on brush and twigs. A snake slithered away, and he retracted his leg just in time. Sardinia did have some poisonous snakes, and Dan could tackle snakes with his kukri, but it was only going to slow him down.

The trees became denser, till the only light was the rays that stole in through the heavy foliage. Dan stopped behind a tree and crouched. It was very quiet, save his own labored breathing. He listened hard. The Scorpion would be making sounds as she moved. But he heard nothing but silence and the odd creak of a branch. It made him uneasy. Where was she?

A tingling in his spine made him move. He didn't know what it was, but years of being hunted and shot at had given Dan an almost extrasensory perception of danger. He turned and went deathly still. The sharp end of a needle was pressed against the soft of his throat, right next to his windpipe.

"Don't move, Dan. All I have to do is press," the Scorpion whispered.

Dan closed his eyes. Her voice sent a shiver inside him, like a wind moaning through a graveyard. She meant what she said. He knew that much.

"I'm not going anywhere."

"Put your hands up in the air and keep them there."

Dan did as he was told. The needle stayed in contact with his skin as her other hand frisked his belt. She threw away the Sig and two magazines then the kukri.

"You have a gun on one of your legs, covered by a sock, right?"

It was useless to argue. He nodded.

She said, "Lie on the grass. Hands stretched in front, facedown." She moved quickly, but Dan had lied about the ankle holster. As soon as the needle left his neck, he kicked viciously with his right leg. It caught the Scorpion by surprise. She fell sideways, and Dan rolled away then sat up to pounce on top of her. He moved his face just in time as the silver flash of a needle darted past his nose, so close it almost touched it. Then he was on her, shoulders knocking her back, hands reaching for her hands to stop her from getting another needle.

The Scorpion fell backwards, but she bent her knees and unfurled a double kick with both legs that slammed into Dan's chest. It gave her time to grab another needle from her rig, and she flung it at him. Dan dropped like a stone, and he got lucky again. The missile whistled past his ear this time. He knew there wouldn't be a third time lucky. Not with the Scorpion.

He lunged at her, this time grabbing her legs as she kicked. She managed to hit him in the face, and he felt the dirt from her boot blind his eyes, and he tasted it on his tongue. But he didn't stop. If she could aim again, he was as good as dead. He moved up her body, covering it with his own. His hands reached for hers as they fell on her belt rig. He pressed her hands down then closed his fingers around them. She lifted her head off the ground, trying to head-butt him. He yanked his neck, and the blow hit him in the shoulder. He had both her hands in his grip now, and he sat on her chest, forcing her arms back over her head. Sweat dripped off his head, falling onto her face. She stared up at him defiantly, ignoring the splatter. She snarled and struggled to move, but Dan held her down hard.

He lifted his ass slightly to let her breathe but didn't slacken the grip on her hands.

"Well, well, Natasha. We meet again," Dan said.

CHAPTER 52

Natasha gritted her teeth and squirmed underneath him. Dan knew her. She hated being subdued, and though he watched her carefully, part of him couldn't deny enjoying this. He was panting with exertion, and he bared his teeth.

"I'm better than you, right?"

"Fuck you, Dan," she shot back. "Why don't you get off me and fight like a man?"

"Did you say you wanted to fuck me?"

"In your dreams," she snarled. But her movements lessened, and the hard glint in her eyes dulled.

"Why are you here?" Dan asked.

He wanted to wipe the sweat that was pouring off his forehead, salting his eyes. He noted the Scorpion didn't seem to mind it. They stared at each other, Dan still holding her hands above her head.

"You don't expect an answer to that question, do you?"

"I know you are protecting the Chechens because that's your job. You came to kill Andreyev. But there has to be something else, or you wouldn't be here."

"There *is* something else," she smirked. "To kill you."

"Not if I kill you first." His jaw tightened. "I could do it right now."

"Then why don't you?"

The answer stood still between them, as if forming a cloud that appeared from the mingling of their breaths. They had come together like this in the past, in violence and heat, but found some tenderness in each other, a little warmth. Dan saw that memory suddenly flash in her eye, like a comet blazing across a desolate, starless sky, the only light that emptiness ever saw, like his own heart, now feeling the sparkles of that warm memory lit in her eyes.

"Shit." Dan sighed.

"Answer my question, Dan. Why don't you kill me, and we can end this."

"Because I don't kill women. You know that."

Her eyes narrowed but not with suspicion. It was more like pain. "This only ends when you or I die. Might as well be now."

Dan's hands slackened. His palms were sweaty, holding hers tight. He didn't let go of her hands, but she moved so fast his eyes didn't even register it. Her legs came up behind his back, hooked over his head and gripped him like a pincer. Dan was between her legs, and the pressure from her hips was immense, crushing him. He used all his strength to pry himself free, pushing her legs apart. He rolled off her but not before he had caught the butt of her Makarov handgun from the belt holster. He came up on his knees as she got to a crouch. He pointed the gun at her. He loaded a round in the chamber. She sat there, staring at him.

"Go ahead," Dan said. "Make your move." His voice was calm, but it hid the turmoil in his heart, the black sea in his soul heaving in a storm. He didn't want to do this. But he was a killer. Could he kill his former lover?

"If you stand in my way, Dan, I will have to kill you. I swear I will," she whispered.

Dan kept the weapon pointed at her. She could move faster than him, and he wasn't taking any chances. Her hazel eyes were low like the turquoise waters of the sea in the evening. Low and restless, as if a storm were raging inside her. Her short chestnut hair, the freckles on her face, all of it reminded him of a different time. He wished it could be different this time. But he knew it wouldn't be.

"What do you have to do?" he asked.

"A big job." She shook her head. "You won't understand."

"Try me."

She didn't reply.

Dan asked, "Where is Roberta and her son, Paolo?"

A steely gaze came over her eyes. The old glint was back. "You don't have to worry about them."

"Paolo was abducted. The Chechens took him, didn't they?"

She shook her head slowly, remaining silent. Her face changed suddenly, registering surprise. She pointed her finger upwards. "Listen."

Dan kept the gun trained on her and glanced upwards for a fraction of a second. It was all the time the Scorpion needed. Dan caught a flicker of movement, and she had moved behind a tree trunk then suddenly melted into the dense emerald forest. He ran forward, swearing to himself, gun pointed. He saw a flash of her body, more imagined than seen, as she went around another tree. Now he saw her, then he didn't. He jerked the gun in that direction, the butt moist in his palm. It was no use. She was gone.

Dan could have screamed in frustration. He kicked the brush at his feet. Then he stopped moving as his eyes fell on the object on the ground.

CHAPTER 53

Dan flinched and fell backwards, scrambling to get as far away as possible. The object was round in shape, and it glistened as it caught a sunray. *A curious object,* he thought as he stared at it from a safe distance. His initial impression had been a grenade on a time fuse, designed to blow his legs off. But it was too bright to be an explosive, unlike any he had ever seen. After two minutes, nothing happened, so he stepped out. The object was partially hidden under a bush. He got closer. It was a rough round shape, baseball sized. He kicked it with his boot. It rolled out in the open.

Dan crouched then picked it up. It had a dull glow to it and the appearance of aluminum foil but cased in dirt. He rubbed at it, and the foil-like consistency was rough and grainy, but the glow was brighter. It looked like silver. He moved the rock around in his hand, his eyebrows creased.

He heard the roar of a motorcycle, the sound muffled in the trees. He stood up, put the rock in his pocket, and went searching for his weapons. He tramped back to the road. The motorcycle was nowhere to be seen. His scooter was lying where he left it, but the tires had been ripped by a knife.

Dan took his cell phone out and powered it up. He called Melania, who promised to send a car once his GPS signal had been received. Dan dragged his scooter back so it wasn't easily visible. He faded into the trees and held out the rock to examine it again. He didn't know much about minerals, but he had seen silver before, and this was similar. His mind went back to the files on Sardinia. He couldn't remember if silver was mined here. But if it wasn't, how did a rock like this end up with the Scorpion? She had picked it up from somewhere and dropped it during the fight.

His thoughts were interrupted by the sound of an engine. He glanced from behind the trees to see the headlights of the now-familiar armored Jeep, a new one. Charlie was driving, and Dan brought him, and Melania on the phone, up to speed on what had happened. Light had faded from the skies, but sunlight still lingered at the edges of the horizon.

"I can't believe it," Melania exclaimed. "You find her, then we lose her for the second time."

Dan hung up, chugged some water down, then closed his eyes for the remainder of the ride. The analyst room was empty when they got back to base, save Jake and Melania. Dan told them the whole story then held up the rock.

"What's that?" Melania frowned.

He explained. Jake busied himself on his laptop, looking for silver mines on the island.

"I need to find that boy, Paolo." The steely determination in her eyes held Dan's attention. "That takes priority."

"I have a feeling if we follow our way to the silver mines, a lot will fall into place."

"But will it help to find the boy?"

"I think so."

"You think?"

"I know you want to find him, but just trust me on this."

Melania stared at him for a while then averted her eyes. She seemed preoccupied, Dan thought. He knew it was getting late to be at the office. It was close to 2200 on his watch. But Melania didn't just look tired—she looked... haunted.

"Are you OK?" Dan asked.

She frowned at him. "Why wouldn't I be?"

"No reason."

Melania turned away as Jake approached them. He had Google Maps open on his phone. Like the phone that Dan had been issued with, jam-proof GPS was installed on it.

Jake pointed at the green dot on the screen, which contracted and dilated in one spot. "A place called Argentarium," he said with a note of satisfaction. "Been mined for silver since Roman times. Silver and coal mining are big businesses in Sardinia."

"Still in use?" Dan asked.

"No. This mine's been shut down for several years."

"How far?" Dan asked.

"Thirty-four klicks from here."

"Great," Melania said. "We go now."

"It's dark," Dan said. "On terrain we are not familiar with. I'm worried about them setting booby traps. Our lights will expose our location as well."

Melania asked, "What are you saying?"

"I'm saying I'm all for it, but I also like a level playing field. I just battled with the Scorpion. She'll warn them, and there's every chance we'll be facing a welcoming committee." Dan looked from Melania and Jake. "Better if we wait till first light. Send a drone out to scan the area. Then move in fast."

Melania hesitated.

Dan said, "Whatever's happening there won't stop overnight, will it?"

She nodded, but Dan noticed the troubled expression on her face only got deeper. She walked out, leaving the two men facing each other.

CHAPTER 54

NSA
Signals Intelligence Directorate
Fort Meade

Chuck Jones gripped the headrest of the analyst's chair and stared at the wide screen. The analyst in question was a black woman called Jennifer Lucas, a senior cryptologist. Jennifer's screen was divided into four boxes on the top and bottom. Eight in total. Each box held a graph. Different-colored lines streaked across each graph.

"What am I looking at?" Chuck asked.

"You told me to collect all the signals from Porto Cervo in Sardinia over the last forty-eight hours, right?"

"Yes. Did the Italians allow you to access their data?"

"Yup, AISE sent me their files." Jennifer pointed to a red line that was thicker than the rest and punched higher on the bottom right graph. She said, "Phone calls, emails, app messages, any and all electronic signals from Porto Cervo are here. I've just arranged them according to frequency levels. But this frequency is the highest."

Chuck bent down lower till his face was next to Jennifer's and he could smell her lavender-and-lilac body perfume. "What is it?"

"I don't know. Not high or broad enough to be from an explosion. Plus, an explosion would have a dampening effect on all the other frequencies. No, this was something precise." Jennifer turned to look at her boss. "Why are we looking at this?"

"Chechen terrorists are hitting the island." He straightened to his six-foot-one height and rubbed his chin. "Can you find out what this is? I need a report today."

"I'll do my best."

179

"What about the drone feed images I sent you? That man's face in particular. Any matches?"

Jennifer clicked a few buttons, and the screen changed to the images that Melania had sent. Jennifer shook her head. "Nope. No matches. Not on our databases, anyway. But I'll keep plugging away. Might be something on other governments' systems, like GCHQ in the UK. But we need clearance for that."

Chuck considered. That level of clearance would have to come from the highest level of CENCOM. It could wait, he decided. He was doing this as a favor to Melania, and he had a hundred other jobs to catch up with.

"Put it on hold for now. But check out the Sardinia frequency and let me know."

Chuck walked back to his office, and Jennifer got busy. The mention of Chechen terrorists had sparked an idea in her mind. Two weeks ago, a high-level fundraiser for the North Caucasus had been caught. His contact network had revealed hundreds of encrypted messaging apps used by terrorist cells in the area between Chechnya, Dagestan, and Georgia. The information load was huge, but that was what MYSTIC and ID-300 supercomputers were used for. They scanned terabytes of internet files and used artificial intelligence to look for patterns in messages, images, credit card or bank transactions, any activity that was capable of being recorded.

Jennifer pulled up the Terambutov files and inserted the data. What struck her was the coded message of violence that had set the DNI, the Director of National Intelligence, on red alert: violence on a scale the west had never seen.

Still, that was old news, and nothing had happened in the last two weeks. Jennifer superimposed the Terambutov files on the Sardinia data and ran a search. The screens remained blank, and the graphs on which the data was displayed were a confusing mishmash of colors. Nothing stood out, like the Sardinia frequency. She knew ID-300 would match images with electronic data. No dice.

She picked up the phone and called Chuck. She told him what she had done. "Any new intel on the threat?"

"No. Seems quiet currently, but that's not a good sign. You know these guys are as patient as hell and plan long-term."

They were both silent, thinking.

Chuck asked, "What about Terambutov's financial transactions? He set up several offshore companies to transfer money to his network."

"Most of them are onions, ending in areas where we have no jurisdiction. Or they're Havala." Havala was the ancient method of transferring money for goods in the Middle East and Asia, a banking system where only cash changed hands. It was virtually impossible to track or shut down.

Chuck hung up and checked his phone. It was evening in the US eastern zone, which meant late night in southern Europe. He decided to try. Melania surprised him by answering.

"Sorry, did I wake you up?"

"No." Melania's voice was alert. "What is it?"

Chuck told her what Jennifer had found.

Melania was silent for a while. She said, "It's a good idea to put this on Terambutov's files and see if we get a match. With the money side, we tracked down the cash we found on the truck driver, Billy Cavalli, right?"

Chuck sat up straight. He opened the file up on his screen. He scrolled down to where Billy had disclosed the deposit box he cashed the money into. It was a local bank in Bethesda, Maryland, called Premier Financial. The owner of the deposit box was a company, but this time they had tracked down the owner.

A man called Shahab Barakat. When Chuck clicked on the name, a red icon displaying MISSING began to flash. He was immediately redirected to an FBI and CIA page for more information, if he had any.

"Shit, I got something."

"What?"

"Billy dropped money into a box that belonged to Shahab Barakat. He's the imam of Hanlon Park mosque in Baltimore. And he's missing."

CHAPTER 55

Chuck hung up and strode into the office where Jennifer was sitting with other analysts.

"Run this name on the jihadi networks. Shahab Barakat. Pretty sure he uses an alias as well, but his real name will pop up somewhere. Do it on the Terambutov files."

Jennifer ran the search. Several pings came from the machine, and a sequence of lines dropped on the screen.

"OK, we got him," Jennifer said. "He uses the alias of Sheikh al-Amriki, or the Sheikh from America." She pointed to the lines that were still appearing on the screen. "Very active on the messaging networks. It'll take a while to get the full intel, but this is a guy who preaches and sanctions jihad."

"A hate preacher."

"You got it."

"Lock him down. I want everything on him. Then cast the net wider. All his contacts, family, friends, going back to high school."

Jennifer raised a thumb and got busy. She went to the Hanlon Park mosque as Shahab's workplace. She collated all the signals within a five-mile radius around the mosque and ran a search. She was looking for a pattern again, any pattern. It took several minutes, but finally the data pinged.

Graphs appeared like thumbnails across her wide screen then grew larger. One graph in the middle caught her eye. A fat red line whose frequency punched higher than the rest.

Jennifer frowned and called up the Sardinia graphs. She superimposed the high-frequency line with the data from around the mosque. A red dot started pulsing in the middle of the screen. Jennifer's eyes widened.

"Bingo," she whispered.

She called Chuck on the phone, and he came running.

"What is it?" he asked, excited.

"The Sardinia frequency is exactly the same as this one from the mosque. It happened from a room inside the mosque, one day before the imam was reported as missing."

"You sure it's the same?"

"The machine won't lie, Chuck. This is a pure, isolated, high-quality signal. Like a satellite communication."

"Or a satellite phone?"

"Yes. A phone call that would be undetected on terrestrial or VOIP calls."

"Run it against all our satellites. I need to call the FBI and DHS about the mosque."

Chuck ran off while Jennifer clicked on her keyboard. She glanced at her watch. Good job her husband had a half day today and was there to look after their two children. She sent him a quick text to say she was going to be late.

The data took a while to load, but none of the domestic or military satellites they had provided a match. Jennifer shook her head and called Chuck.

"No dice. I need clearance to access signals from Russian military satellites. I don't even know if Chechnya has military sats. I doubt it."

"Me too. Hold on, let me get clearance."

Chuck strode to her desk a few minutes later. He used the phone on her desk to call the Charlottesville, Virginia, number.

"INSCOM, this is Chuck Jones, Director of SID. I need a level 4, code red clearance."

Chuck gave his password and waited while he was put through. He relayed the situation to Colonel Sara Dwyer, head of US Army Intelligence and Security Command or INSCOM. He hung up and called the National Geospatial Intelligence Agency and got clearance from them too. Then he lifted the lanyard on his neck, removed his ID card, and pressed it against Jennifer's screen. There was a series of beeps, then a black screen opened with a rectangular white box in the middle. Chuck entered his password, and Jennifer was through.

She called him back in fifteen minutes. "I got it. It's a Lotos S-1 spy satellite that belongs to the Russian military."

"Oh Jesus," Chuck whispered. He hung up and walked over. Jennifer had a picture obtained from the National Geospatial Agency (NGIA) of the satellite in orbit.

"Launched by a Soyuz B rocket from the Plesetesk Cosmodrome, in the far east of Russia. Currently in orbit at five hundred fifty miles above the earth."

Chuck closed his eyes and massaged his temples with one hand. This was shaping up to be a long evening. He stepped back as Jennifer stood up from her desk and flexed her neck.

"Good work, Jenny," Chuck said. "There's no way we can know the contents of that call, right?"

Jennifer grinned. "Even we can't do that, and we're the biggest eavesdroppers in the world." She became serious. "Do you think this Shahab character, the imam, made the call?"

"Him or someone else. I've called the FBI already, and they're putting the mosque on lockdown. But if there's someone with jihadi connections inside the US making contact with a Russian satellite, we've got one hell of problem."

CHAPTER 56

MELANIA – THEN

It was graduation day at Camp Peary. Melania was exhausted but elated. After language classes and interrogation lessons, the twelve-week basic military field training at Camp Peary was backbreaking. The recruits had endured sleep deprivation, mock executions of their colleagues, and prison cell breakouts. It was the hardest part of the CIA special agent training, and some quit at this level.

Melania had made it with flying colors. She rubbed shoulders with her classmates, who had happy, shining faces. From the small podium, the carefully selected class of twenty men and women beamed at the assembled guests.

In the first row was US Congressman Benjamin Wiblin. Cameras weren't allowed inside Camp Peary—indeed, the highways leading up to it were closed to the public. But that didn't stop the proud parents from cheering and waving.

As Melania's name was read out, she glanced at Ben, who stood up. He was a former CIA case officer, and stories of his life in the service of his country had made Melania dream of a life as a CIA agent.

She walked across the podium to where the head of National Clandestine Service was waiting. He shook her hand and gave her the certificate.

"We are very proud to have you join us," the white-haired man said warmly.

Melania had a weird sense this was a dream. Four years of college, endless application forms—like thousands of application forms—day after day of interviews, then all the months of training.

Finally, she had arrived. Special Agent Melania Wiblin.

She had chosen her adoptive parents' name. It came naturally, over the years. Ben had been a concerned, caring stepfather. He was frequently away with work, and since her college years, Melania saw him twice a year maybe. But they remained in close phone contact. He was keenly interested in her career, his pride obvious.

As Melania walked back to her seat, she saw Ben standing and clapping. Everyone else was sat down, cheering and clapping, but Ben was the sole upright figure. Because he knew what it meant to her.

Before she left for college, he told her something she never forgot.

No one becomes a parent by giving birth.

She knew what he meant now. She didn't have a father, but Ben had given her a life she could only have dreamed of in Russia. The daughter of a poor seamstress... she bit down on her lip and looked down. She barely thought of her mama, Aloyna, and little Michka. She had gone to Russia during her sophomore year in college, as early as she could.

No, she didn't find them.

Her nightly prayers, clutching the red hairband with the green dragon on it, continued. She still searched online. She still made contacts in the US embassy in Moscow and sent them emails.

She still believed.

Melania touched the red hairband in her ponytail. It was old now but still intact. Today of all days, she had to wear it.

When the announcements were over, the recruits came down. Hugs and kisses followed. People mingled. Melania walked with Ben down to the canteen. He bought her a drink, and they shared a toast.

"To the future," Ben said, smiling.

They clinked glasses. Melania knew better than to ask about Janice. Ben's wife, and the rest of the Wiblin dynasty, had never been interested in her. In fact, they treated her with disdain. She didn't care. Ben made sure she had private tuition at home and rigorous sports lessons. Her days had been active, physically and mentally.

They talked about Ben's previous life in the CIA for a while. Karl Shapiro, a friend of Ben's, was still working in the CIA. Melania had met Karl and had warmed to him.

She walked Ben out to his car eventually, as he had to leave for Washington.

"There's something I wanted to say," Melania said.

Ben stopped. They were in the shade of a tree, the parking lot several yards away. He looked at her.

Melania struggled to speak. All the emotion she was trying to keep submerged seemed to spill over all at once. Her voice caught. She swallowed, but it was no use.

"You… you gave me a life when I had none."

Ben looked at the ground and didn't lift his eyes.

Melania said, "And all these years, I have never thanked you."

She was crying now, tears smudging her makeup. "So I wondered if you would grant me a wish."

He looked up at her then, and the US congressman's face was contorted, his mouth open, eyes red-rimmed. He breathed heavily, as if he were in pain. He, too, couldn't speak.

"What… what is it?"

Melania stepped closer. Tears blurred her vision, and she made no effort to wipe them. She held his hand and watched him step back. His head dropped back on his chest.

"Let me call you Father," she whispered.

His head fell further on his chest, which was heaving. He turned away suddenly, and she saw moisture glistening on his cheeks. But Melania was holding his hand, and her grip was strong. He stood still, back to her, body shaking.

She stepped up to him. He looked away again. She grabbed his face and forced him to look at her.

"You are the father I never had. You know that, right?"

For someone so powerful, Ben Wiblin seemed like a child. She hugged him and, through her own tears, felt his body shaking with sobs.

CHAPTER 57

MELANIA – NOW
Porto Cervo
Sardinia

Melania hadn't slept well. The call from Chuck Jones had come in late, and following it, she had tossed and turned, debating whether to call him back or wait for it. In the end, she had done neither and drifted off into a fitful sleep. Nightmares tormented her. In one dream, Sergei was chasing her with a long, hooked knife. She knew it was a kukri, the type Dan Roy used. Her mother and baby sister were trying to grab Sergei's legs to stop him. Then Sergei's pale, colorless eyes changed to Dan Roy's brown ones, and his face changed to Dan's as well. Dan jumped on top of her, and she fell to the ground, rocks pressing on her back. Her mother was sobbing. Dan's face changed to Sergei's again, and he lifted the kukri high above his head.

Melania screamed and sat up bolt upright. She was on the floor. *What the...* She looked around the room quickly. It was empty. There was a beeping sound from the digital alarm clock on the bedside table. At some stage overnight, she had come off the bed. Melania got up, embarrassed. She sat down on the bed and slapped the alarm off. She had not fallen off the bed since she had been a child. Dawn light was trickling in through the window shutters. Melania leaned forward, gripping her head.

She felt more disturbed than she had in years. She had seen the face of her tormentor. Sergei. He was older, hair cut shorter, but she knew it was him. Unbelievable but true. A storm raged inside her, revealing old scars. Black ruts deepened inside her heart, leaking out blood that was forgotten, locked inside. It spilled into her veins like acid, corroding her flesh, and she stood up, flinching away from the pain inside her. But she couldn't run from it. This grief had eroded her soul all these years, and now it was back to haunt her.

But it also filled her with a new purpose. She opened the window and watched the sun lift its bold yellow face over the horizon. This time, she would not let him escape. There would be no mercy. Sergei would talk and then get a bullet to the head. Melania showered then sat down at her desk. She took out her two Glock 22s, stripped them, reassembled them, and slapped new mags in each one. She took her six-inch marine hunter knife and put it next to the guns. Then she opened the drawer and took out the red headband. She stroked the green dragon on it. The wings were faded, but the eyes and nose of the dragon remained, mouth yawning open.

"I am so close, Mama and little Michka," she whispered. "When I find him, he will tell me what he knows. That will get me closer to you. I won't rest till I find you." She felt a lump form at the back of her throat, and an unexpected teardrop made its way to the corner of her left eye. She brushed it away.

Melania put the two guns in her belt line and jammed four extra mags in the side pockets of her pants. She stood and put the knife in her left ankle holder. She picked up the red headband and stared at it for a while. She kissed it and opened the drawer. Then she stopped and put the headband in the breast pocket of her vest.

Her cell phone beeped. It was an internal number. Dan Roy's voice came down the line.

"I'm at the station," he said. "Are you ready?"

"See you there," she said and hung up. Dan had slept at the hotel and come around early. Melania locked her door and strode across the compound. When she got into the analyst's office, Dan was staring at a screen with three others. Jake and Charlie nodded at her. Dan straightened finally and looked at her impassively.

"A road leads up to the mine. It's a working road, seems in good condition. But we don't take that route. We come up behind the back." He showed her on the map displayed on the screen.

Melania checked the screen then the drone feed. This time, the drone wasn't too close, to avoid it getting shot down. As a result, the images weren't optimal.

"What's our extraction point?" Melania asked.

"We have to use the road," Dan said. "Unless you have air evacuation."

"That will take time to organize."

"Then leave it. The sooner we hit them, the better."

"Keep snipers located here and here." Dan pointed to two opposite points on the diameter of a circle, with the mine placed at the center. "Those are the two entrances. We have to come out of one of these. Backup stays with the snipers, who join us at the evacuation point."

Everyone had a map on their phone screens, which would act as their GPS device.

Melania nodded at the assembled team. "Let's do this."

CHAPTER 58

Dan was sat behind the driver, and he could see Melania's face from an angle. She wore a blue baseball cap and sunglasses. He couldn't see her expression, but her jaw was clenched tight, and she kept checking her weapons. She was restless and had been that way since she had seen the photo on the drone feed. He knew it was to do with the man she had seen. Time would tell. He had checked his gear already, and this time he wore a tactical bulletproof vest, and his H&K 416 rifle lay on his lap. As the car moved, Dan leaned his head against the glass and closed his eyes.

His eyelids flew open as the car lurched to a stop. His finger curled around the trigger by reflex, and the rifle came up above the window. They had stopped on a grassy knoll. The hill sloped down below them, and he could see the mine shaft and quarries. A black ribbon connected the mine to the main road, which lay over the hills.

The quarries and the mining offices looked deserted. Dan could see the place had not been used in decades. There were three quarries in total. Each of them had a slick of water at the bottom. The harsh summer had evaporated most of the liquid, but he had no doubt that, in the winter, the disused quarries were filled with rainwater.

Dan saw something and asked for the binoculars. He focused on the ground. He now saw the tire marks clearly. More than one truck had come off the blacktop road and travelled down the dusty foreground. He followed the tracks till he saw the covered area. Something lay under camouflage-green tarpaulin sheets. It had to be the trucks, as the rest of the derelict foreground was devoid of vehicles. The tarpaulin was a clever disguise, as it looked like vegetation from the air or on a satellite image.

Dan made sure the rifle was hooked securely on his back. Melania was next to him, spread-eagled on the hill edge, watching the scene below.

"I'm going down," Dan said.

"Not without me."

Dan stopped and shook his head. "It's easier if I do a recon first. I'll give you a signal."

"Negative. No one put you in charge."

Dan levelled a stare at her. "I don't take orders from anyone. That might not have been in my file, but I'm telling you now."

She ignored him and prepared to move. Dan grabbed her arm and pulled her down. Her face turned red, and she turned to him with a snarl. "Let me go!"

Dan said, "Who's that man you saw on the drone feed? What does he mean to you?"

She stopped fighting. Dan held her eyes and detected a crack in the ice, a fissure that allowed some light to fall inside. He detected deep anger and hardness he hadn't seen before. This woman was ready to kill. He could read that because he recognized what he saw in the mirror. He let go of her arm.

"You want him alive, right?" Dan asked.

She nodded in silence. Dan jabbed a finger towards the tarpaulins. "I head down there, you come from the opposite end. Meet in the middle. Got that?"

"Yes."

They did a comms check. The sniper teams, armed with SCAR-H rifle systems, had already left for their positions. There was some tree cover, and Dan scurried from one to the other. He watched as Melania ran out of sight to circle around. Uneasiness stabbed inside him. Should he have let her go? He could tell her mind was disturbed. Dan never lost focus before an op. He was blind to the external world. It was one of the reasons he succeeded. But he knew Melania was anything but focused. That didn't augur well for the mission.

But it was done. She was on her way. He couldn't move forward with regrets, so he put it out of his mind. Tactically, it was the right decision. His watch showed 0600. Dan moved faster, like a ghost in the early-morning light. He stopped when the screen of trees ended. Fifty yards out, he took the Sig in his hand and went to ground. The foreground of the mine was ahead of him, with buildings in the background. He couldn't see the tire marks or the tarpaulin-covered objects from here. He got up and moved to the last tree.

A wind blew dust across the wasted, cratered landscape. Branches creaked above him. Dan lowered himself to the ground again. He could easily run across the open space and get to one of the buildings.

Too easily.

He observed for two minutes. The wind kept up, a cool mistral wind, not the hot sirocco type that scorched Sardinia's hills. He kept his eyes on the hut closest to him, less than fifty yards away. This hut was protected by a mound of soil, and it faced the road directly.

It was then he saw it. A subtle movement at the window of the hut. A rifle muzzle, covered in black cloth so the sun didn't reflect off it.

CHAPTER 59

How many men were there? Sentries normally guarded in twos at the least. The mine yard was large, more than a hundred yards wide and just as long. It was surrounded by hills, with only one road coming up to it. If guards were present in this hut, what about farther in? He tapped his earbud twice.

"Alpha 2, this is Cross 1."

There was a hiss of static and the sound of heavy breathing, then Melania's voice came through. "Reading you, Cross 1. What's the play?"

"I got a man here, guarding the road. Might be more than one. I have to take them out. You might face the same on your way in."

"Roger that, Cross 1."

"Don't—" Dan started, but she cut him off by hanging up. Dan swore to himself. He wanted to tell her not to fire unless needed.

He looked ahead of him. The rifle muzzle had slipped back inside the window ledge, then it appeared again. That was the movement that had caught Dan's eyes. One by one, he trained his eyes on the huts around the periphery. He couldn't see any movement in the ones within reach of his eyesight. They all looked like sentry posts but were probably empty. He clocked the bigger buildings in the middle, with one that looked like a warehouse, next to a broad mine shaft. The tarpaulin-covered structures were right next to it. Somehow, he had to get there alive.

There was a window in the sentry hut that faced him. If someone was watching from it, he was toast. Dan stayed within cover of the trees, and slid towards the middle of the mine yard. He came to another sentry post roughly fifty yards away from the first one. This one seemed empty. He took his chances. Staying low, he approached the barbed-wire fence. The problem of locks and fences had been foreseen, so Dan had a bolt cutter with him. He snapped off the wire to make a square space above and below him. Before he wriggled through, he told the team about the entry point, in case they needed backup.

Dan rolled in then got up fast. The HK416's butt was on his shoulder, and he crossed the space quickly, jerking his eyes left and right. He flattened himself against the timber door. He was about to move when he heard a creaking sound from inside, as if a table was shoved or a chair moved. Then he heard a voice. He recognized the language as Russian.

"...take a look," a bored voice said.

Then he heard the sound of a TV, laughter, and music, all very low, and he strained to hear it. Through the open window, he smelled cigarette smoke. One hell of a job these guys were doing. Watching TV and smoking while on sentry duty? Dan put the HK away and took out the Sig.

Dan raised his head and looked through the window from an angle. Three men at a desk. Portable TV set in front of them. All three had their backs to Dan. He circled around till he got to the door. He took two steps back then tried the handle. It was open. Dan went to his knees and stepped in, staying low. He heard a voice in his direction. Gun pointed, Dan stood up quickly, shooting at the first hint of a shape in front of him. He caught the first guy flat in the chest. He had stood up to investigate the door opening. The heavy round pushed the man back and another one to his neck sprawled him over the table, blood spurting in an arc over him. The next one didn't get a chance to stand. He was halfway up when Dan caught him in his center of mass as well, and he slammed back in his chair and toppled over.

But the other one did what his friend should have done; he dived for the floor. There was a waist-high partition separating the door from the room. The man shot twice, and Dan was saved by the wooden partition as timber pieces broke off and bullets whined. Dan cursed to himself. This guy was holed in now, and his unsuppressed rifle had just alerted the other sentries.

Dan crawled out the door as another round flew above his head. He went to the window as he heard a shout from the first sentry position. Ignoring it, Dan peered in through the window. The man was crouching, swivelling his weapon around. He was in his turn when he spotted Dan at the window and tried to snap back. Too late. Dan's first shot got him in the shoulder, spinning him around, and he cried out as he fell. The next one smashed into the petrous bone of his skull base, exploding brain matter all over the floor.

Dan put the Sig back in its holster and put the HK on his shoulder. He heard the other sentries approach the building. He peered around the corner. Gun pointed, a guy in black fatigues, a similar outfit to the men Dan had just killed, appeared. He was looking at the door. He shouted for his friend then nudged the door with his weapon. Dan stepped out, and he tried to turn, but Dan shot him twice in the ribs then finished with a head shot. Dan caught a flicker of a shadow in the extreme left of his visual field. It was too late to bring his weapon to bear. He dropped like a stone, and bullets smacked into the wooden wall behind him. With no time to aim, Dan fired blindly in the direction of the shadow. He got lucky. The rounds tore into the legs of his attacker, and he screamed. Before he could aim, Dan fired twice, watching the dust and blood rise in puffs from his chest. He sprawled on the floor.

Suddenly, it was quiet. Dan stayed on the ground and scrambled back to the wall of the hut. Panting, he wiped sweat off his forehead and did a three-hundred-sixty-degree sitrep. He figured the sentries were dead, but that was just the beginning. They had radioed in by now, and Dan had lost his element of surprise.

He tried to contact Melania, but she didn't answer. He had to keep moving. Dan came out of the shadow of the hut. Before him, he could see the sprawling warehouse and the mine shaft. His eyes fell on the green tarpaulin, its ends lifting in the breeze.

Movement. A shape appeared then quickly withdrew behind the far corner of the warehouse. Dan didn't want to fire and give his position away, but neither could he get stuck here. He picked up a piece of rock at his feet and flung it towards the warehouse wall. It made a loud, hollow sound. The warehouse was a broad, flat structure, and it faced Dan. The shape he had seen was in the near corner, but a new shape appeared at the far end. Dan fired at the near wall first, his round ricocheting off the warehouse wall. It didn't get his target, but it had the effect of making him seek cover.

His partner now knew Dan's position, and bullets flew in. It was what Dan wanted. He ran backwards in a semicircle, across the hut. The two men were shooting at the spot he had just vacated. Dan threw himself on the ground when the warehouse came into view. He could see the man at the far wall. There were two of them. One of them caught sight of Dan, and it was the last thing he saw. Dan's finger feathered the carbon trigger of the HK twice, and the man shot backwards, slumping against the wall. His partner was still shooting, and he looked up as he registered his partner falling. Dan had time to aim and watched the head explode in a geyser of blood and bone as his rounds found their marks.

Again, it became silent. Dan heard running footsteps and a slamming door. The sound echoed. He got up and made sure he was alone. He ran to the warehouse wall and flattened himself on the ground next to the dead men.

He searched them quickly. They were broad and swarthy, heavy in the shoulders like Russian or Chechen gangsters. Dan pocketed their handguns after checking the magazines were full. He ignored their AK-47s. He had five more mags of the HK on him, and the thirty-cartridge mag was nowhere near finished.

He could hear rattling sounds inside the warehouse. More footsteps. Something was happening inside. The heavy steel shutters of the door were right next to Dan. They were shut, and there was no way he could open them. He ran to the corner where the other shooter had been. This guy had run backwards, so there must be a door. Dan peered around the corner. It was like a passageway between the warehouse wall and the tarpaulin-covered mass. Dan wanted to check under the tarp, but he needed to get inside the warehouse fast—more chances of getting the enemy when they were stuck inside.

He came to a door in the side. It was shut. He pulled the handle once, twice. It was a heavy steel door, and his bullets would be of no use. Neither would the bolt cutter. He glanced above him. To his right, farther up, was a fire escape. The ladder was on the latch. He bent his knees and jumped. After the second attempt, his fingers curled around the lowest rung. He climbed up, the rusty iron creaking in protest. He swung over onto the landing then ran up the stairs. The fire door was shut, but it had a glass panel on top. The time for subtlety had long gone.

He hit it with the butt of the HK, and after three blows, the glass cracked and gave way. He got rid of the jagged ends, crawled through, and landed on his feet. He turned quickly, expecting shots. Nothing came, but the sound of voices was now louder, like a hum. Rifle on shoulder, Dan stepped across the corridor. He scanned the staircase. Empty. In front of him, across a doorway, was a walkway that went around the circumference of the warehouse. The hum of voices was getting louder by the second.

He got to the door and looked down the walkway grill, into the floor of the warehouse. What he saw made his blood run cold.

CHAPTER 60

Melania skirted wide across the hills. She came down the slope and kept going till she found a spot the drone had identified, where a fallen tree had flattened the barbed wire. Her suppressed AR-15 was poised on her shoulder. She looked through the viewfinder and found the hut facing her. She could see the snout of a weapon poking out the window. The gap in the barbed wire was more than twenty yards away. There was a crop of outbuildings to the left of the sentry post, and beyond that, the green-tarpaulin-covered mass and the warehouse in the middle. To her extreme right lay the deep valleys of the quarries.

Melania snuck in through the gap and scurried to the outbuildings. Panting, she took cover against a deserted shack and cocked her rifle towards the sentry. Above her, a signboard in Italian lurched and creaked in the wind. Dust blew in her face, and she averted her eyes. When she looked back, the same still view greeted her. Either the sentries hadn't seen her, or they were coming up behind her.

She turned, peeked around the corner. Empty. She waited for twenty seconds then went across the open area to the next outbuilding. She repeated the process till she was close to the center. The warehouse, a giant, squat structure, was clearer now, with the tarpaulin spread next to it. It clearly covered something big and tall.

Melania stepped out to rush closer to a hut near the warehouse when suddenly the sound of a gun exploded in the silence. It came from ahead, past the warehouse. She hit the ground and, from the corner of her eye, detected movement. A back door at the warehouse opened, and two figures in black fatigues stepped out.

Both ran towards the source of the sound. Melania heard a gunshot again and then some softer sounds, which sounded like suppressed weapons. Dan Roy. It had to be. Pounding footsteps came from the warehouse again, fading away. Dan had created something that played well into her hands—a diversion. She looked behind her, wary of the sentries coming up.

She got up and ran sideways towards the tarp. She was out in the open now and a sitting duck for a sniper. She lifted a corner of the tarp, which was secured tight into the hard earth with pegs. She couldn't lift it much, so she gave up and crawled inside. From her chest rig, she took a flashlight. Giant wheels appeared in front of her, then the rest of the machines came into view. It was a collection of trucks, all dusty with travel. She squeezed her way around them. Twice she ducked as she heard loud and soft gunshots close to her. She took photos of the license plates. Six trucks in total. She took out her Glock and put bullets inside as many tires as she could. It wasted two magazines, but it meant the trucks were going nowhere.

She stood still when she came to the last vehicle. It was a black SUV. She recognized the license plate. It was from Rome, Italy, and the car in which Sergei had made his escape. Her breath came fast and loose. It was locked, but she peered inside with the flashlight. The car was empty, save for a drink carton by the driver's seat. She shot the tires. Behind her, the noises had grown in frequency. There was a gun battle raging. It meant Dan was still alive, but she had to help him.

She came out from under the tarp. Seeing the SUV had sparked disturbing memories inside her. Sergei. He could be here. She tightened her grip on the AR-15. Chances were he wouldn't recognize her. Not without a closer inspection. Well, if she caught the bastard, she would make *sure* he got a closer inspection.

Before she put a bullet in his heart.

Melania took a breath and put the thoughts out of her head. She wiped her palms on her pants and then made a fist, trying to quell the shake. A few feet away, running feet crunched on gravel. When the sound was gone, she poked her head out. Empty. She got out, pointed the AR-15, and ran towards the rear of the warehouse.

She found the door from which she had seen the figure in black emerge. She heard the running steps in front and shrank back just as bullets splattered the ground in front of her. The firing stopped, and she looked out to see the man running forward. She dropped him with a chest shot as he tried to aim again, and kept shooting as another man came up behind him. She pumped lead into the bodies till they stilled. The muzzle of the gun was warm, and smoke rose from it. She kept the gun at her shoulder and nudged the door with her feet. It fell open.

A narrow metallic hallway ended in another door. She could hear muffled voices. Heartbeat pounding in her ears, Melania stepped forward slowly. This door was shut. One hand on the rifle's trigger, she turned the handle with the other. It opened. There was suddenly a din of voices, and a smell hit her nose. It was oddly familiar.

She stepped into a large clearing, the holding space of the warehouse. Her breath left her chest as if it had been punched by a sledgehammer. Pressure grew in her forehead, as if it were being squeezed by pincers, till her eyes shook.

Children. Some lying, some sitting, arranged in groups all over the warehouse floor. Their clothes were ragged, torn, soiled. She caught the eyes of one girl as she turned to look at her. A knife sliced through Melania's heart, ripping it open. The girl was eleven, maybe twelve years old. There was a dull, lifeless look in her eyes, as though she knew her life was over.

Melania leaned against the door, trying to control her heart rate. In a couple of seconds, she composed herself. She shook her head, as if trying to shake the mist that covered her mind. The girl was still staring at her, and now the girl next to her did the same, as children often did. Melania knew that was a mistake. She couldn't draw attention to herself.

She stared back at the two girls and put a finger to her lips. A quick glance left and right told her the coast was clear. But she could see a man way up, patrolling the middle of the floor. He had a rifle strapped to his back, and a handgun on his belt.

Melania was still in the shadows. She kept low and tiptoed to the next column. Bracing herself against the steel structure, she prepared to move again.

A long, cold piece of metal was thrust against her neck. The muzzle of a gun.

"Do not move, or you die," a thick voice said in an Eastern European accent.

CHAPTER 61

Dan couldn't believe his eyes. The scene below him was heart-wrenching. Cold anger spread through him till he snarled in silence. There would be no mercy if anyone stood in his way tonight. So this was the operation. Dan could tell by the children that many were from the Middle East, North Africa, and Eastern Europe. War-torn, conflict-ridden areas where vermin like human traffickers prospered. The warehouse was almost full, and the sad stench of human excrement hit his nostrils. He shook his head. Dan had seen many versions of hell in Iraq and Afghanistan, but this was worse. What sort of human being did this to children?

He caught sight of the central patrolling figures—two men at opposite ends of the sprawling warehouse. The one closest to Dan was standing, alert, looking around with finger on trigger. The moans of a few children reached Dan's ears. Spread-eagled, he went forward till he was looking over the edge of the walkway. Apart from the two men, he couldn't see any more. He had killed six men so far. One had escaped. Where was he?

Dan positioned his HK416 and took aim. The man's head appeared in the viewfinder. He stopped and looked up. Dan saw his eyes widen as he was spotted. A second later, the man's head erupted like a smashed melon, spraying blood high in the air. Dan turned towards the other guard, who was to his right, about thirty yards away.

The guard heard the sound and turned, pointing his rifle. Dan didn't rush. Fast bullets were wasted bullets. Besides, he couldn't afford to hit one of the children.

The guard jerked his head around in panic then scanned upwards. Dan pressed the trigger, his body bent sideways. He didn't go for the head this time. He was shooting at an angle, too risky. He hit the man's chest and lower into the abdomen, twice. The man jerked, tried to lift his head, then stilled.

The children mumbled more loudly and raised their heads. Several put their hands on others' shoulders and stood up. They stared open-mouthed and whispered to each other.

"Hey, you!" a voice shouted from below. Dan had withdrawn from the walkway already, expecting return fire. He didn't expect the voice.

The children quietened suddenly. A man appeared. The children shrank away from him. The man had a body in front of him. It was a woman, and he held a gun to her neck. His elbow was fixed around her neck, and her hands were tied behind her back. Dan's throat ran dry, and his pulse surged.

It was Melania. She was looking up to find Dan.

"Come out now, or I shoot her!" the man shouted. His hair was cut short, and he was bulging at the shoulders, like most of his beefy friends. He pressed the gun muzzle against Melania's neck till her neck was leaning sideways.

Dan appeared on the walkway. He had the HK416 in his hands.

"Drop the gun," the man said.

Dan walked a few feet till he was at the head of a staircase that dropped to the ground. "No. You let her go first."

"Fuck you!" the man shouted. "Drop the gun, or the girl dies."

"You kill her, then what?" Dan shouted back. "You are surrounded. We have men waiting outside. Police are on their way." It was a white lie, and the man didn't know any better.

"Drop the gun, and put your hands in the air!" the man screamed. He rammed the gun harder against Melania's neck. His eyes were wild.

Dan bent down and put the gun down. He got up slowly. The man said, "And your other weapons. On your belt and ankle straps."

Dan took out one Sig from his back belt line, but he had another next to it. He put one Sig down then lifted his leg and took out the kukri strapped to his left ankle. He put all the weapons on the floor. He raised his hands.

"Now come down slowly, where I can see you."

Dan couldn't hear other men. Was this guy the last one? Had he called for help?

As Dan came down the stairs, Melania caught his eyes. She was looking down at the children. One child in particular. It was a boy, and he was slightly older, maybe fourteen years old. Melania was opening and closing her mouth rapidly in silence. It looked weird. She was making a biting movement with her jaws and jerking her head down. She wiggled her eyebrows. The boy she was in silent communication with was looking at her with rapt attention, his mouth open. He nodded slowly.

Dan didn't understand what the hell was going on, but he started talking to attract the man's attention.

"I know who your boss is. Aliev Daurov, right? The CIA are on his tail now, and the Russians are giving him up."

The man's eyes narrowed, then he shook his head. The gun didn't budge from Melania's neck. "Shut up," he snarled. "Keep your hands up."

"It's true," Dan said as he stepped down the long staircase. "Daurov's compound in Grozny is being attacked as we speak. The *Daurovtsky* are being killed, one by one."

The mention of Daurov's personal army made the man think. "What are you talking about?"

Dan didn't look, but he caught movement near the man's feet. The boy Melania was speaking to had crawled to the back and was behind the man.

"Ring Daurov and find out. He won't answer. But ask anyone."

The boy jolted forward suddenly. He grabbed the man's knees, and his teeth sank into the calf muscle of the left leg. The man screamed, and the gun came away from Melania's neck. Dan whipped the second Sig out from his back. Melania kicked back with her leg and lurched forward to present Dan a better target.

Dan shot immediately, his first round finding the man's neck. The boy was lying on the ground, and his friends now reached for him, dragging him back. The man was tough. He clutched his neck and aimed at Dan. The bullet had caught the side of his neck. Dan shot him in the chest twice, and he stumbled back then slammed onto the floor.

Dan ran down the stairs full tilt. The murmurs from hundreds of children were loud. Dan got to the man, looking up and around, jerking his weapon. So far, no one. He frisked the man quickly and found a knife in his belt line. He used it to rip off the plastic ties that bound Melania's hands. She shot him a quick look of gratitude then scrambled to her feet. She took the man's weapon and scanned around, her back to Dan.

CHAPTER 62

The mine yard was buzzing with activity. Sardinian law enforcement officers in red-and-black uniforms and nurses in white uniforms helped load the children into a convoy of ambulances. The children were lining up to board either a bus if they were considered healthy or an ambulance if they weren't. A makeshift medical camp was created, a large tent with a red cross on its side. Children sat on the dusty ground, leaning against one another. Melania, with the nurses, gave them water.

As she did so, she swallowed back the emotion that threatened to overcome her. Each pair of eyes she looked into melted her heart. She knew how they felt.

She knew.

Their lives were snatched from them, and no one knew if they would ever get them back. Uniting them with their lost parents was a gargantuan task and would take time. For many, it wouldn't happen at all.

As it didn't happen for her.

Melania brushed the hair off the forehead of a child. The girl looked up at Melania and said something in a foreign language. Melania turned to the nurse next to her. The nurse shrugged as well, as she didn't understand. Melania stared at the girl for a second then simply leaned over and hugged the child.

She stood up when her cell phone beeped. Her eyes narrowed at the number. It was HQ. She answered.

"Can you talk?" It was Chuck Jones from the NSA.

Chuck filled her in quickly about the military satellite phone being used in Sardinia and Baltimore.

Melania strolled to the barbed wire and leaned against a post. "So you got this imam's bank details from Billy Cavalli, the driver I caught?"

"Yes. They are part of Terambutov's network."

"Have you interrogated Terambutov?"

"It's ongoing. Using advanced techniques. But so far, he has nothing. He's not an operative, so I think he's speaking the truth."

"The only people who know are the ones using the sat phone. Did you track the Sardinia frequency to get a location?"

"Yes. It's offshore, about a hundred yards. Has to be a ship of some kind."

"Send us the GPS coordinates, and we'll visit it today. We have to be quick. Their operation here is a bust now, so they'll be expecting us."

"What did you find?" Chuck asked.

Melania filled him in.

"Did you find that guy from the drone feed?"

Melania gripped the phone tighter. She had been through every dead body in the mine yard. One of the sentries she had shot was still alive. Dan was questioning him, as he was the only one who spoke Russian. She hadn't found Sergei. Either he had escaped, or he was somewhere else to begin with.

"No," she said between gritted teeth. "Did you find anything on him?"

"Negative. None of our programs ID's his face. But we're still looking. There's a lot happening here, Melania. The mosque in Baltimore was a kill zone. Bloodstains were found, with Shahab Barakat's DNA. Other DNA as well, as yet unknown." Chuck continued. "Your boss called. Joint conference call with the DNI and us today, when you can make it."

"Roger that. Give me one hour."

Melania walked over to the medical tent, where Dan was speaking to the wounded guard. He turned as she approached.

"He's Chechen. Spilled the beans when he realized the game's up. There five more camps like these, all in deserted old mines. They bring kids from Algeria, Libya, Tunisia, even as far as Thailand, and store them here before shipping them out."

Melania nodded. It was mind-boggling to hear of the scope. She thought of all the young, innocent lives ravaged, and her sorrow hardened into cold, sharp anger. They went outside, and she repeated her conversation with Chuck.

Dan said, "It has to be Daurov who's using the sat phone in Sardinia.

Unless someone from the SVR is down here. If it's one hundred yards from shore, has to be a yacht. Let's find out if Daurov has a yacht here and then check for a GPS match."

"Good idea."

Dan glanced at her. "You didn't find your guy here, did you?"

Melania took a deep breath. Dan knew what was making her tick, and for a man, he was surprisingly intuitive. "His name is Sergei. Just in case you hear it anywhere else."

Dan stared at her, and she knew he wanted to ask more questions. But he didn't. He said, "Selling children is how these scumbags make their money. But they use that money for something else. We'd better find out soon what that is."

Melania nodded. "This shitstorm is just beginning."

CHAPTER 63

The analyst room was humming with computers working overtime and the soft buzz of air-conditioning units. Melania and Dan stood in front of a laptop whose screen was divided into two. On the left, Chuck Jones and Jennifer Lucas sat next to each other. On the right, it was Karl Shapiro, chief of the Directorate of Operations, and Stephen Polk, Director of National Intelligence (DNI).

Dan noticed the curious looks Shapiro and Polk cast in his direction. Melania introduced them.

Polk said, "So you are the mysterious Dan Roy."

"In the flesh," Dan said drily.

Chuck Jones took over. "Jenny and I have been working on MYSTIC and ID-300 today. Guys, the jihadi networks we identified from Terambutov's files are jumping again today."

"With what?" Melania asked.

"News of an impending attack. They're calling the faithfuls to get ready. One word keeps getting repeated." Chuck spelt it out. "Q-A-Y-A-M-A-T."

Melania frowned. "What the hell does that mean?"

Everybody shrugged, apart from Dan.

Dan said, "It's an Arabic word but used widely in Pashto as well. It means Doomsday or Judgment Day. Like the end of the world. The Taliban used it to prophesize our end."

Silence followed his comment. Eventually, Shapiro said, "What the hell? Jihadi networks are talking about an attack so big it's going to be Judgment Day?"

Polk echoed, "And we have no idea what it is? Gentlemen, that's not good enough."

Shapiro said, "What are we doing about the Russian satellite?"

Polk said, "I alerted the State Department. They are in touch with the

Russian Embassy. But more importantly, I contacted Zemirsky, head of SVR, myself. He denies knowing about it."

"How the hell could he not? Someone knows the frequency of the satellite, and it has to be one of their men. We sure as hell don't know how to make contact with a Lotos S-1. It's a new launch, for heaven's sake."

Dan said, "It could be a rogue agent. This agent is supplying info to the jihadists, maybe for money. Worth checking out."

Polk frowned and pointed towards Dan from the screen. "You saying the Russians have a mole?"

"Not a mole who's on our side, clearly. Zemirsky could tell you which senior SVR agents have contact with Daurov. We know the Russians are sleeping with the Chechens now. There must be a list he can tick names against. If Zemirsky refuses, threaten him."

Polk looked at Dan with narrowed eyes. "Good point. I'll get on the phone."

Melania said, "Is there any feedback from the FBI about the mosque?"

Shapiro said, "Nope. There's reports of a man who was a big donor to the mosque. He was friends with the imam. They were in the same room where we found the blood drops. Chances are this man or the imam made the phone call."

"And then he killed the imam. Or the imam killed him."

"Shahab Barakat, the imam, was fat and slow. I doubt he could kill anyone."

"That narrows it down to this new man in the mosque, then. Any witnesses? How about CCTV?"

Chuck said, "We are trolling through CCTV images from that part of Baltimore. It would help if we knew what to look for."

Melania had a sudden thought. "How about Sergei? The man from the drone feed."

Chuck nodded. "Sure, I should have thought of that myself." He looked at Jenny, who wrote the name down on her pad.

Dan was rubbing his chin. "And let's cast the net a little wider. Anything else happen in Baltimore that night? I mean apart from the usual gang fights and gunshot wounds. Any unusual murders?"

Jennifer took more notes. Melania said, "The time scale on this is our biggest enemy. We need to know and do it fast."

Her attention was distracted by Jake, who was waving to her excitedly. She called him over.

Jake walked over hurriedly. "The GPS coordinates you sent me correspond to a yacht called the *Bolshoi*. It sailed from the Black Sea and is definitely Russian owned. That's where the sat call was made from, to the mosque in Baltimore."

Dan stood. "Then let's bring Judgment Day on the *Bolshoi*."

CHAPTER 64

Apostolic Palace
Vatican City
Rome

The Apostolic Nuncio for the USA, Cardinal Bernardio, stood at the front doors of the opulent Apostolic Palace, situated in the northeast corner of St. Peter's Square. The Apostolic Palace was the home of the Supreme Pontificate, the pope himself, and many cardinals and bishops.

Bernardio stood with his arms behind his back, facing the well-manicured gardens and fountain that faced the internal courtyard of the palace, away from the bustling St. Peter's Square and its hordes of tourists. The courtyard and its gardens were entered through a secret, medieval entrance that connected to the canals of the river Tiber. The entrance ensured the smooth discharge of the pope in case of an emergency, directly onto a speedboat guarded by Italian *Carabinieri* twenty-four hours a day, thee hundred sixty-five days a year. The palace, being the most important dwelling within Vatican City, also had a helipad next to the guesthouse quarters where the pope lived.

Bernardio now watched the figure wrapped in a black Catholic priest's smock as he emerged from the secret entrance. The figure was flanked by two members of the Pontifical Swiss Guard, the Holy See's personal bodyguards. Despite all his years in the Apostolic Palace, Bernardio couldn't hide the faint feeling of mirth when he saw the blue-, yellow-, and red-striped uniform of the Swiss Guards, a uniform that dated back to the Renaissance. But the Swiss Guards were far more modernized today than their uniforms dictated. Trained by Italian Army commandos, they excelled in a variety of heavy- and small-arms weapons. The two approaching him, however, held only their long staffs. But Bernardio knew they had compact submachine guns hidden under the vest of their uniforms.

He stepped forward as the figure in the black smock approached him. The man went down on one knee, and Bernardio smiled and put his right hand on the man's head.

"Rise, Bishop Deakins."

Deakins rose. His face was happy and excited, flushed with the expectation of finally arriving at the HQ in all of Roman Catholic Christendom. Bernardio beamed. He had spent decades at the Roman Curia and acted as secretary to several popes in his time. But the joy of seeing new blood arriving at the palace remained undimmed. After all, the reason why Catholic bishops were chosen with such careful deliberation was a simple one—they had the potential to be a future pope.

As Bernardio smiled at the new bishop, one thing about his face struck him as odd. His eyes were blank, emotionless. Even when Deakins smiled, the eyes remained dead, cold, flat. Bernardio pushed that to the back of his mind.

He embraced Deakins then ushered him inside. The elaborate tapestries on the walls were awe-inspiring, and as expected, Bernardio watched as Deakins tried hard not to stare. Bernardio stopped.

"Our life is not one of material pursuit, Bishop Deakins."

The man looked at him, and his smile faded. Bernardio laughed.

"But life is empty unless one appreciates all that God has created for us to see." He raised one arm and swept it across the tapestries, the Raphael frescoes on the ceiling, and the Bernini sculptures located at the same distance in front of the windows. "All of this is art that God inspired man to create. Appreciation of art brings us closer to God, therefore, does it not?"

Deakins bowed. "Amen."

Bernardio nodded. "Amen." He smiled and took the fortysomething man's elbow. "Don't worry. Soon you'll be walking past these amazing works and not batting an eyelid. Best to enjoy while you can."

They walked down the magnificent hallway, sunlight spilling in through the floor-to-ceiling windows. Bernardio was a slim, fit man in his late fifties, and he walked swiftly. The younger Deakins hurried to keep pace. They went through a succession of small hallways till they reached the *Sala Regia*. The white-and-pastel-marble floors of the chamber gleamed in the light from the ceiling, and its ornate paintings on the wall were stunning. Bernardio swept through the space towards the doors at the end. They were open and allowed entrance into the *Cappella Paolina*, the small chapel in the Vatican that was closed to public and even to visiting dignitaries.

Bernardio stopped at the entrance. So did Deakins, behind him. Deakins's heart kept up a steady drumbeat because he knew who he was about to see.

The portly figure at the head of the chapel, kneeling in prayer, remained so. The figure was clad entirely in white, including the silk skull cap with a raised point in the middle. When the figure straightened, Bernardio cleared his throat.

Pope Luis made the sign of the cross with his hand then turned around slowly. He looked good for sixty-five, and the papal robe did a good job of hiding his girth. The robe also hid the bulletproof vest that all popes were required to wear after the assassination attempt on Pope John Paul II in 1981. The pope's real name was Giorgio Pallini, and he was a Catholic cardinal from Athens, Greece. He stood and nodded at the two figures waiting for him.

Bernardio approached slowly then bowed.

"Your Holiness, may I present the new bishop from the USA, chosen by yourself for a lifetime of service to the church. Bishop Peter Deakins."

Deakins went down on his right knee again and kissed the pope's outstretched hand.

"Rise, my child," Pope Luis said in English.

Deakins got up and met his eyes. They crinkled with good humor, and Deakins couldn't help smiling back. The pope smelled faintly of sandalwood and roses, a nice, relaxing smell.

"How was your journey?" the pope asked.

"Fine, Your Holiness, thank you."

"You must be tired after your long flight."

"Seeing you has lifted my spirits, Your Holiness."

The pope grinned. "How long have you been practicing that line?"

Bernardio laughed, and the ice was broken. They sat down and spoke of the Rome Diocese and what the pope expected of his new bishops, which was mostly austerity. There was no need to take the example of Cardinal Guiseppi, who had recently been removed from his role in the Curia as he drove to work in a Ferrari and lived in a lavish palazzo outside Rome. Deakins nodded dutifully.

He was shown to his quarters by Bernardio, who advised him to be ready for dinner at 6:00 p.m. sharp. When the door was shut, Deakins looked around his room swiftly. It was a small one-bedroom apartment. He went through the hallway, checking the floorboards and cornices, then the bathroom, bedroom, and small living room that looked across an open garden space at the western guesthouse that was the Holy See's private abode.

When Deakins was satisfied the place was clear, he shut the bathroom door in case there was a camera behind the mirror. He flipped open his suitcase and took out a handheld mirror. He teased out the brown contact lenses he was wearing. Dias Dashev blinked his strange, pale, colorless eyes. It was a relief to take those damn things off. Thankfully, the rest of his face bore an uncanny resemblance to Peter Deakins, the priest he had murdered in Baltimore.

He flipped out his phone. "I am here," he said when someone picked up. "I need the material tonight. Meet me at the entrance by the river."

CHAPTER 65

Aliev Daurov leaned against the railing of his nearly five hundred-foot yacht, the *Bolshoi*. Bolshoi meant big in Russian, and Daurov approved. The name fit the bill. The yacht was like a miniship, with three decks and a cargo hold converted into a gym and space for three rigid inflatable boats. Daurov's sleeping quarters were situated in the top floor, above the bridge. There was a helipad next to it. A Sikorsky helicopter sat on the big H, its rotors moving slightly in the mistral blowing off the coast of North Africa. The undulating hills of the Costa Smeralda, or Emerald Coast, lay before him. The jewelled shoreline of Porto Cervo was a collection of Lego houses from this distance. Behind him lay the island of Corsica, visible as a small, dim shape from this distance. Daurov gazed fondly at the gentle turquoise-blue, almost translucent waters below. The vegetation on the seabed changed the color to a darker blue farther ahead, providing a spectacular contrast.

Daurov was pleased with the turn of events so far. He had done the right thing by siding with the Russians, despite the objections of many Chechens. He had more money as a result, and his private army had grown. By helping out Russian forces in Syria, he was closer to the Russian military than ever before. Now, he would fulfil his personal agenda, and no one would be able to stop him. Yes, it would bring the world to the brink of a war. Much worse than Afghanistan and Iraq. Qayamat. A war to end the world. But it wouldn't be easy to apportion blame. He smiled to himself. The plan was nearly perfect.

He heard a sound behind him and turned. His recent casual girlfriend, Tatiana, stepped out. She wore a slim negligee and nothing underneath. Tatiana was a Russian model, and apart from an hourglass figure, she was also amazing in bed. Memories of last night stirred in his mind. Tatiana came closer to kiss him, and Daurov grabbed her butt, squeezing and pulling her against him. She rubbed herself against his hard but bulging belly, giggling. Daurov felt himself stiffening. The beeping of his cell phone spoiled the moment.

215

"Do you have to answer that?" Tatiana murmured and bit his earlobe.

Daurov stared at the number and frowned. It was his right-hand man in Sardinia, Sasha.

"Yes, I do," he grumbled, moving away. He answered. "What is it?"

"Boss, we have a problem." Sasha paused, which infuriated Daurov.

"Well, hurry up, *durakh*, haven't got all day!"

"It's our mines. The silver mine near Porto Cervo was occupied today by Sardinian police. All our men inside are dead, apart from one. He's been moved to the capital, Cagliari."

Color drained from Daurov's face. With one meaty fist, he gripped the railing hard. "How did this happen?"

"I don't know, boss. One of our informers in the police said a man and a woman were at the scene. They're American."

Daurov closed his eyes then blinked several times rapidly. The beautiful scenery in front of him was turning the color of vomit. "Americans?"

"Yes, boss. I don't know where they—"

"Shut up, you fool!" Daurov howled. "How can you not know? They must be from the CIA black camp. The bastards who were guarding Andreyev and who caught the Scorpion."

Sasha was silent.

Daurov raged on. "I want to know how they found out. Who led them to the mines?"

"I don't know—"

"Will you stop saying that? You need to find out. The alternative is a slow death, Sasha. You choose."

Sasha began to stammer. "B-but, boss, it will take a while to find out."

"Then start now. And where the hell is the Scorpion? Never mind. I'll contact her. You get cracking at your end. Give our police contacts more money. Do whatever you have to."

Sasha's voice was dry. "Boss, there's something else."

"What?"

"They got hold of all our mines. The ones down south as well. I've been around all of them. I didn't sleep last night, driving up and down. It's crawling with not just cops but AISE as well."

Daurov felt like throwing the phone into the sea. He gripped his forehead. "AISE?" Italian Intelligence.

"Yes, boss."

"That proves it was the CIA who alerted them." The anger was replaced by reflection in Daurov's mind. "If the CIA is onto us, we need to be careful. There is much more at stake than the mines. I thought after the Scorpion escaped, we would be OK. She told them nothing, and I believe her. But maybe I was wrong."

"Our police informer took a photo of the man and woman at the silver mine. Shall I send it to you?"

"Yes, right now. And shut down the nightclub—Billion. We need to keep a low profile now."

Daurov hung up and called the Scorpion. When she answered, he barked, "Where are you?"

"On the island. Where, specifically, you don't need to know."

Daurov gritted his teeth, pulse pounding in his forehead. "Listen to me, you bitch. We are facing a crisis." He told her what was happening. "How do you think this happened?"

"I have no idea."

"I told you to kill that man who attacked the Billion club. I'd bet my last ruble the man works for the CIA."

"I tried. It wasn't as easy as I thought. I will try again."

Daurov thought for a while. "No, forget it. I want you to leave for Rome tomorrow. But for tonight, I want you to guard the boat."

The Scorpion paused before replying. "Rome? Why?"

Daurov told her. When he had finished, the Scorpion was silent. He said, "You know what happens if you don't follow my orders."

He could hear the anger in the tightness of the Scorpion's voice. "Yes, I do," she said.

CHAPTER 66

Evening was a beautiful time in Porto Cervo. The setting sun lit up the sky in golden and purple hues, which turned the clouds into fire. The heat melted the sky, bleeding blue into the hills till it pulled the dusk into its cavernous ring of sea surrounded by mountains.

Dan Roy stood on the wild beach bereft of any human beings apart from him and Melania. He watched the colors of the horizon deepening, moving into the sea. It was getting dark rapidly. Dan wore a wet suit, and he hated it. It chafed his neck, as his chest was broad, and fitting into them was a nightmare. Although Dan was a strong swimmer, his combat days were spent in the army as a Delta operative, not in the navy. Unlike a DEV-GRU, or Seal Team Six operative, he didn't have a wet suit built to size. But he knew he had to wear it tonight. The oxygen cylinder, mask, and fins were already in the RIB. It was the same RIB and driver who had picked him up when he had landed in the Tyrrhenian Sea three days ago.

Melania said, "I still don't think this is a good idea."

"If I'm in trouble, I'll call for help. But a full-scale assault could turn into a bloodbath. This could well be Daurov's HQ in Sardinia. He can be trapped on the island, but here he can just take off."

Melania shrugged. "All the more reason to send a team in."

"I'm just gonna recon. You have my word." He winked at her.

Melania shook her head.

As he walked on the warm sand towards the sea, Dan turned back. "If you get too stressed, have a fag. They're in my locker."

She didn't reply. Dan knew she was itching to get into the boat with him, and he had no doubt she could handle herself. But things could be different in water. Arms and legs got heavy trying to stay afloat. Panic set in. Dan didn't mind losing his own life, but he didn't want Melania on his conscience.

The driver, Sean, helped Dan aboard the RIB as it bobbed on the water, tied to a rock. Dan waved at Melania, who raised an arm. Then she turned and left for the Jeep at the top of the cliff they had scrambled down to access the wild beach. A drone was hovering over Dan's head, and it gained height as the RIB's powerful twin 250cc engines churned the water. The back of the boat dipped and the nose lifted as, with a growl, the machine surged into the sea.

Wind whipped Dan's eyes with saltwater spray. He put his diving glasses on. Sean had GPS coordinates on, and they were hoping the drone feed they had was correct—the *Bolshoi* hadn't moved from its anchor position. Three hundred yards out, the RIB started to slow down. Dan stood next to Sean and pulled on his NVGs. Everything turned green, apart from the flecks of phosphorus that flared bright. Visibility was reduced to pitch-black more than thirty yards out, which was expected. The boat slowed further as it got closer to the coordinates.

Sean said, "I can't see the lights."

For a yacht the size of Bolshoi, there should be lights, Dan knew.

"Cut the engine," Dan said. The din of the engines ceased suddenly. The rotors whizzed then were silent. The RIB bobbed up and down in a gentle swell. The wind was cooler out at sea. Dan felt it on his face. He strained his eyes into the distance with the NVGs on. He couldn't see a great deal after about seventy-five yards.

"OK, start her up," Dan said, "But go real slow. Make as little sound as you can."

Sean maneuvered the boat expertly. When the GPS location was a hundred yards away, Dan called out for him to stop. The boat drifted.

Sean said, "The currents are taking us closer. If the boat's here, they switched the lights off."

"That's what I'm worried about," Dan whispered back. "No reason why a yacht that size would have its lights off. Unless they're expecting us."

"Why would they?"

Dan didn't answer. He put his fins on and kept his goggles on. He dipped the fins in the water. "Don't drift too far," he said. "I'm going for a swim. If you see lights and hear gunfire, it means I'm in trouble."

"Roger that."

Dan would prefer the boat to cast anchor, but there was no time to lift anchor in a chase. The cold water numbed his face, but he rotated his powerful shoulders and scythed into the sea. After twenty minutes of swimming, Dan rested. He consulted the green dial of his wrist device. The GPS locator was flashing with his location and beeping, and the yacht was supposed to be less than fifty yards out. He couldn't see anything.

He started swimming again and stopped after five minutes. The wind felt different on his face. He strained his eyes. A dim black shape was rising out of the sea, some distance ahead.

CHAPTER 67

Dan swam to the anchor. He grabbed the thick metal chain and rested for a while, listening. The ship was completely dark and silent. Wind whipped around him. An ominous feeling was tingling in his spine. He tapped his waterproof earbuds. Melania answered immediately. Dan gave her a sitrep then hung up. He removed his fins then tied them to the anchor with a nylon string. He raised himself slowly out of the sea and grabbed the chains. He lifted himself up then felt for the kukri knife on his belt. Dangling from his neck was a Watershed anti-immersion water bag. Inside it was an MK23 0.45-caliber ACP handgun, with anti-saltwater coating on the slide. That would keep the barrel from saltwater corrosion, and Dan hoped the gun actually worked if he had to fire it.

The anchor was long, and Dan stopped frequently, listening. He got to the top rung of the chain and grabbed the railing of the lower deck. With both hands grasping the railing, he hung for a while. He couldn't hear the RIB, which was good news. Dan pulled himself up then vaulted over, onto the deck. He ran across to the nearest shadow cast by a chimney pipe sticking out in one corner. He unzipped the bag and took the suppressed MK23 out. He slid the safety off and put a round in the chamber then scurried over to the cabins. A passage wrapped around the cabins. Dan patrolled around it. His uneasiness was growing by the second. The deck was empty.

Why would Daurov leave his yacht in the sea? Was it a trap? It had to be. Dan had three extra mags for the MK23, then it was him and the kukri. Well, he had asked for it. Now he would deal with it.

He came to the stairs that led up to the deck above and stopped. The dark tomb of the silent ship rose high above in a pyramidal shape. He saw no movement. But he didn't take the stairs. He went out to starboard and climbed on the railing. He gripped the metal railing sticking out from the deck above. It was enough for him to get a grip. His feet were slippery on the railing, and he wobbled. The drop was more than twenty feet, and the splash would be a noisy one. A noise he couldn't afford.

Dan tightened his hold and deadlifted himself. He managed to rise enough to hook his right leg over. He tumbled onto the pelmet and rolled to a stop against the railing. He lay there for a while, breathing heavily. This deck, too, seemed empty. He got up and padded towards the main cabin. By its long glass window and the space in front, he guessed it was the bridge. There was no one inside. Dan tried the door handle. It was locked. This level, too, was deserted.

Dan leaned against the railing and looked up. There was no pelmet this time. He would have to take the stairs. He held the weapon out in front of him, scanning in the darkness. Hairs prickled the back of his neck. There was something here. He could feel it. He put his foot on the first rung, tested it, then climbed. The MK23 was pointing vertically up.

He climbed onto an open deck. It was windier now than before. That meant a restless sea and more drift for Sean. Dan put the thought out of his head. Starlight shone down on him, but the moon sailed under a cascade of clouds. He could see the white structure of a cabin before him in the middle of the deck. He figured this would be where Daurov lived.

Dan stopped. His breathing was faster. He did a three-sixty then approached the main door quickly. It was a bifold glass door, and it was locked. Dan felt in the pocket of his wet suit and took out a lockpick. He fitted it into the lock and jangled the key.

He kept his eye on the glass. That saved his life. A shadow loomed behind him, and he ducked at the last minute. A blow shattered the glass into a hundred pieces, showering him with glass fragments. Dan didn't hear a suppressed round—the impact was from a blunt instrument. They wanted him alive. He knew the next blow would be directed down, so he didn't fall to the floor. Instead, he leaned back quickly, into the arm that wielded the weapon.

He cannoned onto the figure, twisting and grabbing onto their midriff. He drove them backwards, looking to bash the figure against the railings. The hammer came down again and landed on his lower spine, sending a jarring pain down his legs. Dan winced, and his knees folded. But he continued driving the person back. They smashed against something metallic that twanged, sending a tremor through the deck. Dan grabbed his attacker's legs and flipped them up, and that was when he knew.

It wasn't a man; it was a woman. The Scorpion.

He flipped her sideways, but she grabbed his hair and pulled him down with her. He landed on top of her. She had a needle ready, and he jerked his head away. The tip went past his nose, and she punched him with her left arm. Pain mushroomed inside his head, and he realized she was wearing steel dusters on her knuckles. She pushed him off her, and Dan rolled several times to get away. He heard the needle hit the floor several times. Then he was up on his knees, eyes dimmed, pain roaring in his brain. It made him feel numb, unfocused. He saw her circling him, hands loose.

"Natasha," he cried out hoarsely. "Why are you doing this?"

"It's my job, Dan."

"I don't want to kill you."

"Really?" Her voice was taunting. "Then why are you on this yacht?"

"To find out who Daurov called in Baltimore."

It might be his imagination, but he thought the Scorpion stopped for a while. "I don't know anything about that."

She got closer, and Dan took his gun out. He locked on her.

She said, "Take your shot, Dan."

He shook his head. "This might sound weird right now. But I miss you. You..." He gasped, wondering where the words were coming from. "You know me, Natasha. And I know you."

She was still coming forward but slower, he noticed. He couldn't see her features in the faint glow of the starlight.

He said, "If you want to know the truth, that's why I came. To find you again. I needed to find you." Dan straightened and stuck the gun in his belt. He felt a calm descend upon him. He spread his arms. "I can't kill you, Natasha. But I won't let you kill me either. What's it going to be?"

"You don't know me, Dan. And you never will."

With a scream of fury, the Scorpion thrust herself at him. Dan was ready.

He crouched and grabbed her forearm. He lifted her on his back in a jujitsu move and flung her across the deck. But he was close to the railings, and she went sailing over them, into the dark void of the sea and wind.

Dan gripped the railing and stared down. He heard the splash then nothing but the moan of the wind.

CHAPTER 68

The powerful lights on the RIB focused on the waves that rose and fell. The machine churned as Sean reversed and cut across in a slow circle. Dan leaned over the side of the RIB, pointing a handheld light into the choppy waters.

"You sure she fell around here?" Sean yelled.

Dan nodded. It was a long way to fall, and though the Scorpion had protective gear on, the collision with water could have hurt her. If she was knocked out... Dan saw a light flashing on his wrist device. He waved at Sean to cut the engine. It was Melania, and her tone was urgent.

"A boat is moving away from you at high speed. The drone just picked it up. It's headed for the Italian mainland."

Dan's mind clicked. The boat was the Scorpion's getaway vehicle. He gave Melania a sitrep then got back on the yacht again. He went straight up to Daurov's pad on the top floor. The glass of the bifold door was smashed, and he stepped over it. He felt for the light switches and turned them on. He was in a living room with a bar. A door at the end connected him to a luxurious bedroom. Dan opened all the wardrobes in the room, finding them empty. There was a study next to the bedroom with glass walls looking out over the sea. Dan found the desktop empty and the drawers bare.

Over the next half an hour, he searched methodically. With the kukri, he ripped into the mattress, lifted panels from the wardrobes, and ransacked the place. When it was done, he was covered in sweat, but he had found nothing. He flopped on Daurov's chair behind the study desk. The place was a mess. Dan had turned the table upside down and taken its legs off to find secret compartments. Again, there was nada.

He shook his head and rubbed his eyes. He stood and scraped the chair back. On the floor, he noticed a business card. Its ornate gold borders caught his eye, and he bent to pick it up.

Cardinal Bernardio Giacometti
Apostolic Nuncio (Stati Uniti d'America)
Apostolic Palazzo
Citta del Vaticano

Dan stared at the card. He didn't know much Italian but was pretty sure the last line meant the Vatican City. The card belonged to a cardinal, whom he guessed was pretty high up in the pecking order to be in a palace in the Vatican.

The golden border winked in the light. A flicker of thought winked inside his mind as well then vanished. His eyes narrowed, and he sat down heavily. There was something here, just out of his grasp. He could feel it. He stared at the card.

He screwed his eyes shut, forcing himself to think back to the source. Terambutov. Renowned jihadi banker, risked himself when he came to USA. For what? To ensure money was available for an important cause?

Daurov calling the mosque… jihadi networks… Qayamat… Judgment Day… Judgment Day…

Dan shot upright suddenly. A cold sweat broke out on his forehead, and his heart hammered against his ribs. His mouth was dry. He stared at the card for a second then called Melania.

"Call SISMI. The Vatican is under attack. This is what they mean by Judgment Day!" Dan blurted breathlessly.

"What? Dan, slow down. How did you get that?"

"I'll explain when I see you. We need to take a flight to Rome right now. I've got a bad feeling something big is going to happen inside the Vatican."

He heard her voice become lower. "You mean like a bomb?"

"Or even worse," Dan whispered, suddenly halting in his tracks. "Oh shit."

"What?"

"These nutcases think this is a religious war, right? Who could they take out to strike the biggest blow of all time? Inside the Vatican?"

"Oh my God. It's the pope."

CHAPTER 69

Dan jumped off the RIB and helped Sean drag it to shore. He had seen the headlights of the Jeep shining from the cliff top as the RIB roared in from the dark sea. Melania was waiting for him on the beach, waving her flashlight. He ran up and grabbed her elbow.

"I'll explain in the car. Did you sort out the bird?"

"Yes," Melania said as they jogged over the sand. "The Rome CIA station is sending a bird. It's going to land at the Porto Cervo airport's helipad. We're heading there now."

Dan grunted with exertion as he ran up the slope of the cliff. He paused to help Melania, who was out of breath.

Between gasps, she said, "Alerted Chuck Jones and my bosses as well. They're calling SISMI."

They got to the top and collapsed against the side of the Jeep.

"What's the matter?" Dan panted. "Not used to running slopes?"

"Matched you for pace," she shot back, ignoring Dan's raised eyebrows.

The Jeep took off with a screech of tires. Jake drove like a madman, and Melania held on as she made a flurry of phone calls.

When she hung up, Dan explained his thinking to her and showed her the card. "The Scorpion also left for the Italian mainland. She must be heading for Rome."

Melania nodded. "That's where the last drone feed placed her." She looked at Dan. "She still didn't manage to kill you?"

Her tone made Dan turn his head. He looked away without speaking.

Melania said, "You know her well, don't you, Dan?"

"No," he said.

"No? It's weird that she gets you on her own twice, but neither of you seems to be able to hurt each other."

"She's good at her job."

"You have quite the high impression of her."

Dan didn't reply again.

Melania said, "I need to know if you're in this one hundred percent, Dan. Are you focused?"

Anger flared inside Dan. He ground his teeth together and got his face close to Melania's. She didn't move away and glared back at him.

"Listen, lady, I'm not a case that you can analyze. Keep your opinions to yourself. Next time you question my focus, think about yours."

"What the hell does that mean?"

"Who's that guy in the drone feed? The one you hoped to find in the silver mine?"

It was Melania's turn to be quiet.

Dan smirked. "You got focus, right?"

Melania grabbed hold of Dan's shirt and pulled him towards her face. "You want to know who that guy was, Dan?"

"Yeah," Dan said, his face inches from hers. "Tell me."

"He was the asshole who stole me from my family and then trafficked me to the United States. Happy now?"

She let go of Dan, and he fell back in the seat. The car was roaring down a side road and screeched as it made a sharp turn on the main street of Porto Cervo. Melania had the window down. The wind was blowing her hair back in a stream. Dan noticed she had her Glock out on her lap.

"I'm sorry," he said.

She shook her head, still looking out the window. "Just leave it."

It was a balmy night in Porto Cervo, and tourists packed the sidewalk. The crowd spilled onto the road, and cars stopped, honking. The glitz of the bars and expensive-car showrooms lit up the street in a neon glaze.

Jake leaned on the horn. "Watch out!" he yelled. He swerved to avoid hitting a drunk man, but the brake lights of an SUV loomed large in front. Everyone shouted as Jake spun the wheel like crazy, and the tires lost control of the slide. The Jeep slid sideways. Dan was slammed against the window, with Melania on top of him. Jake went the other way, and the car crashed against the side of a sedan, glass exploding on impact.

"Fuck!" Jake screamed. He revved the gas, and the Jeep responded. A man had come out of the sedan. He waved his hands, trying to stop the Jeep.

Dan heard sirens behind him. He looked to see flashing blue lights. "Uh-oh. You did warn the Sardinia cops, right?" he asked Melania.

"Yes, I did."

The red-striped BMW SUV was getting closer, siren blaring. Dan said, "Looks like they didn't get the message." He slapped the headrest of the driver's seat. "Go, Jake!"

But the man was standing in the middle of the road now, gesturing to his car angrily. Dan took the suppressor off his Sig, leaned out the window, pointed the gun to the sky, and pulled the trigger. The blast of the 0.45-caliber round was loud. People screamed and ran for cover. The road was clear for Jake, and he floored it. The Jeep smashed against the side of another car, ramming it sideways, then it was free, streaking down the road towards the airport.

Dan jerked his thumb at the police car in hot pursuit. "When's the bird arriving?"

CHAPTER 70

The Jeep had a 4.0-liter, 16-valve engine, and its gas tank was full. Jake put pedal to metal, and the car roared down the road. Melania had her phone out again and was speaking feverishly. Dan kept an eye behind them. The police SUV had now been joined by another one, and both were keeping up, lights and sirens active.

"How far to the airport, Jake?" Dan shouted.

"Another five K," Jake said.

Dan thought. If this procession arrived at the airport, it was almost guaranteed they would be stopped, despite their creds. It could result in them being arrested first and asked questions later. All of which led to loss of critical time.

"Did you get my duffel bag?" Dan asked.

Melania nodded. Dan leaned over to the rear hold and heaved his bag over. He took out the HK 416 and attached the night sight to the Picatinny rail then screwed a suppressor on.

"Slow down," Dan said to Jake.

Melania had the phone to her ear, but she put it down. "Our bird's arrived. It's an MI-17 with a two-man crew. We have permission to carry weapons on board."

Dan nodded, focusing on his weapon. Melania caught his sleeve, forcing him to look up at her.

She asked, "What the hell are you doing?"

Jake was still maintaining current speed. He glanced at the rearview to catch the conversation. Dan glanced at the headlights that were looming larger through the rear window.

"We need to get them off our tail."

"We cannot shoot law enforcement officers here, Dan. They're cooperating with us."

"Looks like the order's not filtering through."

Melania clicked her tongue. "I am trying, damn it."

Dan shook his head. "Not your fault. I'm not gonna shoot them. Don't worry." He caught Jake's eyes in the rearview. "Slow down, bud."

Jake took his foot off the gas, and the Jeep decelerated.

"Now stop!" Dan shouted.

Jake slammed on the brakes, and Dan opened the door and got out quickly.

He crouched by the side of the Jeep. The police vehicles were approaching more slowly now, and Dan located them on the viewfinder of the HK. The butt was solid against his shoulder, and he was stable on one knee. The headlights from the cars lit him up. He aimed, allowed the time lag for the moving vehicle, and pressed the trigger. The front tires of the first car exploded. Dan changed angle, aimed, and fired again. He missed the second car, bullets picking up dirt on asphalt. The car realized Dan was aiming for the tires and tried to slow down more, changing lanes. Dan had to fire three times more to hear the sound he wanted. The second car lurched forward then braked to a stop as it tilted on the roadside.

Dan was back up in the Jeep, and it screeched away before the first cop came out of the car.

Melania said, "They have a bird, but I'm hoping it's not in action."

"Cut the lights," Dan said. "It's how we used to drive in Iraq. It's dangerous but worth it."

Jake hit the lights, and sudden darkness enshrouded them. The road wasn't visible anymore, or the white line that divided the lanes. After fifteen minutes of driving, Jake flicked the lights on. The turning for the airport had arrived, at a traffic junction. The lights of the airport were gleaming in the middle distance.

"Sure as hell we get in," Dan said.

The airport was small but busy. It worked for commercial flights mainly and had a private section for the billionaires. Melania showed her creds, and they were kept waiting till a sergeant came and checked them over.

Dan fumed with impatience. He decided to go for the direct approach.

He stepped in front of the sergeant. "I know you're trying to do your job, but I'm trying to do mine. There could be a terrorist attack in the Vatican." He repeated the last sentence as the man looked up at him. "If you don't let us through to our flight, the worst could happen. Get me?"

The sergeant stared at Dan's intense eyes for a few seconds then blinked. He gave the creds back to Melania and waved at them. "Follow me."

CHAPTER 71

The black MI-17 helicopter was like a glass tomb, and the noise inside was deafening. Ernie Feltz was the pilot, a member of the 160th SOAR. He was on Dan's comms channel. Dan pressed a button on his radio and got his attention. They were still flying over the dark expanse of the Tyrrhenian Sea, and land wasn't visible.

"ETA into Rome, Ernie?"

"Forty-five minutes in this weather. Thirty if the wind dies down."

"Roger that."

Melania nudged him, then her voice came to life on his channel. She spoke into her headphone mic, and Dan could see her lips move.

"I'm hooking you into this call. It's from Chuck Jones at the NSA."

Chuck's voice came on the line. "Jenny, our analyst, found something interesting."

"What?"

"Not sure if there's any bearing, but on the basis of what Melania has fed back to me, it could be. A priest was killed in Baltimore two days before the phone call to the mosque. Father Peter Deakins. He was the parish priest in a suburb seventy miles northeast of Baltimore but lived close to the city. We decided to cast the web wider to see if any unusual cases turned up. This was one of them."

Chuck continued to tell them about Deakins's recent appointment as a bishop. "It's not easy becoming a bishop, folks. Highly competitive, in fact. The Apostolic Nuncio of the USA has to vet you, then the pope has to personally agree." His voice went quiet. "And I heard what you said about that Cardinal Bernardio. He is the Apostolic Nuncio for the USA, right?"

"Right," Dan said, "but why kill the priest?"

Melania said, "So the killer can get into the Vatican posing as him?"

Dan frowned. "I'm sure the Vatican have checks in place. And this guy

233

needs to look the same or very similar." A wave of cold fear washed over him. "What if that *is* true?" he whispered almost to himself.

Melania asked, "You mean, like a body double? Is that even possible?"

Dan shook his head. "It's not that uncommon, and you know it. Saddam Hussein had a doppelgänger, and so does—"

"Daurov," Melania whispered. Her eyes widened as the realization hit her like a speeding train. "Maybe that was their plan all along. To find someone who looked similar to a bishop or cardinal either in the Vatican or about to enter…" Her words trailed off. Her mind grappled with the enormity of it.

Chuck said, "Hold on. Are you saying we need to look for Bishop Deakins in the Vatican?"

Melania and Dan looked at each other. Dan said, "Yeah, I guess so. At the very least, we need to find out if the newly minted bishop has reported for duty."

"Oh shit," Chuck exclaimed. "The FBI said his passport and other IDs were stolen."

Melania said, "Then do we know if the passport has been used again?"

"I'll check and get back to you."

"While you're at it, email me Deakins's photo," Melania said.

Chuck hung up, and Melania's line beeped on another channel. It was Ernie.

He said, "The DNI needs to speak to you."

"Put him through." When Polk came on her line, Melania said, "Dan Roy is with me on this call."

"Fine. Is this all true?"

Dan said, "We need to pursue it, as this has the worst outcome. The fact that a bishop was killed makes it more likely." He told the DNI about Deakins.

"Yes, Chuck has briefed me on this already. There's something else the FBI fed back to me. Ballistics from Deakins's body came back. They're .45-caliber rounds, fired from a Makarov pistol, likely modified for Special Forces use."

Dan asked, "Do we have any ballistics from the mosque?"

"Nope. No bodies have been found from the mosque as yet. Still searching for the imam."

Chuck came back on the line, joining them. "Got some news. State Department confirms Peter Deakins boarded the 0900 flight to Rome from Thurgood Marshall yesterday."

There was an appalled silence inside the MI-17. Dan heard the roaring of the rotors in his ears, replaced by a different sound in his mind—waves of panic, thrashing against his skull.

"He's already inside. Oh God." *That pun was not intended,* he thought as he screwed his eyes shut.

Polk said, "I'm calling the Vatican authorities. Hold on."

CHAPTER 72

Apostolic Palazzo
Citta del Vaticano
Roma

Dias Dashev, disguised as Bishop Deakins, smiled cordially as another bishop walked past him in the hallway. Dias was dressed in a black smock, with the traditional red sash on his waist, and a red skull cap. He crossed the internal entrance to the Sistine Chapel, which was devoid of any hubbub of voices from tourists at this time of the night. He slowed his pace as he got to the *Cappella Paolino*. The door to the *Sala Regia* was open, and he could see a light shining from inside. It meant someone was praying, and it could well be the pope. Would the pope be alone or with some of his cardinals? Pope Luis was well known for making impromptu visits to the *Cappella Paolino*. It was his favorite chapel in the entire *Vaticano*.

Dias clenched his jaw and checked his watch. It was past eleven p.m. He was going to be late if he got held up here. If the pope was not alone, then questions would be asked about what he, a junior bishop, was doing up this late. Most of the staff in the Apostolic Palazzo went to bed at ten p.m. to ensure they rose when the pope rose, at 4:45 a.m. sharp.

Dias went downstairs and stopped at the gates that led to the courtyard. A Swiss Guard was patrolling the grounds. The courtyard was large and well lit with fluorescent yellow lamps that stood between the trees. Still, there were plenty of shadows, and it was possible that Dias could sneak through to the ancient, heavy oak door that guarded the passage to the River Tiber. But Swiss Guards always worked in pairs. He needed to locate the other one before he went out.

He waited for a while, standing still against the heavy brocade curtains that hung from the ceiling to the floor. Light spilled in from a lamp outside.

236

Dias checked his watch again and glanced nervously down the wide hallway. The famous tapestries and paintings seemed to watch him. Unlike the rest of the Vatican, lights in the Apostolic Palazzo were always turned off in evening. What Dias really didn't need was another priest coming up on him and asking awkward questions.

Through the glass panels of the door, he saw the other Swiss Guard appear. He must have gone for a toilet break. The guard went over to speak to his friend. They were standing right in the path of the oak door, and that was no coincidence. For centuries, that great oak door had stood as a secret known only to insiders at the Apostolic Palazzo. Other staff in the Vatican didn't know of its existence.

Dias glanced down the dark hallway once again and made his mind up. He couldn't be late for this appointment or else all was lost. He opened the door and stepped out.

"Help! Help!" Dias shouted. Not too loud, as he didn't want to alert the occupants of the bedrooms in the floors above. He waved as he ran forward. His actions had the desired effect. In the stillness of the yard, his voice carried easily to the guards. They stiffened and turned to him.

"Cardinal Pettrino has collapsed in the corridor. I need help to get him up." Dias gasped as the guards abandoned their positions and ran towards him.

He led them inside the hallway. It was still deserted. He unsheathed the knife from the vest inside his black robe. The Swiss Guards fell in behind Dias, expecting him to lead them. Dias waited until they were a few paces in then turned on them swiftly. He stabbed the guard on the right in the neck, the knife entering the windpipe, dissecting it as he moved it up and down. With his left leg, Dias kicked the other guard as he tried to take his weapon out.

Letting the wounded one collapse, Dias rammed his body into the other guard, propelling him backwards. They tumbled to the floor. Dias raised his knife and stabbed the man in the face, hitting his eye. Blood spurted up, and the man howled in agony. Dias clamped on his mouth and, with the other hand, throttled his neck. He squeezed with both hands, veins standing out on his forehead as he increased the pressure. Soon, the guard stopped struggling, and his eyes stared out vacantly.

Panting, Dias stood up swiftly. He looked for witnesses and found none. He took the large ring of keys from one of the guard's pockets. He pulled the dead bodies behind the curtains and covered them the best he could. They wouldn't be visible to any casual passerby till the morning. He went out into the garden, walking unhurriedly, like a man out for an evening stroll. When he got to the door, he paused.

There was a bench next to the door, and he sat down. He observed the windows above him, many of them lit. To his left, beyond his own room, he could see the western guest house, the living quarters of the Holy See. All the lights were ablaze, and he wondered if the pope was inside. Satisfied that no one was observing him from beyond a twitching curtain, Dias stood up and unlocked the door using the keys. He had observed the guards closely when he came in the day before. They used a long silver key that stood out from the other brass ones.

Dias locked the door then hurried through the passageway. The ancient, moldy brickwork smelled of moss and damp. It was dark, too, pitch-black. Only the flashlight in Dias's hand showed him the way. The passage was also narrow. No more than two men could walk side by side. It sloped downwards as he advanced, and the bricks beneath his feet became slick with mud. The smell of damp increased, and the whisper of flowing water entered his ears. A rat scurried on the ground, and he stiffened, reaching for his knife. He moved again, feeling fresh air on his face.

The rustling of water increased. The passage sloped down to the river's edge, and the muddy gray waters soon became visible. The cobbled bricks were now covered in mud. In high tide, the river came inside the tunnel. The mouth of the tunnel where it met the riverbank was wide to allow water to collect and not flood the interior.

Dias lifted his smock, his shoes and socks now wet. He got out of the tunnel and climbed up the small flight of steps to higher ground. A jetty poked above the water. Dias stood on it, feeling the planks creak under his feet. The boat manned by the Carabinieri was bobbing in the water, tied to the jetty. It was a fifty-foot RIB with a cabin built in the middle where the pope could sit if needed. There wasn't a light on in the cabin, but Dias knew an Italian commando was there, armed with a submachine gun.

He approached the boat. He looked at the opposite bank, where the high walls rose to the traffic-riddled roads of Rome. His eyes scanned down to the bank again. Eventually, he saw it... a light that blinked on and off. It was a rubber dinghy, waiting for his signal.

Dias glanced at the RIB again. The lights remained off still. He took out his flashlight and pressed it on and off three times in quick succession. He couldn't hide the signal from the commando in the RIB. The honking of cars filtered down from above, and it masked the machine of the dinghy as it set off from the opposite bank.

Dias stepped closer to the RIB.

"*Ciao!*" he called out loudly.

He had to call again before a shape shifted inside the cabin. A light went on. A figure stepped out, dressed in green fatigues. Dias looked over the whispering dark waters. The dinghy was black, and it remained almost invisible as it putted across.

"*Va bene, Signore,*" Dias said.

The soldier had a flashlight, and he pointed it at Dias. He exclaimed loudly. "Ciao, Your Excellency," he said, mistaking him for a senior cardinal. It was one of the reasons Dias was dressed in a cardinal's robe. "Is everything OK?"

"Yes, of course. I just came for an evening stroll. Felt like seeing the waters."

The soldier stared at him and rubbed his jaw. Dias knew what the man was thinking. It was rare, if not unheard of, for a cardinal to come down here at this time.

Dias said, "I look for divine inspiration everywhere, my son. Sometimes, there is only peace in solitude."

The soldier bowed his head. The sound of the dinghy's motor grew louder. The soldier turned his neck around, following the sound. Dias saw his finger caress the trigger. The boat was two yards away from the jetty. Dias jumped.

He slammed into the commando, who was taken by surprise.

The knife was ready in Dias's hand. It sank deep into the commando's neck then withdrew and stabbed repeatedly around the face and neck. The last thing the shocked commando saw was a cardinal staring at him in the face as the knife came down for the killer blow.

The dinghy docked against the jetty as Dias stood up, sweating. His smock was covered in blood.

The man shining the flashlight said, "You did well there, brother."

Dias picked up the commando's submachine gun, flicked it to automatic mode, and made sure it was a suppressed weapon. He would need this later.

"Are you Nifas?" Dias asked.

"Yes, I am," Nifas replied. He was a radicalized Tunisian youth who had illegally entered Italy to claim asylum.

"Do you have the material?"

"Over here."

Dias helped Nifas move the twenty kilos of TNT explosives from the dinghy into the jetty. It was inside a backpack, and Dias opened it to check. He stood.

"You did well, too, my brother," he said to Nifas. "Tomorrow the world will change. Victory will be ours."

"Yes," Nifas said fervently.

Dias said, "Heaven awaits you, brother."

Nifas blinked. "What do you mean?"

Dias pointed the weapon at the young man's chest and pulled the trigger. A stream of steel flew out of the muzzle, driving Nifas into the RIB, and his blood-soaked body came to a rest next to the dead commando.

"That's what I mean," Dias said.

CHAPTER 73

Via del Corso
Roma

Like every head of state, the Italian prime minister had his own residence. This being Rome, the residence happened to be an actual sixteenth-century palace, Palazzo Chigi. It sat across the river from Vatican City, almost directly opposite. The busy piazza overlooking the city-based palazzo had a host of small meandering streets around it. But one street was ramrod straight and wide. This was the Via del Corso, where many of the Italian cabinet had apartments they worked from and housed their mistresses in.

In one of the apartments of a stately terrace on Via del Corso, the phone began to ring. The Italian Secretary of State, Paolo Noleggio, had just fallen asleep. He had recently gotten back from Berlin. His current mistress, an ambitious young opera singer, had worn him out, and he was having a pleasant dream. The incessant ringing of the phone strained his consciousness. He thought it was part of the dream.

His lover elbowed him in the ribs. "That will be for you," Valentina said sleepily.

Paolo grumbled and reached for the phone, just to stop the damn thing ringing.

"Who is this?" he asked roughly.

It was his secretary.

"Do you know what time it is?" Paolo said angrily.

"Sir, this is an emergency. The US ambassador is on the line, asking to speak to you."

Paolo woke up. He raised himself up on one elbow. "The US ambassador? Signor Denison?"

"Yes, sir. He says the head of SISMI also wants to speak to you."

Paolo swung his legs down to the floor. "Put him through."

The call was patched on to Anders Denison, the US ambassador. His voice came in crisply. "Good evening, Mr. Noleggio. How are you?"

"Anders, what time do you call this?"

"Sorry to disturb, but this is important."

The tone of his voice made Paolo pause. "What's going on?"

"The CIA has reason to believe there is an imminent attack against the Vatican."

"What sort of attack?"

"A terrorist one."

Paolo sighed. "Anders, if you knew the number of prank calls we get about attacks on the Vatican—"

"This is different. It involves a bishop from the USA who has travelled to the Vatican recently."

Paolo stood up. He was naked, and he walked over to his dressing robe. "Hold on." He put his robe on then walked to the next room and shut the door. He was completely awake now. "Which bishop?"

Anders told him the whole story.

Paolo listened without interrupting. Then he shook his head. "This sounds almost preposterous. Impossible."

"Truth can be stranger than fiction, Paolo," Anders said. "Think about what's at stake here. Do you really want to take the chance?"

Paolo considered for a few seconds. "Does the prime minister know?"

"No. You are the first member of cabinet I am calling. The SISMI director was told by the CIA director, Stephen Polk."

"What do you propose?"

"You let the CIA team that made the discovery handle the operation, with your help, of course. Give them access into the Vatican."

Paolo rubbed his cheek. He was an experienced politician, and he seldom missed a trick. He could see the headlines already. *American team saves the Vatican.* Not Italian. He knew what the prime minister would say. More importantly, he could sense what the proud Italian public would think.

"Italy is a sovereign nation, Anders, just as America is. I suggest you hand over the intelligence to us and let us handle the operation from here."

Anders sighed down the phone. He had been the US ambassador to Italy for more than a decade now. He knew the politicians well. "This is not about scoring points, Paolo. You can take the credit. That's how we sell it to the media, all right? But my guys are warm on this. They know who they're chasing. Let's not waste time."

"Anders, you know better than me the media love nothing better than a scandal. They will get wind of this. And we all know how much you Americans love to boast. Do you really think this will remain a secret?"

"My guys have their lips sealed."

Paolo opened his drinks cabinet and poured himself a dash of red wine. He swirled the crimson liquid before taking a sip. "Your president is down on the polls for the midterm elections, isn't he?"

There was silence. Then Anders said in a guarded tone, "So what?"

"So this looks good on him. The president of the USA directed the CIA team to save the Vatican from a terrorist attack. The pope himself blesses the president. We could even have an official state visit for that purpose. There are a lot of Republicans in your country who would love that. Might turn your president's political fortunes around."

Silence again. Anders said, "The polls are not in our favor because of the recession. People are unhappy—"

"People?" Paolo snorted. He drained his wine glass. "Since when have you cared about the people, Anders? Come on, what is this about really?"

Anders's voice now had an edge. "Damn you, Paolo. This has the potential to be a disaster. OK, I am thinking about my angle. Can't blame me, right? We have a lot of loonies in the right wing of our party. You know that. If this blows up, we're looking at another war. And believe me, no American wants that now. I mean, not even us. But if this shit hits the fan, we can't control them. Hell, even you won't be able to stop the fanatics in your party."

Paolo took a deep breath and let it out slowly. He tapped his glass. "OK. But I will not allow a full CIA paramilitary team into the Vatican. No way. Two or three CIA operatives only. The rest have to be Italian. *Capisce?*"

"Loud and clear. I need a green signal."

"Let me speak to the Vatican secretary of state first. Cardinal Benito. If they refuse, then no power on earth can get you inside. You know that better than I do."

"And you know Rafal Benito well. Why the hell do you think I'm calling you and not another member of cabinet?"

"Flattery will get you everywhere, my friend."

"Just get me inside the Vatican."

CHAPTER 74

The armored Fiat was speeding away from Fiumicino Airport. Dan was seated with Melania and the Deputy Director of AISE, Marco Bianchi, in the rear of the car.

"What's the delay about?" Dan asked.

Marco Bianchi was a slim, soft-spoken man in his fifties. His cheeks were sallow, and the hair on his scalp was thinning. His face had a hangdog expression, as if he was tired of the tricks life had played on him. Only his black eyes were watchful, and he spoke in a measured, slow tone. "Our Secretary of State has to ring his counterpart in the Vatican and get his permission. Until then, we cannot enter the Vatican." He glanced sideways at Dan then at Melania. "Also, I am instructed to tell you that a maximum of two or three CIA operatives are allowed inside. The Arma dei Carabinieri, or Italian Military Corps, will run the mission."

Melania frowned. "Wait. The mission is ours because we got the intelligence. Frankly, without us, you wouldn't know what the hell was going on. So I suggest you let our full team in."

Marco sighed. "I wish I could. But our secretary of state is also my boss and handles our budget. I cannot disobey a direct order."

Melania said, "That's ridiculous. Now we have to brief the Carabinieri and work with a different team?"

Marco raised his eyebrows. "What if this were the White House and we had the intel?"

"I see your point. But the White House is an American institution, whereas the Vatican is not Italian—it's actually a state in its own right. Surely they can make their own minds up."

"That's happening now. Let's see what they say." Marco settled back in his seat.

Melania met Dan's eyes, and he shook his head sideways slowly. The message was clear—stay out of it. The Fiat sped down the road, ignoring traffic signals and taking corners at high speed. It had a red lamp flashing on the hood and a siren with it. In half an hour, they had reached the US embassy, based inside the Palazzo Margherita in Via Vittorio Veneto. The location of the CIA station was not publicly known, but it was somewhere inside the sprawling palazzo. The name was on a stone outside the magnificent building. Lights glowed from the third-floor roof of the Greco Roman building.

As Dan walked in, he leaned over to Melania and asked, "Do they name all their palaces after pizzas?"

Melania didn't respond. Her mind was tied up in knots, trying to piece together the details. The bishop's death in Baltimore and then the use of his passport bothered her more than anything else. She wondered where Sergei fitted into all this. She knew he did. The black SUV he escaped in was under the tarpaulin at the silver mine. She'd found it herself. But Sergei had escaped. She felt sure of it. All the mines had now been shut down in Sardinia, and the trafficked children were in safe hands. Daurov's men had not been found, and neither had Sergei. The yacht had been left as a trap, and Melania was thankful that Dan hadn't died in a booby trap.

The Scorpion was also here. Maybe she knew where Sergei and Daurov were hiding.

The lobby of the palace was gigantic, stretching almost the whole length of the building. Melania smiled as she saw the figure of her boss, Karl Shapiro, striding forward to meet them.

"Got us all shook up, Mel," Karl said with an attempt at a grin, but his smile was fake, and his eyes were drawn with anxiety. "But this is really happening, right?"

"You bet. May I introduce Marco Bianchi?"

The two men shook hands, and they went upstairs into the embassy then through a series of corridors and stopped at what looked like a janitor's cupboard door. Karl lifted the lanyard on his neck and held out a red plastic card. He touched it to the keypad of the door, and it buzzed. There was nothing but darkness inside, but when Karl stepped in, a series of lights blinked to life, showing a wide corridor stretching as straight as an arrow.

The door shut behind them. They went past rooms filled with humming servers. Karl pressed his card again on a door thirty yards down the corridor, and it swung open to reveal a large open-plan office. It was dark, lit only by the light of computer screens. Karl directed them to a desk. He opened up a laptop as the others sat around him.

Melania asked, "Do we have a photo of the priest? I didn't get it as we were on the bird."

"Should be in your email now."

Melania had checked but not seen anything. Karl secured access to the FBI site then clicked on a link. The passport photo then some photos from Peter Deakins's parish came up on the screen. Melania stared at the images of the dead bishop with a frown on her face. He seemed oddly familiar.

She glanced at the others. Their faces were lit only by the laptop screen. She caught Dan looking at her.

Melania said, "I feel like I've seen this guy before." She bent her neck, thinking. A thought struck her suddenly. She said, "What sort of visuals do we have on the Chechens in Sardinia and Terambutov's contacts?"

Dan replied, "I don't know what you have on the database, but we know Daurov's face for sure. The only other images I can think of are from the drone feed."

Melania nodded. "Karl, can I access our files from here? I need clearance."

"Sure thing," Karl said. He got up to let Melania sit.

Her fingers flew over the keyboard. She picked out Daurov's image first and planted it next to Peter Deakins's passport photo. There was no resemblance whatsoever. She finally got to Sergei's image from the drone feed. Her heart kept up a steady drumbeat, rising to a crescendo as she clicked on Sergei's face. Her breath was tight, and she could feel her palms become moist.

With trembling fingers, she put Sergei's face on a close-up and blew it up next to Peter Deakins's. A sudden pain lanced through her chest, and she couldn't breathe. She hunched forward as though someone had stabbed her in the back. Waves of nausea shook her body, but she couldn't stop staring at the screen as if it had grabbed her eyes, forcing her to focus.

Dan saw it as well. "Shit," he said.

The man known as Sergei was almost identical in his looks to Bishop Deakins. The resemblance was uncanny, apart from the eyes. Deakins had brown eyes, whereas Sergei's eyes were pale and almost devoid of color. There seemed to be no expression in his features at all.

Karl pointed at Sergei and asked Melania, "Who is that?"

There are so many ways I can answer that question, Melania thought. As she often did at times of acute stress, her fingers went to the pendant on her necklace. The gold pendant, a gift from Ben Wiblin, bore the Wiblin family insignia.

"Mel?" Karl raised his voice.

She cleared her throat. "A suspect in Sardinia. He escaped." She composed herself then turned around to face Karl. "As you can see, we just found the double of Bishop Deakins. This is the man who's inside the Vatican."

CHAPTER 75

The Scorpion crouched in the shadow of the wall. She had stolen a car in the coastal town of Ostia, where the boat had dropped her off. The forty-mile ride into Rome had taken her less than an hour.

She had parked on the outskirts of Rome then hiked to her designated point. As she walked, she realized how hungry she was. She had some money and stopped to buy slices of pizza from a late-night cafe. The food slowed her down, but she needed her energy for tonight. As she got closer to the river, the lights of the Vatican rose into the murky sky like a halo. The river Tiber bent as it flowed past just south of the Vatican. The Scorpion got to the riverbank and stared at the almost invisible but rustling waters below her. The drop to the river was steep. She found a set of stairs, and the gate was locked at night. She vaulted over the gate and went down the stairs swiftly.

The sounds of the river grew. She took out her phone and checked she was in the right place. Her landmark was the Ponte Principe bridge, which hulked against the night sky ahead of her. On the opposite side of the bridge and fifty yards away from it stood the secret entrance. It was painted like a brick wall to disguise it, and only the presence of the wooden jetty gave it away.

She got to the riverside. Water sloshed around her ankles. The bank opposite was shrouded in darkness. The tide swirled the waters into a frenzy as they swung around the posts of the massive bridge, now way above her.

Her phone beeped. She stared at the screen for a few seconds before answering.

"Are you in position?" Dias Dashev asked. The Scorpion had never met the killer whom Daurov valued so highly. His right-hand man. But she knew his reputation.

"Once I get across the river, I will be."

"How will you get across?"

"Swim."

There was silence. Then he spoke again. "OK. But don't be late, and don't keep me waiting. I'm in contact with Daurov. If you don't make it, then you know what happens."

"I do. Don't worry. I will be there. How long is the tunnel?"

"A mile, roughly. When you get to the other end, knock three times quickly on the door. I'll be there."

"OK."

"One more thing."

The Scorpion waited.

Dias said, "Tonight is the night when the world ends. Remember what is at stake here."

At stake for you, asshole, she thought. "I know."

She hung up, put the phone in its waterproof case, and checked her chest rig. The needles were in place, arranged according to size. The Makarov was snug in its shoulder holster. And on her back, the kukri knife, a gift from Dan Roy.

She waded into the water then started to swim with powerful strokes.

She only knew she was at the other bank when her hands touched reeds. She stood and found herself in water waist high. Ahead, she could make out a dim shape. It was a boat, and she waited for a while to see if it was occupied. She swam around the boat then heaved herself up on the jetty. For a while, she panted, breathless. Her eyes got used to the darkness. The dull glow from the city lights helped. The RIB was unoccupied, she realized after a while. Silently, she stepped on it. She got inside the cabin and rummaged around the seat. Shelves were built into the wall. She found a flashlight. Cupping the front and pointing it down, she switched the flashlight on. She came out and looked around the RIB. She knew how to operate this boat, but without switching the engine on, she couldn't tell if the tank was full.

The deck was covered in blood, but she couldn't see a body. She stepped off the jetty, feet squelching in mud. Rats scurried off in the darkness as she located the door. She stepped inside the tunnel and started walking rapidly. It rose upwards, narrowing as it did so.

When she got to the end, she was gasping. She leaned against the sodden brick wall, getting her breath back. Her watch said she had been more than half an hour. Dias Dashev was waiting.

She knocked on the door three times. There was a heaving sound then a loud creak. The beam of a light danced into the darkness.

"Who is it?"

"It's me, the Scorpion."

"Come this way."

CHAPTER 76

On the fourth floor of the Apostolic Palace, almost directly above where the Scorpion entered, a hand knocked on a door. Then it hammered loudly. The hammering continued for a few seconds, then a light came on inside the room.

Cardinal Rafal Benito, secretary of state for the smallest sovereign nation on earth, opened the door with a bemused expression on his face. He was dressed in a white bathrobe with the Vatican's insignia on it. He blinked then stared at the Swiss Guard standing outside his door.

"What is it?"

The guard held out a phone. "Paulo Noleggio, secretary of state, called our HQ. He wishes to speak to you urgently about a security matter."

The cardinal took the phone, nodded at the guard, then closed the door. He went and stood near the window that looked down at the well-lit but deserted St. Peter's Square.

"I'm very sorry to disturb Your Excellency," Paulo said. "But I had no choice."

"What is it?"

"I must apologize if this sounds far-fetched. But there is a new bishop from the USA, inside the Apostolic Palazzo, who is a terrorist."

It took a few seconds for the message to filter through. Cardinal Benito was in his sixties, but his mind was as sharp as a razor. Even then, the weirdness of what he was hearing hit him hard. His tone was sharp. "What are you talking about?"

Paolo explained in a hurry. He let the cardinal digest it then said, "We need to get a team inside the Vatican right now, Your Excellency. The terrorist networks are buzzing about a Qayamat, which means—"

"Judgment Day," Benito said, frowning. "It's mentioned in the Bible and the Torah as well." He shook his head, thoughts jostling around. "This sounds so bizarre."

"But true, Your Excellency. We need to get a team inside. I implore you."

Benito thought for a moment. In his thirty years at the Vatican, he had never heard of anything so extraordinary. "Paolo, the Apostolic Palazzo is a place of peace. Everyone is asleep. This will cause a great disturbance. And what if this bishop you speak of is not even in his room? Indeed, what if all of this is just coincidence and hearsay?"

"Then if we check it out, we can sleep in peace."

Benito stroked his chin. He made up his mind. "This decision is not mine alone. I need to discuss with the Holy See himself. And we can conduct our own check on this new bishop. Let me do our own investigation, and then I will get back to you."

"Your Excellency, the Holy See's life could be in danger. And the future of the Vatican. I beseech you—"

"If that were to happen, it is God's will, Paolo. This is what He is telling me to do. I must honor my sense of duty."

Paolo's voice was desperate. "Please, Your Excellency, I beg of you."

Benito stood up. His voice was gentle like the moonlight on the dome of St. Peter's Basilica. "Men have always threatened violence against each other. But we are still here. Fear not, my child."

Paolo was still speaking when Benito hung up. He opened the door and called to the guard standing outside.

"Call the Holy See. We need his guidance tonight."

CHAPTER 77

Dan paced the office floor in Rome's US embassy.

He glanced at Melania, who seemed to be lost in her own world. He wanted to question her about the past but knew that was precisely what occupied her mind. Was it a coincidence that the man who had abducted her all those years ago was now a terrorist and inside the Vatican? Dan didn't believe in coincidences. But why would anyone target Melania? It didn't make sense.

Karl Shapiro came off the phone. He swivelled around to them. "Just spoke to Anders Denison. The Vatican secretary of state wants to conduct their own investigation. Then they'll let us in."

Dan slumped. Melania's eyes met his. She was shaking her head.

Dan said, "Look, Karl, they're not getting the urgency of this. We're dealing with a nutjob here. He's going to do something really bad, and we'll have to pick up the pieces."

Karl's eyebrows were knitted together. "You don't think I know that? But our hands are tied. The Vatican is a sovereign state. We have to wait."

Melania's phone beeped, and she answered. "Ok." She put it on speaker mode so the others could hear.

DNI Stephen Polk's voice said, "Is Dan Roy there?"

"Yes, sir," Dan said.

"Well, I owe you. I threatened Dzemirsky with making this public and throwing out the Russian diplomat. The White House supported me." Polk chuckled. "The bluff worked. I told him to check with SVR agents who were in close contact with Daurov. Turns out a senior ex-GRU agent called Colonel Borislov took a load of cash from Daurov via unknown sources."

"Could be Wahhabis or Salafists," Dan said.

"Yes. We're checking the money trail."

Dan asked, "Has the military sat phone been used again?"

"Yes. Once again in Sardinia, ten hours ago. More recently, in Rome, in the last hour."

"That would've been just before Daurov left Sardinia. Probably called from his boat again. Now he's in Rome." Dan couldn't stop the hint of urgency in his voice.

Polk's voice was tight. "What's happening down there?"

Karl explained.

Polk sighed. "Guys, this is wasting time. We need results."

Karl said, "No can do, Stephen. You know that. Can't go against the Vatican."

Polk said, "I'll contact Anders Denison again. If needs be, this needs to be elevated to POTUS level. I'll be in touch. Good luck, gentlemen." He stopped then added hurriedly, "And lady. Sorry, Melania."

"That's all right, sir."

Polk hung up, and Karl looked at both of them in turn. "Nothing to do but wait."

Dan said, "Right." He stretched. "Do you know where the driver's gone? He had a light and I"—Dan produced his pack of cigarettes—"have some smokes."

Karl said, "I don't know."

Melania picked up the phone next to her and dialled reception. She spoke for a while then hung up. "Driver's in the parking lot, at the back."

"Can I get down there?" Dan glanced at Melania then Karl.

Karl said, "I don't know how."

Melania was looking at a floor map on the wall. "It's through the basement. Elevators are just outside. My creds will work." She stood and joined Dan as he walked out the door.

Once they were out in the corridor, Dan whispered, "Have you got your weapons on you?"

"Yes."

In the elevators, Dan checked he had his two Sigs and extra ammo. He touched the kukri knife at his back.

Melania asked, "What are you planning?"

"We need to get out of here. Karl can't do anything. By the time we hear from the Vatican, it might be too late." He read the conflict in Melania's eyes. She was a CIA agent, after all. This could cost her career. "You don't have to do this," Dan said.

The elevator came to a stop, and they stepped out into the dim lights of the basement. A sign on the wall directed them to the car park. Melania didn't move.

She said to Dan, "Do you know how long I have waited to see Sergei's face?" She looked away from him. "He ripped my life apart. Now he's here, by some strange twist of fate. Son of a bitch." She closed her eyes and breathed deeply.

Dan put a hand on her shoulder. "It's gonna be all right. I want you to get the past out of your head. Focus on this moment, right now. You can do that, right?"

Melania opened her eyes. "Right. But I want to kill that bastard."

"He'll pay for his crimes. I promise you that. But don't let the anger cloud your judgment. Think of what's at stake here."

Melania nodded. "OK. Let's do this."

They came out into the parking lot and found the driver near the gates, chatting to one of the guards. Dan did a quick sitrep. He could see one armed sentry at the bar. The other was in front of him. The bar was lowered, and the road went up a slope to join the main street outside. There could be more guards outside. Dan bit his lower lip. He had stormed out of difficult situations before, but this was the embassy.

He went up to the driver, who recognized him. "I left something in the car. A folder, and it's important."

Melania and Dan followed the driver, walking on side by side behind him. When they got close to the car, Dan nodded at Melania. He shoved the driver against the side of the car and thrust the muzzle of his Sig into his back.

"Don't move. I'm not going to hurt you, but you have to do as I say. Open the car."

The terrified guard did as he was told. Melania got into the back seat and pulled her Glock out.

"Now get in," Dan said. He kept the gun against the driver's side as he took the wheel, and Melania took over. Dan ran around and got into the passenger seat.

Dan said, "Do you know how to get inside the Palazzo Apostolico?"

The man was shaking. He wiped sweat off his forehead. "Very difficult. You have to go through the Bronze door which is on the right of St. Peter's Square. The Square is guarded by armed Carabinieri 24 hours. The Bronze Door by armed Swiss Guards."

Melania had a map of Vatican City open on her phone. "Wait up," she said. "If St. Peter's Square is the front of Vatican City, at the back, you have acres of gardens, right?"

"*Si, signora.* Almost the whole of the Citta del Vaticano's rear is made of sculpted gardens."

Melania was still engrossed in the map. She looked up. "OK, take us to the Viale Vaticano that hooks around the gardens. I think that's our best way in."

Dan said to the guard, "You're gonna drive us out of here and take us to the spot. Make any funny moves, and you're a dead man. Got it?"

"Y-yes, Signor," the man stammered.

Dan kept the gun pointed at the driver but folded his arms across his chest, hiding the weapon. The guards stopped them but waved them through when Melania flashed her creds.

"Go fast," Dan ordered when they were out. The car hurtled down the deserted night streets. They crossed the river, and Dan caught a flash of the famous St. Peter's Square in the distance. Soon they were on the curving road called Viale Vaticano that went around in a semicircle across the city-state. Dan looked at the walls, and his heart sank. They were enormous, like the ramparts of a castle.

He turned to the driver. "Stop the car." When the vehicle pulled over, Dan said, "Look, we are the good guys here. There is a bomb inside the Vatican. The pope's life is in danger. Only we can stop it."

Melania said, "The politicians are fighting over who can be allowed entry, Italians or Americans. We don't have time for that."

The man looked at both of them. He nodded slowly.

Dan asked, "Do you know if we can get over the walls anywhere?"

"Yes, there is a place where the slopes are high enough, and there are holes in the wall you can use to climb."

Melania hooked an eyebrow. "Really?"

The man smiled. "This is Italia, Signora. Everything is possible. But the climb is a dangerous one. If you fall, you can break your bones." He looked at Dan. "On the other side, you can walk around the top till you find steps. Be careful, as these will be guarded."

"Thank you," Dan said. He put his gun away. "I'm sorry I had to threaten you."

"I believe you," the man said. He made the sign of the cross. "God bless."

He drove for another two minutes till they got to the spot. Dan saw it—a bank in the slope that climbed almost halfway up the wall. Opposite, there were modern Greco Roman homes. Melania and Dan climbed up the slope on all fours. Dan pointed his flashlight up the wall. He could see the holes in the wall, but they were too high for him to reach.

Melania said, "I can stand your shoulders and reach them. Let me go first." She watched Dan hesitate and nudged his arm. "Come on. There's no time to waste. It's a long way through the gardens into the palace."

CHAPTER 78

The halogen lights of the courtyard were just enough for the Scorpion to see Dias Dashev's face for the first time. His eyes seemed to be two blank holes, and a shiver shook her spine as she stared at him. She had never seen eyes like that on a human being. A dead fish, maybe.

"What are you looking at?" Dias whispered.

"Nothing." She swallowed and massaged her neck. "What do you want me to do?"

He walked to a large potted plant next to the oak door and pointed at the ground. The Scorpion saw a stack of brick-like objects. Dias shined his light on it, and she recognized C4 plastic explosives.

"Carry these up the main staircase, into the Sala Regia, then the Capella Paolino. I will direct you."

"And then?"

She thought Dias smiled, but it was hard to tell on his strange, expressionless face. "Then we have some fireworks."

*****

Melania's hand grabbed a hole in the solid stone wall, and she pulled herself upwards. They were not mere holes, she realized. They were slits for eyes and weapons, built in case of a siege. Wind whipped around her face, pushing hair into her eyes. But she had no time to fix it. She wasn't good with heights. She didn't want to look down and appreciated the fact that Dan hadn't called up to her and was silently climbing directly below.

Pulsing with adrenaline, she kept moving. Thankfully, the holes were not too wide apart. There was a blast of wind suddenly, and it forced her hand off the nearest grip. She slipped and swung off the wall. She cried out, the sound stolen in the wind. But her left hand was still secure, as was her left foot. She felt a hand grip her right foot from below. It was Dan. She flailed, trying to

259

regain her balance. Dan tried to direct her foot into the right space, but what helped her was the strength in her left arm. She swung herself back, right hand groping against the wall in the near darkness. She found the gap, and her fingers slid inside.

Panting, she reached the top and swung her burning legs over. The wall was double layered, with a narrow walkway in between. She slid down in the gap, trying to catch her breath. Dan climbed in beside her. He was the first to get up and helped Melania to her feet.

Dan pointed his flashlight once then started moving, crouched low. They hurried over as the wall dipped and rose, following the ground. Dan lifted a hand, and they stopped. A flight of stairs led down the wall, the bottom lost in blackness.

"Stay here and hide till I signal," Dan said.

Melania flattened herself against the wall. She looked over the silent gardens, aware that the Swiss Guards patrolled this area.

Dan took a step down, then another. When he was halfway down, he beckoned at Melania, and she walked down swiftly. Dan pointed to the lights far ahead, towards the river. The dome of St. Peter's Basilica was rising like a moon from the clump of trees.

They moved swiftly from tree to tree. Both heard the sound at the same time. It came from a distance then grew louder. The barking of dogs.

"Run," Dan said.

They took off like lightning, sprinting towards St. Peter's Square. The gardens were beautiful, with long stretches of topiaries and shaped hedges around large fountains. But they had no time to appreciate their beauty. The moon came out, bathing the gardens in silver shine. The barking was louder by the second.

"We need to split up," Dan panted. "You head for the Apostolic Palace. I'll hold them."

"No, we go together."

"Negative. Raise the alarm. That's the best thing we can do. Now go!"

He pushed her gently, and they stood for a second, washed in moonlight, staring at each other. Then Melania turned and ran for her life.

Dan stood his ground. The barking was around the corner of a hedge. At least two dogs, he guessed. Dan had grown up with dogs as a child, and he used to love them. But these dogs were different. They were trained to hunt thieves as animals to be eaten alive. And Dan wasn't about to become dog food.

Two snarling beasts came at him, saliva frothing at their jaws. The first one leapt at Dan, who remained stock-still. He moved at the last minute, hearing the dog's jaws snap inches from his face. He punched the dog in the soft of its belly, and it yelped, rolling away. The second one was almost upon him, and he caught sight of another pack behind it. Maybe two or three. He didn't have a choice. These were German Rottweilers, and there were more than he could handle. He took out his Sig and shot the dog as it prepared to jump on him. He shot the one behind it, too, then turned and ran. He needed distance from the beasts because their masters weren't far behind.

The gardens grew sparse, and a huge building loomed ahead. The giant dome of St. Peter's Basilica was right behind him, so Dan knew from the map this was the Vatican government's palazzo, with the Santa Maria Cappello in front. He stuck to the right, the path leading to St. Peter's Square.

The sound of the dogs had become fainter as he ran, and his feet pounded the ground loudly. He didn't see the black shape that streaked out from a hedge and slammed into his midriff.

CHAPTER 79

Melania stopped in the shadow of one of the colonnades that surrounded St. Peter's Square like maternal arms. The huge basilica lay to her left, the obelisk that Emperor Nero carried from Egypt, to her right. The whole square was eerily silent, washed in the hush of pale moonlight. Way behind her in the distance, she heard the faint baying of dogs. Her thoughts returned to Dan briefly. She focused. As Dan had said, there was a lot at stake tonight.

She ran across the empty square, pressing closer to the Basilica, its massive shape now looming over her. She took her flashlight out, not caring if she alerted the Carabinieri, whose cars were visible at the mouth of the square. She shone the light on statues and monuments carved on the wall. The tall door set back in the wall got her attention. She didn't know what the Bronze Door looked like, but if she had to guess, this was it.

There was only one problem. The Swiss Guards had the key, and she sure as couldn't ring a bell. She ran down the side till she saw a row of windows. The ledges were large enough for her to climb onto. Melania made her mind up. Her Glock 21 had 0.45 ACP cartridges. It was heavy enough to break armored glass if fired repeatedly. Then she had to kick the glass. She guessed this glass would be armored or heavily laminated, at least.

She took a few steps back, crouched, and aimed. She fired three times. With each shot, jagged shards spread sideways from the point of impact. Armored glass, Melania thought. It made sense. These windows, albeit at the extreme corner of the square, still faced millions of tourists every year. She emptied the magazine. With the last two shots, a round gap exploded in the glass, and the bullet went through. An alarm started blaring, and lights came to life on the wall.

"Forgive me," Melania muttered. She took off her vest and wrapped it around her left elbow. She jumped on the ledge and slammed the glass with her elbows till the remaining shards came off. Shouts came from the

Carabinieri, and she could hear running footsteps pounding on the cobblestones.

Melania put the vest on, ducked her head, and scrambled inside. Her palms bled from rubbing against the shards. She was in a hallway, and to her right, she could see a broad flight of stairs. Halogen lights had come on, illuminating the walls covered in art and the ceilings. Melania ejected the magazine, slapped a new one in, and chambered a round. She ran for the stairs. They were broad enough to fit a herd of elephants walking side by side. After several landings, the staircase turned to the right. She came to a set of massive doors set deep into a wall full of carvings. The door was firmly locked.

Melania heard voices from below. The good thing about the staircase was that the wall arched over it every fifteen to twenty steps, at the landings. This created large alcoves that she could hide behind. A chair was placed on each side at every landing. The staircase was long, and it made sense that some could get tired from the climb. Melania ran behind an alcove and peered out. The distinct yellow-and-blue-striped uniform of two Swiss Guards came into view. They were still at the bottom of the staircase, debating which way to go. More of their friends arrived. Melania snuck out and went down the staircase quickly. She stood behind an alcove two landings from the top of the gigantic staircase and peered down again.

Three of the Swiss Guards were jogging up the stairs, submachine guns in their hands. She was trapped.

CHAPTER 80

The force of the blow flung Dan against a hedge. It took him by surprise, as it came from the side. He let himself fall. The hedge supported him, and he hooked his right palm against his attacker's chin. Dan pushed up then punched into the jaw as he thudded into the ground, the man falling on top of him. Dan saw the man get ready to punch him, and he could do nothing but parry the blow with his arms. The punches came thick and fast. Dan knew he couldn't just keep blocking. He had wide hips, and he buckled them, dislodging the man enough to grab his neck. Dan pushed up hard, raising the man's neck, arching his back.

In the dim light from the building, he realized he was fighting a Swiss Guard. Dan had no wish to kill the man. But he had to get away. He twisted, and they rolled on the ground. Dan head-butted the man, and his face rocked back, teeth flying out on impact. Another blow to the jaw sealed it. The guard collapsed. Dan was up and running again, breath rasping in his chest.

He came up to the square and skidded to a halt when he saw the armed Carabinieri running around. An alarm was blaring, and he saw a group of blue-uniformed men outside a window to the extreme right. The glass had given way. Dan smiled to himself. Melania had gotten through.

But would he? His eyes darted around. Security would now be heavy. It was what he wanted, but Melania was in trouble, and she needed his help. Dan heard footsteps. A Carabinieri officer was running up the colonnades. He hadn't seen Dan hidden behind a colonnade pillar. His size was right for Dan. He reached out and grabbed the man by his collar. Dan pulled savagely, bashing his head against the stone pillar. The man fell in a heap. Dan dragged his body into the shadows and, working quickly, dressed himself in the man's uniform. It fit, including the shoes.

Dan took the man's weapon and ran for the damaged window. He didn't want to get too close to the Carabinieri, as he didn't speak Italian. Luckily, they dispersed as he arrived. One of them waved to Dan and shouted an order. Dan nodded and raised his hand. He was being asked to stay and guard the window. Just him alone. Divine intervention? Dan thought so. As soon as the officers had turned the corner, Dan grabbed the ledge and lifted himself up. He jumped down and straightened, right in the face of two confused Swiss Guards.

Dan spread his hands, turning his lips down in an apology. *"Non parlo Italiano.* I'm new and from the USA."

He knew the Guards spoke English perfectly well. They frowned and looked at each other.

There was a sudden scream from their right, near the grand staircase.

CHAPTER 81

Melania watched the two guards jog past her. They followed the staircase up and turned right. One of the guards said the words, "*Sala Ducale.*" She knew *sala* meant *chamber*. When she glanced down the staircase, there was a knot of Swiss Guards, but they were all looking away. She took her chance. She went from one alcove to the next till she veered right and came to the massive doorway. One of the Guards had a large ring of keys, and he was opening the door. Both of them had to push one door. The other remained shut. They stepped inside, leaving the door open.

Now or never, Melania thought.

She crouched by the door then looked inside. The interior of the large chamber was simply stunning. It was large enough to be a ballroom, and magnificent paintings hung from the wall. Halogen lights lit up the ceiling, which was covered in frescoes. The two guards were in the center of the room, looking around. Melania caught a black shadow at the back of the room, near another doorway. She pointed her weapon, but the guards were in her way.

"Get down!" Melania shouted, running inside the marble-floored space.

The Guards turned as one. They saw her weapon and thought she was trying to shoot them. Before Melania could open her mouth again, the sound of two suppressed rounds ruptured the silence. One guard's face blew open, and the other toppled forward, the back of his head smashed. Melania dived to the floor and rolled around as rounds spit up chunks of marble on the floor. When she pointed her weapon, it came to bear on the figure of a woman dressed from head to toe in black.

"Put down your weapon," the figure commanded in English.

Melania didn't. Through gritted teeth, she said, "So. The Scorpion reveals itself."

"I said put down your weapon now, if you want to live."

Melania's senses were razor sharp. She could hear every sound, see every

266

detail on the Scorpion's face. The chestnut-red hair, hazel eyes. From her neck hung a necklace with a pendant.

A pendant...

Melania's stomach suddenly lurched, and her heart seemed to stop beating. Pressure built behind her eyes till she thought her eyeballs would explode.

The pendant was the same as hers. It was a gold heart with the Wiblin family insignia.

How was that possible?

As she watched with trembling breath and shaking eyes, the Scorpion lowered her weapon. She kept her eyes fixed on Melania and reached behind her head. She shook her hair free and produced a hair band. Saying nothing, the Scorpion stepped forward. Her eyes were ablaze, cheeks contracted, sweat glistening on her forehead. She held the hair band in the air as if it were a peace offering.

Melania glanced at it. Her breath froze in her chest. Her hands shook, the gun wavering. The pressure behind her eyes spread to her brain. Her mouth opened, but she still couldn't breathe.

The hair band was red, with the green image of a dragon wrapped around it. The green paint was flaking, but it was still present.

The Scorpion crouched low, kissed the hair band, and slid it across the floor. Melania gasped as she picked it up. There was no doubt. It was the exact same as hers. With wide, shocked eyes, she stared at the Scorpion.

The Scorpion said, "Marinochka, my sister. I found you at last."

CHAPTER 82

"Stay here," the Scorpion whispered. She ran to the door and pushed it closed. It was hard work, and Melania watched her, powerless to move. She was sitting now, holding the hair band. She held hers in her other palm and stared at both in wonder. They were exactly the same.

The Scorpion came and crouched in front. They searched each other's eyes, face, noting every angle and corner, searching for a truth, a peace that had eluded them all their lives. Their ripped, torn, damaged lives.

It was the Scorpion who spoke first. Her chest was heaving, but she composed herself. "We don't have much time. We need to move. The explosives are ready to detonate. Dias is waiting. Just listen."

Melania couldn't do much else. She felt paralyzed, rooted to the floor of the Sala Ducale.

"Daurov showed me your photos and adoption certificate. Benjamin Wiblin adopted you because he is your real father. And mine."

Melania's eyes flared up, and sudden jolts of emotion jarred her whole body. Tears pricked the backs of her eyes. What was happening? What else would she learn tonight?

"Aloyna Karmen was our mother. She moved to Moscow after you disappeared. She looked for you everywhere. But you were gone. She contacted our father, Benjamin. He searched and found you were abducted. Yes, by the same bastard who's here today. Dias Dashev."

Melania whispered, "Sergei."

"That might've been a fake name. Anyway, I grew up without you. Daurov showed me your documents and your old and recent photos, and I knew it was you. Benjamin Wiblin also told me before he died."

Melania found her voice. "You knew I was alive?"

The Scorpion shook her head. "Only recently. Our father died three months ago, right?"

Melania nodded, feeling as if her head were wrapped up in a cloud, and she was hearing her sister's voice from the heavens above.

Was this even real? Or was it a cruel dream?

The Scorpion said, "Daurov blackmailed me. If I didn't do this, they would kill you."

Melania's eyes widened.

"I hated every minute of it. But I had to it. All that time in Sardinia, I kept an eye on you. But I still had to show them I was doing my job. I shot at you in that hut but missed on purpose. I left the silver rock with Dan because I knew he would trace it back to the mine."

Melania shook her head, her tongue and words still blocks of granite. There was a sound from the door then hammering.

The Scorpion stood up. "We need to move."

Melania said, "Mama... what happened..."

At the mention of their mother, the Scorpion's face was downcast. Grief, the type that lay in your soul like a wound, hidden but never healing, rose like poison into her eyes. She put a hand on Melania's shoulder.

"We'll talk later. Mama died. She was broken after you were gone. She didn't cope."

There was more hammering from the door and shouts. Melania stared at the Scorpion's face and saw the deep scars left behind by the ravages of a cruel, indifferent fate. Tears blossomed in her eyes and cascaded down her cheeks. For the first time in her life, someone had told her. Her mother, Aloyna, was dead. Her beautiful mama with her dancing dark eyes.

Melania didn't even know this woman, but she saw a single teardrop bloom from her eyes. The Scorpion pulled her into an embrace, and although it was from a stranger, it felt like a benediction, warmth that seeped deep into her bones. And suddenly Melania knew. She felt the truth reverberate like a volcano in her soul, shaking the core of her being. She wanted to hug this woman all her life. Because she had hugged this body when it was little, barely three years old. She had held these hands, kissed that face. She had stared deep into those hazel eyes and laughed when she smiled. Melania didn't know how she knew.

But she just knew.

And she couldn't stop crying, tears falling as though a dam had burst inside her. Even the shattering sound of a gun behind her couldn't tear her from the Scorpion. Melania had lived this long, and she would gladly die for this moment, if only she could hold on for a while longer. Because it was easier to die in contentment than live a life walking wounded, riddled with pain.

"Move!" the Scorpion screamed, pulling her towards the other doorway at the back of the Sala Ducale.

CHAPTER 83

Melania and the Scorpion ran through the doorway. They went through a hallway then up a staircase.

Melania had composed herself and had her weapon back in her hand. She rubbed the red tip of her nose as she ran up the stairs. This staircase was narrow and led up to a small landing. The door coming off the landing was small, and she had to duck in order to get in. The room she stepped into seemed to be from another world. Simple in itself, the walls and huge ceiling above her were full of large-scale, elaborate frescoes. There was an altar before her, and the room was easily fifty yards in length. Wooden panels on the walls came up to head height. Halogen lights were shining in the room. But the effect of the giant frescoes was overwhelming. It made her feel small.

"This way. Hurry." The Scorpion pulled her hand.

As Melania ran, she gazed up at the ceiling once again. Two fingers met in the middle. She had seen the painting before. She was in the Sistine Chapel. There was no time to appreciate her surroundings. The Scorpion was running ahead of her.

A shot rang out suddenly, and she saw the Scorpion jerk and fall.

"No!" Melania screamed, running forward. She held the Scorpion and scanned around with her weapon. She couldn't see anyone. There was a partition in the room, at the other end, made of a fenestrated wooden screen. She jerked her weapon in that direction. Nothing.

She transferred her attention to her sister. A bullet had hit her in the left shoulder. Melania looked at the wound closely. It was in-and-out, a flesh wound. The shoulder bled, but it wasn't a mortal blow.

"I'm OK," the Scorpion said. She held her shoulder, her hand turning crimson.

"Michka, where is he?" Melania asked.

"Close by. Help me get up."

A voice rang out close to them, from the back of the room. "I wouldn't do that if I were you."

Melania jerked her weapon up. A figure had crept within twenty yards, holding an assault rifle that was pointed right at her. The man came closer.

"You can shoot me, but I'll kill you both," he said. His voice sent shivers down Melania's spine.

The Scorpion cried out, "Don't shoot, Dias. I'm coming. Leave her alone."

Dias Dashev lowered his weapon a fraction but kept it pointed at them. "Oh look," he mocked. "Isn't this sweet. Two sisters reunited."

Blood turned to ice in Melania's veins. She recoiled as she recognized the face. Those pale, colorless eyes—she would remember them till she died.

"Sergei," she whispered. The gun trembled in her right hand. She swallowed and tried to steady her arm, but it was no good. Her left hand was pressing on the Scorpion's shoulder.

"I have many names." Dias smiled. "But it's not important. Tell me, who wants to die first? Time is short—barely five minutes."

As she stared at his face and listened to the way he spoke, horrible, old memories resurfaced like knife wounds scraping her flesh. Anger suddenly pulsed inside her, suffusing her with hate.

"You son of a bitch. You destroyed our lives."

Dias nodded. "Yes. But I didn't finish the job. Now, it's time." His eyes held Melania's. "You first, as you are older."

"No!" the Scorpion screamed. "Dias, take me."

But Dias's eyes never left Melania's. They were almost hypnotic. Melania bared her teeth. She lifted her weapon up and in the same instant saw something silvery fly from below her and hit Dias in the chest. He fired, but his shot went wild, high over Melania's head. She fired at the same time and watched her bullet hit just below the needle sticking out of his vest. She kept firing, watching his body shake and jerk as lead pumped into it.

The door behind her burst open. She turned to see Dan Roy at the head of a group of Swiss Guards and Carabinieri. He ran forward and crouched by them.

"Natasha, are you OK?" Dan asked, addressing the Scorpion.

She nodded, and Dan looked at Melania.

The Scorpion said, "Dan, we need to find the C4. Dias told me to bring it up here. He's set it on a timer."

Melania said, "And it's got five minutes."

CHAPTER 84

Dan straightened as uniforms filled the room.

"Where did you stack them?" Dan asked.

The Scorpion waved her good arm. She was still lying on the floor, head cradled in Melania's lap. "Behind the partition. Hurry."

Dan ran to the rear of the Sistine Chapel, through the opening in the partition. He looked around wildly. Chairs were arranged in the corners. He pushed them aside, looking under them. The paintings on the walls looked down at him as he moved every piece of furniture, sweat pouring down his face.

A table covered in black cloth caught his attention. A flower vase rested on it, under a painting. He lifted the tablecloth. Nothing.

"Three minutes left!" Melania shouted from behind them.

"Tell the Carabinieri to get a car ready. We need to get it out of here as soon as I find it."

If I find it, he thought. Panic suddenly surged in his chest, an alien emotion for him. He had to find it. The alternative was unthinkable.

"Natasha!" he yelled. "It's not behind the partition. Any ideas?"

"I don't know."

"OK. Everybody, get the hell out in case this thing blows. Tell the cops to keep the car revving outside."

"What about you?"

"Just go. Go now!"

Dan checked the time on his watch. Another thirty seconds gone. He heard the others getting up and filing out of the Sistine Chapel. Dan swivelled three hundred sixty degrees, eyes darting around. He had checked everything on the floor. Apart from pulling up the floorboards, there was nothing to be done. He looked behind him, at the front of the room. His eyes fell on the altar. It was small, made of wood, and painted black. In the magnificence of the room, it was easy to miss. Unless someone was praying at it. A cardinal, maybe.

Or the pope.

Dan ran full tilt towards the altar. It was stuck to the floor, and he couldn't move it. With effort, shoulders heaving, he ripped it off. Then he saw it. At the base of the altar, stacked like bricks, were layers of C4 explosives. The timer was on, and the red numbers glowing on it showed two minutes left. Even as he watched, the countdown changed to 01:59. Dan snatched the top brick with the timer and shoved it into his pants pocket. He cradled the rest in his arms and ran out of the room like a madman.

The Sistine Chapel was right next to the Sala Duca. Dan burst through the doors, shouting his head off, but the room was empty. He got to the main staircase and saw the Swiss Guards at the bottom.

"Get the car ready!" Dan hollered. "Less than two minutes left."

Dan had never moved so fast in his life. He sprinted down the stairs. On the last few steps, he slipped and fell, crashing to the floor. He picked up the explosives and ran again. The huge portcullis of the Bronze Door was open. Dan stormed out of it. A blue-and-white Carabinieri car was waiting for him at the base of St. Peter's Basilica. He took a moment to register that the car was, in fact, a Ferrari.

The engine was on, and a driver was in place.

Dan bundled himself inside and yelled at the driver, "Let's see how fast this thing does zero to sixty!"

The words had barely left his lips when the driver, a Carabinieri officer, slammed on the gas. The Ferrari shot forward like a rocket, pressing Dan back into the seat.

"To the river!" He knew the river was close by.

"Si, Signore!" the driver shouted back.

The car hurtled down a pedestrian street after the square. Dan sneaked a look at the timer.

One minute left.

His breath came in gasps. Damn, he was going to die. And he had dragged this innocent driver along with him. Still, calamity, Qayamat, the end of worlds was avoided. The Vatican was safe. The world wouldn't mourn the loss of Dan Roy. Natasha, a.k.a. the Scorpion, would be sad, and maybe McBride. But that was it. Dan closed his eyes. At least he would die knowing he had saved the world.

The Ferrari swerved, pressing Dan against the side. It flew down another empty street then jerked to a stop. Dan was out immediately, along with the driver.

Thirty seconds left.

The cement balustrades came above his waist height. The muddy waters of the Tiber rippled far below. Dan chucked the pieces as fast as he could. Then he wrenched the last piece, with the timer attached, from his pants pocket.

Ten seconds left.

He hurled the piece as hard as he could. Then he pivoted, grabbed the driver, and ran behind the Ferrari.

The ground shook, and the blast shattered the windows of every parked car. The Ferrari was lifted from its wheels and turned around as Dan felt the heat of the explosion on his back. He was flung forward as an orange-yellow ball mushroomed above Rome's skyline, tremors passing through the bowels of the ancient city.

The Ferrari smashed down, its body buckled, windshield and windows blown. Dan covered his head as debris rained down on him. There was cloud and dust everywhere, and dirt choked his mouth. He could barely breathe.

A body lay next to him. Dan crawled then shook the figure. It moved and raised its dusty head. It was the driver. Dan helped him to move to the sidewalk then collapsed again next to him. The sky swirled with dust, and the smell of cordite and gunpowder choked his nostrils.

CHAPTER 85

In St. Peter's Square, a line of cars and ambulances stood with lights blazing. The media had turned up, and two vans with satellite dishes stuck on top were unloading camera crews.

Outside the Bronze Door of the Apostolic Palazzo, Swiss Guards had formed a cordon, cutting off the entrance. Inside it, there was a similar group. Only the ambulances were allowed in, bringing out the bodies in gurneys.

The courtyard in the middle, *Cortile San Damaso*, or the San Damasus courtyard, was relatively quiet. Against the shadow of a wall, two figures were slumped, facing each other.

Melania said, "I used to call you my little *lapochka*."

Natasha smiled. The ambulance crew had stitched her wound up. She had refused to go to hospital.

Melania said, "Mama used to call you that too. We used to play with you." Tears rolled down her cheeks.

Natasha reached out and wiped them.

Melania whispered, "Did Mama suffer?"

Natasha nodded. She told her sister how Aloyna's depression destroyed her, forcing her into a life of drugs and prostitution.

Melania gripped her head and sobbed. While she was building a new life for herself in America, her poor mother was sliding towards death. Melania knew her mother had chosen to die. She killed herself with drugs. Melania knew that because she felt the same way. Not knowing. Not having any closure. She, too, had been the walking dead. Until tonight.

Natasha said, "Although my life was harsh, I was spared what you and Mama went through. I'm sorry."

Melania dried her eyes. She now knew what Natasha had to endure, on her way to becoming the Scorpion. "Your life wasn't exactly a bed of roses."

Natasha shrugged.

Melania said, "So Benjamin, our father, must have pulled strings to get me delivered to him." She recalled how she was taken off the ship and transferred to the boat that took her to Boston.

Natasha said, "Before Mama died, she told me. She called him. He used to work for the CIA then. An internal agent in Moscow. But he was back in the USA by the time I was born. He used his contacts to find what happened to you. Guess it worked out."

"He saved me but not you," Melania said.

Natasha smiled. "But he did come back. By then, it was too late." She took Melania's hand. "Mama left a letter for you. I have it with my stuff back home. But I don't understand something."

"What?"

"How did Daurov get hold of your documents? Adoption certificate, recent photos, you name it."

Melania shook her head. "I don't know. Dan might. I have to ask him."

At the mention of his name, the sisters looked up at each other.

Melania said, "No. Nothing happened between us. But I know something happened between you and him."

Natasha sighed. "Yes. We were lovers. Sometimes I think he's the only man I ever loved."

"Then get back with him."

A pained expression came over Natasha's face. "It doesn't work like that." She hung her head.

When she looked up, Melania saw tears glistening. She gripped Natasha's arm. "What?"

"You have to kill me."

"What? Wait. Why?"

"Don't you see? They'll keep using you to blackmail me. They now know we are sisters. This only ends if I die."

Melania felt her heart had stopped beating. Her mouth went dry. "No, my little Michka. I've only just found you. There is no way I'm letting you go."

Natalia grabbed her sister's hand, feeling a weight pressed against her throat. "But what can we do?"

A voice came from a few feet away. "There is something you can do."

Both of them startled then saw the tall figure standing in the shadow of an alcove. He stepped out. It was Dan Roy.

CHAPTER 86

The three SUVs rolled to a stop outside the Palazzo Margherita. The security detail was noticeably heavier. Two armored cars stood at either end of the building, with armed guards patrolling around the block. Helicopters crisscrossed the sky overhead, searchlights pointed at St. Peter's Basilica and Vatican City. The whole of Italy was on alert. News of an explosion just outside the gates of St. Peter's Square had spread like wildfire.

The armed commando unit manning the gates checked the drivers' IDs then let the cars through. Melania and Dan alighted, and another armed unit came out of the other two cars. They stayed in the basement while Melania and Dan went up in the elevator.

The analyst room wasn't dark this time. The lights were on, and although the room was nearly empty, the large screen at one end was alive, with the face of Chuck Jones and Stephen Polk clearly visible. The screen was divided into four boxes, and Dan didn't recognize the two faces at the bottom. But he had already spoken to McBride and given him a debrief of the operation.

Karl Shapiro, Jake, and Charlie were standing, waiting for them. They shook hands.

Karl had a warm smile on his face. He said to Melania, "I guess this is the first time I congratulate you for disobeying an order."

Polk said from the screen, "No, I guess not. All of us owe you a great deal. May I introduce the White House Chief of Staff, Ty Parsons, and Anders Denison, our ambassador to Italy."

Dan and Melania took turns to explain exactly what had happened.

Polk said, "Paolo Noleggio, the secretary of state, is furious. He wants to know why an Italian team wasn't there."

"Tell him there was—they just didn't speak Italian," Dan said.

Everyone laughed.

Chuck Jones asked, "Where is Daurov? The sat phone has not been used again."

Dan shook his head. "We don't know. He wasn't inside the Vatican. We know that much."

"But the bishop lookalike is dead."

"Yes. His name was Dias Dashev," Melania said. "I killed him."

Polk said, "They had a female operative, right? The one who escaped from our black site in Sardinia. Dan saw her on Daurov's boat. What happened to her?"

"She's dead too," Dan said. "She made it out to the riverbank and tried to kill me. I threw her with the explosives."

"Are you sure?" Karl asked. He was standing next to Dan.

Dan nodded. "Yes. She's dead."

There was silence for a while. Then Anders said, "We are all done, then? I don't need to remind all of you that there will be a media crowd outside early tomorrow, if not already. Under no circumstances do we release any information."

Everyone nodded.

Then Melania said quietly, "There's only one problem."

Polk's eyebrows met in the middle. "What's that?"

"We have a mole."

Polk did a double take. "What?"

Dan spoke up. "Think about it. Only DOD-cleared personnel have access to a military satellite phone. It's not possible to carry it through an airport unless it's a military flight. Dias Dashev was using that phone with impunity. It's like he knew he was protected."

Melania said, "Dias also had all my details. My photos, CIA employment file, even my adoption certificate. The SVR agent, Colonel Borislov, gave it to him."

Chuck raised his eyebrows. "But why your details?"

"Because someone ordered Dias to finish me off as well. You see, this someone thought I knew about him. He's the mole. He thinks I knew about him. He was scared."

Dan looked around the room then at the men on the screen. "This man had access to all of Melania's files. He also sent her here."

Melania and Dan turned to face Karl. His face was ashen. He took two steps back towards the door. His hand dived into his pocket and came out with a Glock. He pointed it at the four of them.

"Karl!" Polk cried from the screen. "What the hell are you doing?"

Karl didn't answer. His eyes were bulging, nostrils flaring. He fired his weapon. The hammer clicked on an empty chamber. Karl's eyes bulged further, and he breathed heavily.

Dan opened his fist and showed the cartridges from the gun. Jake had removed them while Dan was on his way back from the Vatican.

Dan said, "I knew it was you, Karl. It had to be. No one else knew as much about Melania as you did. You're a close family friend of the Wiblin family and knew Melania as she grew up. You knew about her past life. You gave her files to Borislov, who sent them to Daurov."

The door opened behind Karl, and two of the commandos marched in. They grabbed hold of Karl's hands. He gave Dan a stare full of hate.

"You'll die for this, Dan Roy."

"I wish I had a dollar for each time I've heard that," Dan said. "I'd be a very rich man."

CHAPTER 87

The Costa Smeralda's lunar crescent of sea and mountains was resplendent in the setting sun. The golden orb seemed to vaporize and sizzle as it settled over the horizon.

Melania and Natasha were standing at the edge of the villa built into the mountains of Porto Cervo, watching the glorious scene. Natasha had escaped via the secret tunnel. She had swum out into the Tiber. She was met by Dan the next day, and now they were all back in Sardinia. The two sisters had talked the whole night through. Melania still felt like pinching herself. One half of her had always been dead, decaying. Now she was whole again, alive. The fading sunlight, the wind from the sea, tingled her skin like never before. She hadn't grown tired of hugging Natasha. She never would.

Natasha said, "I want to see Daddy's grave." Melania nodded.

Natasha turned to her. "You knew him better than me."

Melania said, "At least one of us did. But I never knew what a strange, conflicted man he was." She sighed. She would never understand the strange heart of human beings. Of men.

Natasha asked, "What do you mean?"

Melania looked towards the glorious colors in the sky. "When I graduated as a CIA agent, I asked him a question. If I could call him Daddy. He didn't answer and got emotional." Melania shook her head. "If only I had known."

Natasha said, "He couldn't tell you the truth, even then. Guilt ate into his soul, all his life. But bringing you back was his way of atoning."

"Atoning," Melania echoed. They were silent for a while, then Melania said, "I didn't see him that often. But when I did, I could tell he was genuinely happy. Like—"

"Like he loved you."

"Yes."

Melania said, "It's Mama I feel truly sorry for. I wish I had listened to her more. I wish—"

"Don't." Natasha stepped closer and covered her sister's hand with hers. "It's no good. You were a child. What's happened is in the past. Let's live for this moment."

Melania stared down at their entwined hands. Her voice was a whisper in the mistral wind. "Yes."

They stood like that for a while in silence, their past and present wrapped around them like the colors of the fading sun.

*****

After a while, Natasha glanced down. She pointed at the road that snaked up the hill to the villa. "Who's that?"

A figure was coming up the drive, slouched low. He wore a black coat and a black fedora hat. They saw Dan Roy open the gates to let the man in.

Soon, Dan came up with his guest. He introduced them and said, "This is an old friend. Jim McBride."

McBride was staring at Natasha intently. "The Scorpion," he said in a quiet voice. "Your reputation precedes you."

Natasha glanced at Dan, then back at McBride. "Who are you?"

McBride raised an eyebrow. "Dan just said—"

"I know what he said. I don't want your name."

McBride smiled. "An old man who still fights for his country. That's all you need to know."

Natasha said, "You knew my name, but it's the wrong one. Scorpion is dead. My name is Natasha Karmen."

"Really?"

Dan interjected. "We have a problem, McBride. The Russians, Chechens, Arabs, everyone in fact, knows the Scorpion is alive, and that she has a sister. They will use Melania to get to her."

Melania stepped forward to join the group. She said, "Or the reverse. Pressure me to give up classified information, or they kill Natasha."

Dan said, "So, the best solution is to spread the news that the Scorpion tried to escape. She drowned in the Tiber and died."

McBride said, "There's no dead body. The sort of people who hire the Scorpion are no fools."

Dan had an idea. "The carabinieri on the boat, at the end of the secret passage. His body must be floating around somewhere."

"It's a man, but maybe I can arrange something," McBride said.

Dan nodded. "Pay off someone at the morgue to do a switch with a Jane Doe. Whatever. Just get it done."

"I'll see what I can do."

They spoke for a while, then Melania and McBride went downstairs to get a drink. Natasha and Dan were left alone on the roof. Dan followed her as she walked to the balustrade and leaned over with her elbows on it. Neither of them said anything.

"Weird how things work out," Dan said.

Natasha glanced at him. "Have they?"

Dan raised an eyebrow. "You found your sister."

"That's not what I meant."

They stared at each other for a while, searching. Natasha came closer. She lifted her hand to Dan's face and traced her fingers down his cheek. He caught her hand and held it against his neck. His arm snaked down to her waist.

His voice was husky. "What did you mean?"

"This." Natasha leaned forward, and their lips met in a kiss.

THE END

FROM THE AUTHOR

If you've read this far, I'm hoping you enjoyed this book. I am a self-published author, and I don't have the marketing budget that big publishing houses possess. But I do have you, the person who has read this book.

If you could please leave a review on Amazon, it would make my day. Reviews take two minutes of your time, but inform other readers forever.

Many thanks
Mick Bose.

WANT TO READ MORE?

Join the Readers' Group and get Hellfire, a novella introducing Dan Roy, FREE!
Visit http://www.subscribepage.com/p6f4a1

HAVE YOU READ THEM ALL?
Hidden Agenda (Dan Roy Series 1)
Dark Water (Dan Roy Series 2)
The Tonkin Protocol (Dan Roy Series 3)
Shanghai Tang (Dan Roy Series 4)
Scorpion Rising (Dan Roy Series 5)
Deep Deception (Dan Roy Series 6)
Enemy Within (A stand-alone thriller)

Made in the USA
Lexington, KY
07 November 2019

56724986R00177